THE GOLDEN HOUR

L.M. HALLORAN

COPYRIGHT

For all the fierce women raising fierce daughters,

and for the men who aren't afraid to love them.

SOUNDTRACK

"Gemini Feed"—BANKS
"Young & Unafraid"—The Moth and the Flame
"Critical Mistakes"—888
"lovely"—Billie Eilish
"I Don't Give A..."—MISSIO
"Be Your Love"—Bishop Briggs
"Love is a Bitch"—Two Feet
"Beautiful Wreck"—MØ
and more...

Listen on Spotify

PREFACE

Finn

The first time I saw her was in a crowded courtroom on the last day of her father's trial. She wore a frilly white dress and had a ridiculous pink bow perched on the side of her head. Granted, she was maybe five years old and didn't pick out her own clothes for the occasion.

She sat next to her stepmother in the first row behind the defense, her face pale and expressionless, her eyes huge and glassy.

She looked drugged, which I later realized might have been the case. What five-year-old chooses to sit still while a judge lists their father's crimes and sentences them to life without parole? A doctor probably gave her something. Or her stepmother, who had the same dreamy, detached look as the little girl.

That's what she was—little. *Tiny.* Doll-like with her dark hair, porcelain skin, and huge eyes.

They sat motionless, the two of them, holding hands as the sentence was read and the courtroom erupted around them.

I erupted too. With fierce cries that issued straight from my eleven-year-old broken heart. Justice was done. The man who murdered my father—who the media once hailed as untouchable—was going to jail for the rest of his life.

It was a good day for my family.

Not a happy one—those were gone—but a good one.

———

Three years later, I saw her face again on the news. One of her uncles had just been gunned down outside one of his restaurants, and paparazzi staked out the elite private school she was attending, waiting for her to emerge.

The clip was short—a few seconds as she was ushered outside by bodyguards and whisked away—and her face was only visible for a moment. Startled, tearful eyes. Pale white hands gripping the strap of her backpack. Somehow regal despite the circumstances.

The perfect picture of a helpless victim of ongoing violence and tragedy.

A tarnished princess.

I turned off the television before I could feel any sympathy for her.

None of what happened was her fault, obviously. But she was still the daughter of the man who destroyed my family.

I didn't see Callisto Avellino again for eighteen years. When I did, I nearly made the biggest mistake of my life.

Callisto

"NO ONE MOVES to the Oregon coast to make something of their life."

"Mmm," I hum noncommittally, not looking up as I continue wiping the bar top with smooth, circular strokes.

Old Freddy takes a noisy sip of his beer, then wipes his upper lip with his sleeve. I focus on a smudge, well aware that he's just warming up. It's the second Wednesday of the month, after all, which means Fred's social security check came today. He'll spend the next six hours slowly drinking his weight in beer, eating onion rings and bar nuts, and some well-meaning person will drive him home. Until next month.

Sure enough, after a muted belch, he continues, "If you're born here, you leave, and if you come here, you're either vacationing or running from something. Ain't that right, Mol?"

Out of the corner of my eye, I catch Molly's eyes rolling upward and compress my lips to stifle a smile. She was born here fifty-some years ago, never left, and owns the town's only bar, motel, and restaurant.

"Sure thing, Fred," she chirps, barely glancing at him from her stool where she's reviewing the books.

"What about you, girlie?" asks Fred, his rheumy eyes squinting at me. "Don't think you've told me what brought you to Solstice Bay."

Even though Fred is harmless, the space between my shoulder blades tightens.

"Mind your business," Molly chirps, her sharp eyes piercing Fred from above her bifocals.

I throw her a grateful look, then clear my throat for the standard answer. "I'm here because I love it. There's no story."

His squint grows pronounced, stubby eyelashes almost swallowed by wrinkled lids. "Sure, it's a pretty place for the rich to spend some money, but a young, single woman such as yourself? Nothin' for ya here, I'm sorry to say."

"Maybe life is about more than climbing some imaginary mountain of success," I reply, more to hear myself say it than out of a need to convince anyone.

Isn't that why I'm here? To find out what life is all about?

This is the time of day when Fred gets melancholy. Normally it doesn't bother me, but I'm off-kilter from reading the day's headlines on my phone before my shift.

I look questioningly at Molly. At her discreet nod, I grab Fred's empty glass and draw him another pint, then slide it back over the bar. His grumbled thanks is lost in the sound of the front door opening and closing.

The raucous group of men veers away from the restaurant and toward us, the bar-side of the building, peeling off jackets and beanies as they walk. Regulars, they bring with them loud chatter and the fresh tang of the sea... and the not-so-fresh tang of fish. I'm still glad to see them, because they're the heralds of the evening crowd. From here on out, I won't have time to think about anything but work.

Sure enough, as soon as I've filled their drink orders, the front door opens again. More men enter, this time carrying the scent of the only other industry in town: lumber.

Pinned between a dense forest and a turbulent Pacific, Solstice Bay is a town of under five hundred people, most of them over forty. For eight months of the year, the weather is just shy of miserable. Cold. Rainy.

And the location?

The definition of remote, and the perfect place to hide for the rest of my life.

AN HOUR BEFORE CLOSING, the crowd finally thins. The only group left is the fishermen, celebrating a large haul of coho salmon. I know exactly nothing about different types of salmon, and my experience with fish is limited to ordering sushi. But the men don't require me to understand, only to act excited for them and keep their pitchers full.

Back at the bar, I pause to stretch my aching back before starting the closing routine. Come spring and summer, I'll have help, but the winter months are by necessity run lean and mean. It's the only way for us to stay open long enough for the tourist season to breathe vitality back into an economy on life-support.

I'm loading up a bin with used glasses for the morning kitchen staff when the front door opens with a groan of damp wood and a blast of frigid air. The cold hits my bare neck and I shiver as I turn to see who's come in, praying it's an earlier customer who forgot something.

It's not.

My initial flare of irritation—I was hoping to shut down a bit early—morphs to curiosity as the newcomer drags down the hood of his coat.

Men aren't supposed to have mouths like that.

Not the most dignified thought, but impossible to avoid. This man doesn't belong here. He's too chiseled. Otherworldly. He belongs on the covers of magazines, not in a backwater bar in the middle of nowhere, Oregon.

He scans the dim barroom, bright blue eyes watchful and slightly haughty. Those remarkable eyes meet mine briefly, flit away, then snap back to my face. Now they reflect surprise.

I don't look like I belong here any more than he does. I've certainly been told it enough in the year I've been here.

Frozen, I'm stuck in a movie of my life as he walks toward me, eye contact an electric thread between us. Not until he settles on the barstool directly in front of me do I blink and slam back to reality. His scent teases my nose. Something warm and tingly. Like a hug—preferably the naked kind. I glance at his hands. Strong and sinewy. Then his shoulders, broad and muscled beneath a soft flannel.

"W-what can I get you?"

Smooth.

"Whiskey neat," he says in a rich, melting baritone. A slow smile lifts the corners of his mouth. "Do I have something on my face?"

The casual acknowledgment of our staring contest zings through my body. I haven't been looked at the way he's looking at me in a long time—not counting the handful of lecherous old men in town.

I've forgotten what it feels like to be seen.

"No," I finally answer. "Do I?"

His smirk blooms into a smile that makes me dizzy.

"Nothing but glasses." His eyes flicker to my mouth and back up. "Can I get that drink?"

Heat sizzles in my cheeks. "Yes, sorry."

It's a relief to turn my back to him and reach for a bottle on the top shelf—Single Malt Balvenie—because I know he'll appreciate it. Going by the watch on his wrist, he can easily afford it.

I pour the drink and slide it to him. Before I can retract my fingers, he covers them with his own.

My breath hitches. My stomach drops. My fingers linger, frozen in space, after he pulls the glass away. Mortified, I tuck my hands quickly in my half apron.

He takes a sip. Sighs. Licks his lips. He must know his every movement drips suggestion. Men like this don't have to work for sex. Willing partners flock to them, hoping for permission to touch and be touched, already shaping their hearts into arrows and lobbing them one after the other, praying one lands.

The thought is a shock, instantly dousing my newly woken libido.

"Thanks," he says, eyelashes fluttering as his gaze returns to me.

I nod, stiff now, my body cold from the swift fleeing of desire. "You're welcome. We close in a half hour. Let me know if you'd like another."

I turn to make my escape.

"What's your name?" he asks behind me.

"Grace," I lie effortlessly and keep walking.

I'm not quite five steps away when he murmurs the name I've given him. It lands against my back like a feather, soft and drifting. A touch imploring.

Then it bounces away.

2

Finn

I WATCH the bartender stroll away from me, petite hips in an understated swing, her dark braid swinging against her back. When I walked in here, I was expecting the atmosphere of a dive and all that came with it, including a surly bartender named Mo or some close variation.

Instead, I found Nerdy Snow White in a surprisingly modern space that could go toe-to-toe with any big-city establishment.

I'll admit I was taken aback by the sight of her, slow to recover. When her rosy lips parted on a gasp, and I realized she was equally shocked by me, my head went straight to that plush mouth swallowing my cock. A forceful reminder that it's been weeks since I've sunk into a woman's heat and felt respite from my demons.

The little bartender doesn't know she's the first

woman I've found appealing in months. Maybe longer. The first to make me forget, even for a few seconds, what brought me to Solstice Bay.

The Balvenie glides down my throat, coating it with heat. I roll my shoulders up and back, willing them to let go of the tension they've carried for nearly forty-eight hours of travel. It's no use. My muscles scream for a massage and rest. My entire body is coiled like a spring, my foot tapping incessantly on the rail beneath the bar.

"Kitchen's closed, but we have some mixed nuts if you're hungry."

Her voice, a unique cross between melodic and raspy, wraps around my chest like a band. Something like relief sits in my throat—she ran away from me like a startled doe, but she came back. I'm hoping she couldn't help it. That she feels this chemistry like I do.

I take my time looking up, framing her in pieces before appreciating the whole. Delicate fingers with short, unpainted nails. Small wrists and arms encased in a long-sleeved black shirt. Narrow shoulders—high and tight like she'll run again any second—and a slender throat that swallows as my gaze touches it. Her jaw is tight with tension, the line sharp, almost feline. Two spots of color sit on her cheeks, highlighting cheekbones people pay money for. Dark, sloping brows. Straight nose with a slight point.

I save the best for last. Her eyes. Irises of starless black, or a deep brown only full sun would reveal, and tilted up just slightly at the edges. The thin black frame of her glasses enhances rather than detracts from her allure.

My fingers clench around the tumbler, bereft without a camera. Another first in a while—the desire to photograph something. Or rather, *someone.*

And her skin... I close my eyes, imagining that pale canvas red from my hands. Captured on film. Glowing against crimson silk.

"Are you... feeling okay?"

The soft question opens my eyes, taking my focus away from my stiffening cock. I'm being a lecherous asshole. And rude. My mom and sisters would box my ears if they knew what I was thinking, a thought that nearly cripples me—I shove it into a metal box and slam the lid closed.

"I'm sorry," I say, shaking my head. "I've been on planes or in airports for two days. Severe jet lag. Ignore me."

Don't ignore me. Let me mark you with my teeth and fuck you so hard you see God.

I shift on the stool in an attempt to discreetly adjust my erection. This woman is turning me into a teenager. Months of stress and worry have rendered me incapable of self-control.

Leaning back on the barstool, I rub my face roughly with my hands. *When was the last time I ate?*

"I need to sleep," I say, only partly for her benefit.

"Why don't you?"

Her voice comes from directly before me. Curious, but also hesitant, like she doesn't want to talk to me but can't help herself.

She might be the answer to my unvoiced prayers.

"I'm avoiding responsibility," I tell her, a bit surprised by the truth coming out of my mouth.

Dark, limitless eyes flicker over my face. "Family?" she guesses.

With a wry smile, I nod. "What else?"

"Do they live here?" she asks, then blushes. "I'm sorry, it's none of my business."

"A few of them," I answer, then tilt my head. "Isn't it in your job description? To chat with customers so they stay longer and spend more money?"

She looks down with a small, stilted laugh. "Then I'm not a very good bartender. I don't normally make small talk. I'm not good at it."

"You're doing fine right now," I tell her, mostly to see if I can make her blush again. Pride swells my chest when her cheeks darken.

When was the last time I made a woman blush? Or even tried to seduce someone?

I can't remember. Most of the women I meet in my line of work are models and actresses. Jaded. Confident. Predatory. I take their photograph, and in many instances, also take them to bed. The transactions are always mutually beneficial, but they're just that... *transactions.*

Void of emotional intimacy.

"What are you frowning about?" asks Snow White.

Taking your photograph.

Your skin in the soft light of dawn.

Avoiding her eyes, I finish my drink. There's honest, and then there's straight stupid. I need to pay and leave, crash for a solid ten hours, think about tomorrow. About who I have to see.

But I can't make myself move.

"I was thinking about my mom."

Jesus Christ. What the fuck happened to my filter?

"She lives here?"

I nod, my lips clamped shut. Clearly the whiskey on an empty stomach was a bad idea.

"How long has it been?" she asks, gentle but direct, like she's unused to asking such personal questions.

Maybe she *is* bad at small talk. It's kind of refreshing, even though her question sends heat marching up my spine. Part of me wants to snap at her, tell her to leave me in peace. If there's one thing I don't do—with *anyone*—it's talk about my family.

But there's something about this woman. Or maybe about this place, shrouded in mist and sea spray. And the night outside—true darkness born of minimal streetlights and family-owned businesses that close at sunset. When I drove into town, I felt weirdly enveloped, as though I passed into another time in a world not my own.

"About eight years," I answer my unsuspecting confessor. I offer a pitiful smile. "Don't judge me."

"You won't find any judgement here. Would you like another drink?"

God, her voice. It drips with sincerity, smooth as silk with a hint of barbed wire. More intoxicating than any whiskey.

"Yes, please." My own voice is rougher than intended, sharp with the effect she has on me.

She blinks at me, eyes large and startled. My head spins. She looks familiar suddenly, like a half-remembered dream just outside my reach. For a split second, I'm convinced I've met her before.

Then she spins away, dark braid swinging, and reaches up for the bottle of whiskey, and all I can think about is the gentle flare of her hips and the way her perky ass would feel in my hands.

3

Finn

GRACE AVOIDS me for the next half hour—not an easy task in an almost empty bar. But between tending the final booth of customers, sweeping the floor, and restocking napkins and whatever else, she stays busy.

I almost convince myself to leave three or four times, but instead I nurse my drink and think about what it would take to seduce Snow White. My half-drunk head spins fantasies of feeding her juicy red apples and tying ribbons around her neck.

Eventually I become aware of movement behind me. Heavy boots, rustling coats. The front door opens with a soft squeal as the last customers leave. I listen with half an ear as Grace bids them good night, thanks them for coming in, and try not to think about the fact we're about to be alone. Or that she might be about to ask me to leave.

Out of the corner of my eye, I see her approach the bar and me, and brace myself to be kicked out.

A pair of boots clomps our way and a gruff, grandfatherly voice asks, "You want me to stick around, Grace? Make sure you get home safe?"

The undercurrent of mistrust tells me he's speaking for my benefit. I almost laugh—she's more of a threat to me than I am to her. But I don't say anything, just watch a series of emotions cross Grace's face like a slideshow. Confusion, understanding, embarrassment, gratitude...

Up until this moment, I knew exactly nothing about this woman except her voice gets me hard and I want her beneath me. Now I know she's innocent in a way I hadn't imagined. And probably a lot younger than I originally thought.

I still want her.

She has to be at least twenty-one to be working here, right?

"Twenty-one," I mutter, head in my hands, "I'm out of my mind."

"What?"

In my mental lapse, the well-meaning grandfather said his goodbyes and left. Grace is down the bar from me with a rag in her hand and a dreamy look on her face as she stares at me.

Even though I care less than I should, I make myself ask, "How old are you?"

Her cheeks bloom with red, a sight I'm becoming irrationally obsessed with.

"Why?" she asks, high and breathless.

Screw it. I'm desperate.

"Because I want to invite you back to my motel, but twenty-one is too young for me. Same age as my baby sister."

Grace blinks rapidly. "I'm twenty-five. Twenty-six next month."

A smile tugs my lips and her gaze dips to my mouth. She swallows hard and her lips part. My mouth waters. I can already taste her.

Game on.

I stand up and walk down the bar until we face each other. Vaguely, I realize my body doesn't hurt anymore. Like an addict, I've relaxed because relief is coming. And I know this fix is going to give me what I need and then some.

Turning on the charm to lethal levels, I smile broadly and offer her my hand. "Hi. I'm sorry I didn't introduce myself before. I'm Finnegan McCowen, because apparently my parents didn't think the last name alone was Scottish enough. But everyone calls me Finn."

It works. Her lips twitch, eyes alighting with humor. "Nice to meet you, Finn."

After a small hesitation, her palm slides against mine. My fingers curl, greedily soaking in the feel of her soft, warm skin. My hand dwarfs hers, as I know my body will. I can't stop staring at the contrast of masculine to feminine, large to petite, and it makes me feel weirdly protective. Like I should warn her off from me.

I squash the thought—I fucking need her.

Looking up, I find a similar expression of want on her face and feel like shouting in victory.

"Come home with me."

Her pulse beats madly beneath the nearly translucent skin of her throat. I want to nip that trapped flutter of life. Suck it. Roll it between my teeth.

She stares at me, dark eyes glistening with a heady mixture of surprise and lust. I want to ask if she's ever felt this kind of instant, intense attraction, but I'm sober enough not to. No use giving her any ideas about seeing me past tonight.

Though I'm expecting a nervous laugh and some version of *I've never done anything like this before,* she blows my mind by simply nodding.

"I'm almost done closing."

Her hand leaves mine, robbing my fingers of her warmth. A moment later, a rag hits my chest. I catch it instinctively.

"Make yourself useful, will you? Wipe down the tables and clear that booth."

When the words register, a rusty chuckle emerges from my chest. Another surprise. Snow White has spunk.

I give her an exaggerated bow. "I'm your willing servant."

She smiles fully for the first time, and in my lust-filled haze I decide I wouldn't mind making her smile every day forever. It transforms her from ethereal to mischievous. And far sexier than any woman has a right to be.

I want her with a whole-body intensity that scares me.

Grace tilts her head, brows drawing together in a cute little frown. "Maybe you should get some sleep instead?" she asks, and my mind is wiped of everything but the drive to peel off her clothes with my teeth.

"Hell no."

I hustle across the room, grinning at the sound of her tinkling laughter following me.

4

Callisto

TRUE TO HIS WORD, Finn does everything I ask him to for the next twenty minutes, including taking the trash to the dumpster out back. I'm sure it's because he thinks he's getting laid, which should bother me.

I'm not sure why, but it doesn't.

Maybe it's that for all his self-assurance and practiced charm, he has kind eyes. Honest eyes. And where I come from, that's exceedingly rare to find in a man with a face and body like his.

I haven't felt this reckless—or free—in my life. And really, why shouldn't I let loose for a night? There's no one here to judge me. Punish me. Drag me through hell as penance for daring to have fun. For attempting to be a normal woman.

I've been celibate for over two years, more due to

circumstance than choice, and I miss being touched. Besides, when's the next time an opportunity like this will land in my lap?

Tonight, I'm just a woman answering the call of her blood for the touch of a man.

"Here we are, m'lady. The Presidential suite."

Finn unlocks the door to his motel room, flips on the bedside light, and invites me inside with a playful bow.

Widening my eyes, I gaze around with feigned awe. "My God, I've never been anywhere this fancy."

When he doesn't laugh, I turn to find his eyes on me, his jacket caught half down his arms. "You deserve more than this." The words seem to surprise him more than me, and he turns away, yanking his jacket off and throwing it over a nearby desk chair.

"No, I don't," I tell him frankly. "Besides, my boss owns this motel, and I know for a fact that the sheets are new, the mattresses are soft, and carpets are steam cleaned once a month."

A rough laugh bursts from him, the sound oddly forlorn. He drags a hand through his dark hair, sending the strands into orbit, then focuses his blues on my face.

There's no question of what he wants or when.

Me.

Now.

My nipples tingle, hardening as he closes the distance between us. The single light by the bed casts most of him in shadow, but his pale eyes glint. Wolfish and hungry.

He stops so close to me I can feel the heat of his body. Then he reaches up slowly, like he doesn't want to startle me, and removes my ten-dollar, prescription-free glasses.

"Can you see?"

I nod, struck mute by his tenderness. He smiles and sets the glasses on the nearest surface—the two-seater table by the window—then returns to me. Hot fingertips feather over my cheekbone, trace the slope of one eyebrow, and lower to clasp the back of my neck beneath my braid. He effortlessly tilts my head back, drawing me forward until my breasts meet the wall of his chest. I'm too aroused to be embarrassed by my small, needy whimper.

"I'm going to kiss you now," he says, but doesn't wait for a response.

As I'm learning quickly with this man, there's no use anticipating what he'll say, or in this case, do. Because when I think he'll kiss me softly in introduction, teasing me with promise of more like most men would, he does the opposite.

He takes my mouth like he's starving for it, and I let

him in like he's coming home, sucking in the scent of him and the faint, seductive tang of whiskey.

But the savagery of our kiss isn't enough. We claw at each other's tops, yanking and tugging with no care for abraded skin. My bra tears at the clasp and is discarded. When his flannel and undershirt sail to the floor, I glimpse tattoos. *A lot* of tattoos, some colored, some intricate and dark. His body is a map of his life, and I want to visit each stop.

Finn has other plans, distracting me with a searing, open-mouthed kiss that I feel all the way to my toes. Before I can recover, his hands slide beneath my thighs and I'm sailing upward. His eyes gleam as they trace my bare breasts, now situated before his face, while my fingers sink into his hair.

"Thank you, God," he whispers.

I laugh, the sound dying in my throat as his mouth covers a nipple. I'm lost in the soft flicks of his tongue, the burn of his teeth, and the way he rocks me against him like I belong here. Like I'm made for the thick, hard length of him still trapped in his pants.

I'm sparking, a live wire, the friction and stimulation borderline unbearable. When he switches attention to my other breast, I mewl out my need.

He laughs with strain against my skin. "I know what

you want, and you can't have it yet. You're going to come at least twice before I fuck you senseless."

Holy hell. The filthy promise zips straight to my core. I clench on nothing, gasping at the ache.

Mindless, I beg.

"Please, Finn. Please."

He bites my breast, sending electric pain to mix with pleasure. I moan and yank his hair.

"You're fucking perfect," he whispers, relenting, letting me guide his face up. "How wet are you?"

"Find out for yourself."

His eyes smolder at the challenge and he wastes no time, setting me on my feet and yanking my jeans to my ankles. I squeal, half laughing and off-balance, as his hand dives between my legs and shoves my panties to the side. Two merciless fingers sink inside me, stretching and staking their claim.

A shuddering breath leaves his lips, currently grazing my forehead. "You're soaking. So small and tight. I'm afraid I'll break you in half. Afraid of how much I want to."

Why does that sound so good? I clench around him, my hips jerking, seeking relief for an arousal that's become excruciating. His fingers pump slowly, and his thumb begins to rub slow circles on my clit. My eyelids closing, I see stars falling in the blackness.

"Let go," he demands. "Take it."

Then I'm climaxing, searing pleasure exploding from my center, stealing my breath and igniting tiny storms down my limbs. I fall apart, messy and open—too open—and I forget everything except the desire to be myself.

"Finn," I gasp, "my name—"

Slow, drugging kisses trail down my neck as he guides me onto the bed. His shoes hit the floor, then pants, and *finally*, he settles between my open legs. Nothing between us but heat and the intimacy I feel—that I hope he feels, too.

Tattooed biceps tickle my vision as he grins down at me. Unfairly gorgeous, a god of art and fire. "I know your name, Grace."

I shake my head. "It's Calli."

He blinks, confusion clouding his eyes before they sharpen oddly, scanning my features like he's never seen me before. "Did you say *Calli?*"

I nod, biting my lip.

For a pregnant moment, his smile holds. When it fades, it's like watching the sun sink into endless night. His body stiffens above mine, fingers clenching into fists by my shoulders. Unease awakens inside me, slithering its way down my spine.

Finn shakes his head like he's waking from a dream. "No. Not possible. Please tell me you're joking."

I cover my naked chest with my arms, fighting the urge to shove him off me. "Grace is my middle name. I just thought—I wanted you to know—"

"Stop!"

The shout freezes me in place. Not because of the rage in it—of which there's miles—but because of the panic. Absolute, full-blown *panic*. Finn rockets to his feet, lurching backward until his back thuds against the wall. He slides to the ground, his eyes ablaze, and stares at me like I've sprouted horns.

I've made a grave mistake. One that could cost me my life.

Shaking with humiliation and blossoming fear, I scamper off the bed and grab my shirt, yanking it on, then pull on my jeans sans underwear. I have no idea where my panties are and I don't care. Snatching my glasses, shoes, and jacket, I edge toward the door.

Later, I'll fall apart about the *potentially* best night of my life blowing up in my face, and mourn the impending loss of the first place I've called home in years. But not now. Not yet. Not until I'm behind a locked door with my gun in hand.

I grab the doorknob, ready to bolt, but something

makes me look back. Misplaced nostalgia. A twisted need to see him one more time.

Finn sits against the wall with his head on his knees, his fingers clasped behind his neck. His whole body trembles. I fight an illogical urge to comfort him.

I shake my head. "Don't follow me, or I'll kill you."

He laughs, and it isn't pretty. Dark and half-deranged. When he looks up, the fury in his eyes makes my blood run cold.

"That's rich. But I guess that's how you operate, isn't it? Everywhere you go, you leave dead bodies."

Stunned, I sputter, "You don't know anything about me, asshole."

"Oh, that's where you're wrong. You're Callisto Avellino, and you're supposed to be dead."

5

Callisto

SUPPOSED TO BE DEAD.

How right he is.

Letting myself into the shadowy, silent house where I rent a room, I avoid the floorboards that creak as I make my way upstairs. Adrenaline in full swing, my skin crawls as I slip into my bedroom and lock the door, then freeze, listening to make sure I didn't wake Molly. Other than the usual groans of the old house, I hear nothing.

I don't turn on the light as I kneel next to my small bed and reach beneath for the comforting metal of the lock box. Huddled in the corner of the room, hidden from the door, I unlock the box with the small key I keep taped under the nightstand. Relief sags my shoulders as I lift the gun from its padded casing.

My uncle taught me to shoot, against the family's

wishes. That small rebellion wasn't what led to his assassination; rather, it was merely one straw among many that broke the camel's back. Or, more accurately, ignited my family's innate, vicious nature.

We live, love, and die for the family...

My heart thumps against my breastbone, reminding me that I'm alive on borrowed time. I knew it when I ran —that they'd find me someday—but it was worth it to live a little outside the family's rule.

Her rule.

Moonlight chases shadows across the floor, the tree outside my window bending and swaying in the wind. An owl hoots. My stomach rockets to my throat, my fingers spasming on the gun.

Now that there's some distance between me and what happened in the motel, I realize it's unlikely Finn was sent by my stepmother. He would have recognized me immediately, and his shock at discovering my identity had been genuine. But the fact is, he still knows who I am—my name, anyway—and the vitriol pouring out of him could only mean he has history with us.

With my blood-soaked, wicked family.

It also means I'm no longer safe in Solstice Bay.

Adrenaline makes way for thick, slow tears. I didn't lie to Fred—I do love it here, and the thought of leaving is a physical pain, mirroring the severing of the precious, tenuous roots I allowed to grow.

Caught between the forest and the sea, bordered to the north and south by uninhabited coastline, this sleepy town was my dream come true. I'd allowed myself to feel hope for my future. To believe I might live past thirty.

My mistake.

Roughly wiping my tears, I consider my next move. I don't have a valid passport, so leaving the country is off the table. I have no contacts outside those who'd like to see me six feet deep, no old friends I can call for help.

Mentally cataloging how much cash I've hoarded working at the bar, I surmise I can drive for a week straight before having to stop. Maybe I'll go south, to New Mexico or Arizona.

"Stupid. So stupid," I hiss at myself.

I should have dyed my hair. Cut it. Bought colored contacts. Done a thousand small things to protect myself. But I hadn't, vanity and naiveté my Achilles' heel.

I can almost hear my father's laughter, his mocking voice telling me, *"You're not smart enough to be on your own, my pampered princess. So shut your mouth and do as you're told."*

When all was said and done, I couldn't do what was required of me. And if there's one thing you don't do as an Avellino, it's run from your responsibility to the family.

SOUNDS from the kitchen downstairs jolt me awake. My neck spasms as I lift my head from the floor where I passed out just before dawn. Blinking the grit of dried tears from my eyes, I groan as I straighten my near-numb legs. At least I had the sense to put the gun back in the lockbox, though I left the lid open just in case.

I normally sleep right through Molly's morning routine of making tea and feeding the cats, but my sleep was restless, laced with darkness, poisoned by fear.

Sunlight streams through the window over my head, a stark contrast to my lingering nightmares. Last night's winds blew off the clouds, and though we're a good month away from spring, you wouldn't know it by the birds chirping and seagulls squawking.

But I won't be enjoying a nice run this morning. No lunch at my favorite café or sketching down at the cove before my evening shift. I'll be packing my belongings and sneaking out of town.

Pushing to my feet, I make my way into the en suite bathroom for a quick shower, then throw on jeans and a sweater. My duffel bag comes out of the back of the closet, and twenty minutes later, it holds everything I own in the world.

I hoped Molly would be gone by the time I was finished, but when I crack open my bedroom door, I can hear her humming downstairs.

With everything she's done for me, I dread having to bail without so much as a goodbye. Of course, the other option is to lie to her, but I'm too tired and heartsore to think of an excuse for my sudden departure. Either way, I'll be leaving her in the lurch at the bar. I'm not sure I can handle her disappointment on top of my own.

I shift, and an ancient floorboard groans.

"Grace, is that you? Just brewed a pot of coffee. How about oatmeal for breakfast?"

"Yes, sounds great, thank you."

Her kindness stings, a reminder that until meeting Molly, I'd never known the unconditional care of a mother. Something so simple for her—offering me coffee and oatmeal—is as foreign to me as hugs and lullabies.

I swallow the lump in my throat, grab my glasses from the nightstand, and make my way downstairs. By the time I reach the kitchen, there's a steaming bowl on the table for me with an assortment of toppings. Brown sugar. Cream. Strawberries, blueberries, and diced banana.

Molly turns from a counter with a mug of coffee,

nearly black—just how I like it. Her smile of welcome morphs to concern when she sees my face.

"Good God, Grace, what's wrong?" Depositing the mug on the table, she rushes to me, taking my shoulders in her hands. "Whatever it is, we'll handle it. Just tell me."

I wipe my welling eyes, mortified by my weakness and how pathetic it is that I fall apart so easily. Still, after all these years, after all I've seen and lived through, simple kindness undoes me.

"You're too soft, Little Bear. Harden your heart. Otherwise that viper will chew you up."

"And spit me out?"

My uncle's eyes soften with sadness. "No, little one. She'll swallow you down."

"And digest me? Gross."

He shakes his head, sighing at my eight-year-old attempt at humor, but I can tell he's laughing on the inside.

"All right, let's go another round. I want to see that target in shreds."

Lifting the rifle to my shoulder, I take aim.

"Grace!" Molly gives my shoulders a shake. "What's going on? You're starting to scare me."

"I'm leaving," I blurt. "I'm sorry, but I have to go. Today—now. I'm not safe here anymore, and I don't want to put you in danger."

Molly's eyes narrow and her lips form a thin line. "They found you?"

My heart jackknifes in shock. I've never spoken a word to her about why I'm actually here. All she knows is that I have no one and wanted a fresh start.

"What?" I gasp.

Her expression gentles. "Sit down and eat some breakfast. We should talk. And you can take off the glasses—I know you don't need them."

6

Finn

DEAD.

She's supposed to be dead.

Callisto Avellino went missing six years ago from her dorm at Brown University. Her room was torn apart. Police found traces of her blood and hair torn out by the roots. The entire nation assumed she'd been kidnapped for ransom.

But there was no ransom.

I remember the press conference three weeks after her disappearance. Her stepmother behind a podium, tearful as she pleaded for the public's help in finding her *fragile daughter*, and the other two girls, Callisto's half-sisters, sobbing nearby.

The heir to one of America's most controversial royal families was never found, and two years ago, the family held a massive funeral for her. Televised—of course—because Vivian Avellino wanted the nation to see her as a grieving mother hell-bent on justice for child killers.

The perfect platform from which to launch her political career.

She's supposed to be dead.

I can't fucking believe I didn't recognize Callisto immediately, glasses or not. Sure, she's changed in the six years she's been off the grid. No more sparkly veneer of youth and wealth. She's a woman now. Sharp edges and lush curves. Once pretty, now beautiful.

And I almost had sex with her.

I haven't even begun to process that fact, or the self-loathing I felt after, when I realized how scared she looked as she fled. Or how fucking perfect she felt in my arms.

If there's one thing to be grateful for in the grand fuckery of the last twelve hours, it's this morning's disaster making it impossible to think much about Callisto.

I barely slept, which made for a miserable visit with my mother, which is why I'm now dragging my feet up a walkway to a quaint, bright yellow house—to the only other person who might be able to help me get through to the stubborn matriarch of the McCowen family.

"Please be home," I mutter as I knock on the white door.

A few moments later, the door swings open on my aunt. Though it's been eight years since I last saw her, time has barely touched her. Tall and sturdy, she has crazy brown curls and big blue eyes with only the faintest of lines around them. Her mouth drops open at the sight of me.

"Finnegan McCowen, what the holy hell are you doing here?"

A tired smile tugs my lips. "Nice to see you too, Aunt Molly. Can I come in?"

She glances over her shoulder, then darts onto the porch and pulls the door closed. "No, actually. I have company."

"Ahh." I smirk. "Good for you."

"Not that kind of company, you dolt." She grabs my arm and drags me to the bench beside the door, shoving me down. Exactly like I'm five years old again and about to be put in a time-out.

"You do know I'm an adult now, right?" I mutter.

She settles beside me, angled toward me so she can scan my tired features like an X-ray machine. "You look grown, but not like an adult. Adults don't avoid their families for a decade."

"Christ." I drop my head into my hands. "I shouldn't have come."

"Oh, don't pout." She gives my shoulder an affectionate squeeze. "I'm glad you're here. You look like shit, though."

I heave a self-deprecating laugh. "Thanks. I feel like shit." Steeling myself, I meet her gaze. "I need your help."

Before the sentence is out, Molly's shaking her head. "Nuh-uh. I'm not mediating between you and your mother. That's your business."

My bubbling frustration boils over. "*Please*, Aunt Mol. This isn't a game, or some family squabble. If we don't stop them now—"

"I'm sorry, Finn," she interjects gravely. "I know you've suffered at the hands of the Avellinos, but Meredith suffered, too. She lost your father, too. I had a front-row seat to the heartbreak almost killing her. It was for you—you and your sisters—that she let go of the hate and chose forgiveness. You can't ask her to hate again."

The words burn, swallowed by the dark fury I've carried since I was eleven and watched my father's casket being lowered into the earth.

"He didn't even serve the whole sentence," I say, my gaze unfocused on the small, lovingly tended front yard.

"He's dead," my aunt says simply. "I'd say justice still found him."

My fingers curl into fists. I don't look at her, afraid the venom inside me will spill out, that she'll never look at me the same way after knowing what lives inside me.

"Am I the only one who doesn't want to see Vivian Avellino become the fucking Governor of California? She announced last week. It's all over the news!"

"No, you're not." The soft, wavering voice comes from behind Molly, where the front door stands open.

Callisto steps onto the porch, hugging a thick sweater over her chest. The glasses are gone. Her hair is in a messy topknot, her face clean of makeup. Dark shadows ring her eyes. A shaft of sunlight finds her face, and gold flares in her irises.

I'm on my feet before my brain fully processes the movement. "What the hell is *she* doing here?"

"Sit down," snaps my aunt. "If you can't behave yourself, Finnegan, you can leave. Calli is my guest."

My rage funnels to a savage point, directed at my aunt. "You know who she is? You've been harboring her? For how long?"

Molly's eyes narrow. "I'm not *harboring* anyone. She isn't a criminal. Quite the opposite."

"Bullshit," I snarl, slicing my gaze to Callisto. "What

about your high school boyfriend? David Whoever? I wonder if he'd counter your statement."

The gold in her eyes dims. I feel a pinch in the vicinity of my conscience, right before I realize she isn't hurt. She's furious.

"Who the hell do you think you are?" she seethes, her breath short, chest rising and falling in swift rhythm and momentarily distracting me. "Like I said last night—"

"Last night?" asks Molly, but Callisto's on a roll and doesn't hear her.

"You don't know anything about me! So you've read a few articles, watched some trashy exposés on nighttime TV?" She laughs, harsh and dry. "That makes you some kind of expert on me? On my family?"

I'm on my feet, the porch-railing creaking under my clenching fingers. "Your family is full of crooked elitists and murderers. You've got a lot of nerve coming here, staying with my aunt." I turn to Molly. "And you. What the fuck, Aunt Mol? Her father killed your brother-in-law. My *dad*."

Callisto goes pale, shoulders deflating. "I didn't know," she says, slanting a glance at Molly. "Not until a few minutes ago. I would never have—"

"Okay," snaps Molly. "That's enough, both of you.

Get your asses into the house before the neighborhood starts taking notes."

"I'm sorry," whispers Callisto aimlessly, then turns and slips through the front door.

When I don't follow, Molly growls, "Five seconds or I call your mother."

I drag my feet inside.

7

Callisto

I'VE DIED. This is Hell. And the Devil wears the face of a murdered man's son.

Did my father kill Finn's father? Maybe. Maybe not. But there's little doubt in my mind he was responsible. And if not him, another Avellino. My family is a deep-sea octopus, many-armed, all of us poisonous.

I don't remember much about the trial that put my father in prison. I was young, obsessed with dolls and ponies, and he was often away on business, so extended absences weren't unusual. The only time I was in the courtroom was the final day, and I later found out that Vivian gave me drugged milk so I stayed calm during the reading of the verdict. Her children—my younger sisters —stayed safe at home. They were insulated from the media storm, the cries of the victim's family, while I heard it and felt it all, albeit through a haze of codeine.

Even then, I was merely a pawn in their game.

Was Finn there, too, that day in the courtroom? He must have been, must have been cheering in victory as my father was guided out in handcuffs.

If he was, I could hardly blame him.

It hurts, thinking about how Finn and his family must have suffered eight years ago when my father was released. The sentence overturned on appeal. A technicality. Lies.

A gigantic payoff.

I wish there was something I could say to ease his pain —*I hate my father, too*—but really, I'm just as responsible as anyone. After all, I'm an Avellino. My blood is corrupt.

Molly and Finn are in the living room, their voices low and tense. I'm perched at the top of the stairs, caught between the desire to grab my duffel and run and the need to hear what they're saying.

"You don't know that."

"I do," insists Molly. "Until today, she had no idea who I was. She came to town a year ago, skinny as a stick and traumatized as all hell. I don't know what she's running from, but I can guess."

Finn scoffs. "You think, what, that her family tried to

silence her? Come on, Mol. The Avellinos are psychos, but they wouldn't kill one of their own."

Wrong.

Closing my eyes, I see my uncle's face. His tired eyes, bushy eyebrows, and stern mouth. The fear, the mania, and eventually, the resignation in him.

So much of what I saw while visiting my uncle as a child only makes sense now. Closed doors and whispered conversations in Italian. Cash exchanged in manila envelopes. The two, one-way plane tickets to Italy I found in his coat pocket when he sent me to fetch his phone.

He was planning to take me away.

One visit—one of the last before his death—he brought me to his workshop to clean and oil his guns. There was whiskey on his breath and a mad light in his eyes.

"I'll keep you safe, Calli. They won't ever find you, I promise."

This wasn't the first time he'd spoken this way. "Who?" I asked, not expecting an answer. But this time was different.

"Your father and that woman he married."

My hands stilled in their task and I gazed up at

*him, utterly confused. "But... they're my parents. Why
wouldn't you want them to find me?"*

*Midnight eyes glittered on me, dense with secrets.
My father had the same eyes. So did I. Molten black,
deepest bronze only in direct sunlight.*

*He tapped his temple, smearing oil near his
receding hairline. "Because of what's in your head."*

I trusted and loved my uncle.

But he scared me, too.

"I don't understand," I whispered.

*"Not now, but you will." He nodded at the scarred
table—my cue to get back to work.*

"Tell her to leave."

Finn's voice lifts downstairs, scattering my
thoughts.

"Not happening," comes Molly's calm reply. "Whatever reason she's here, it's a good one, and I won't turn
her out just because you're being a brat."

Finn groans. "Dammit, Mol."

"Now why don't you tell me what really brought you
here after all these years?"

He's silent for long moments, then, "I'm tired of
living a lie, pretending everything is fucking rainbows.
Dad's dead because of that family, and no one cares.
What's that famous quote? 'The only thing necessary for

the triumph of evil is for good men to do nothing'? I can't sit back and do nothing anymore."

"And the Bible says 'Judge not, and you will not be judged; condemn not, and you will not be condemned; forgive, and you will be forgiven.' Hate is a heavy burden to bear, Finn. It's changed you. You were such a wild, joyful child."

"Your dad being murdered changes you," he says rigidly.

"Of course it does, honey. I'm not saying you should forget the past. But you need to decide what you want from the future. What kind of life you want to live."

"One without Avellinos in the top levels of government."

She sighs. "Fine. Then do something. If it's revenge you want, use all that money you've earned taking pictures and hire investigators to dig up dirt on Vivian Avellino. If you really think she's a criminal, put a stop to her political aspirations."

My heart picks up speed. *Maybe...*

"I already hired people," replies Finn, and my rising hopes crash and burn. "Two, actually. Top-of-the-fuck-ing-line PIs. One of them disappeared and the other one came back with nothing, then promptly retired to a tropical island."

My head thuds against the stairwell wall. While I'm

not surprised, the reminder of what I escaped from is still shocking.

"That's suspect," murmurs Molly.

"You think?" Finn snaps. "Please, help me get through to Mom."

"That's why you came?" Molly's voice is hard and cold. "You want your mother to be some sort of figure-head for your anti-Avellino campaign?"

"Fuck, when you put it like that—"

"It sounds horrible, doesn't it? Because it is, Finnegan. Your mom is in a good place right now, and you want her to unearth all that pain just to satisfy your hate for Rafael Avellino? A dead man? Not happening. Don't make me bring your sisters into this."

"Aunt Mol—"

"I will protect this family," she declares, "even from you. Now get out of my house. I need to cool off before I say something I regret."

A few moments later, the front door slams.

"You can come down now, Calli."

My heart hammering, I descend the stairs to the living room. Molly stands near the picture window, gazing onto the street. Likely watching her nephew storm off.

"I really handed him his ass, didn't I?" she asks,

smiling sadly as she turns toward me. "Go ahead, ask me why."

"You said why. For your sister."

I look outside. Across the narrow lane, Finn gets into his rental car. He doesn't turn it on but merely sits there, staring out the windshield with his hands clenched on the wheel. And though I try not to feel anything, sympathy rises in me.

"That wasn't the real reason," says Molly on a pensive sigh. "Meredith would have no problem telling him no herself—if she ever gives him a chance to ask. He has some serious groveling to do before that even happens."

Surprised, I look at her. "Why, then?"

"Honestly? I don't know." Her troubled eyes meet mine. "The poor boy is hurting and I sent him away with angry words."

"You're scared," I tell her bluntly, glancing outside to see that Finn has driven away. "And you were right to discourage him. It's no accident his investigators failed. He doesn't have any idea what he's up against."

Molly gazes at me like she's seeing me for the first time. "Then it's all true? The Avellinos are modern-day mafia?"

I shrug, my stomach leaden. "Not really. I don't know. They might be worse."

She draws a slow breath. "If he keeps after this..."

I nod, confirming her worst fear.

"You have to talk to him, Calli. Please. Tell him whatever you have to. Make him drop this."

I think of my uncle, the fever in his eyes as he plotted against his family. Finn's eyes held the same light.

He won't stop until he's dead, and if I've learned anything in my life, it's that there's absolutely nothing I can say that will sway a man hell-bent on righteous revenge.

But I owe Molly, so I tell her, "I'll try."

8

Callisto

SOLSTICE BAY IS A SMALL TOWN, and there are only so many places to go. I check the motel first, but his car isn't there, so I drive through the center of town, then to the cove. It's not much—a small stretch of grass and a weathered stone bench sitting above a tiny, rocky inlet. The larger bay, which most of the town's economy depends on, is four miles south.

The weather has taken another turn, the winds picking back up. The sky is a distressed, gunmetal shade. No rain yet, but dark clouds sit ominously on the horizon.

Perfect for a doomed conversation.

Finn sits on the bench, elbows on his knees as he stares at the intersection of the sky and his thoughts.

I park behind his rental car and get out before I can

49

L.M. HALLORAN

talk myself out of what I'm doing. *It's for Molly. I owe her.*

But as I walk toward him, my hood up against the cold wind, I can't help but notice the broad swath of his back, the powerful shoulders, and I can't help remembering the way he kissed me, like he was staking his claim on more than my body.

By the time I reach him, I'm not cold anymore. Even though he hates me, is disgusted by my very existence. Even though he'll never touch me again... my body still wants to finish what we started last night.

He looks up as I enter his line of vision. Steeling myself, I meet his cold blue eyes. Sadly, the vitriol pouring out of him isn't the turn-off it should be.

I clear my throat. "Can we talk?"

"I don't have anything to say to you." Gravelly, tired voice, thick with resentment.

"Okay, but I'd still like for you to hear me out."

"About what, exactly?"

"My fucked-up family, for starters, and that going after them is a bad idea."

His eyes narrow. "Molly sent you."

I nod, then gesture to the bench. "May I?"

After a moment's hesitation, he scoots down—*way down*—until most of the bench is empty and he's perched on one corner. He's gone back to staring at the

50

horizon, a clear indicator that whatever I have to say won't affect him. Probably true, but I have to try.

Settling on the bench, I shift to face him, my gaze wandering shamelessly over his chiseled profile, the generous lips currently pressed into a thin line. *Why does he have to be so tragically beautiful?*

It takes effort to pull my gaze away, to focus my thoughts and decide what to tell him. I haven't spoken of the past in so many years, it feels odd—and frankly, frightening—to tell the truth.

A memory swells, hitting me like a wave.

"When I was eight, my uncle took me to visit my father in prison. My father was livid when he saw me. We—his children—weren't allowed to visit him. I thought it was because he didn't want us to see him in a position of weakness, but looking back I realize he was afraid. He and my uncle fought in the way they did—in hushed, rapid Italian. I didn't understand most of it, but what I did hear was the threat. My father told my uncle to *be careful on the slippery road.*"

"Where are you going with this?"

Tucking my shaking hands in my pockets, I continue, "Three weeks later, my uncle was dead from a supposedly senseless drive-by shooting."

More memories—the suited men showing up at my school, pulling me from class. The sympathy in my teacher's eyes. My stunned classmates. The flashing lights of paparazzi outside as I was guided into a car. My stepmother, waiting inside to break the news... and the small white envelope she handed to me, with two, one-way plane tickets inside.

A message that even at eight years old, I understood.

"No one talked about his death. There was no wake, no funeral, no reading of a will. One day he was there, and the next he was gone. Erased from the family."

"If your point is that the Avellinos are dangerous, you can stop talking. In case you've forgotten, they killed my dad."

Each word is a little zap of pain to my chest.

"I'm sorry, Finn. Truly I am." Looking up from my lap, I meet his stormy gaze. "I have three uncles, but Uncle Anthony was everything to me. He died because he was going to take me away, and he was arrogant enough to think no one would figure out what he was planning. After he was killed, I knew I would do everything in my power to get far, far away from them."

"Why did your uncle want to take you away?" The question is angry, like he's annoyed he feels compelled to ask.

Swallowing hard, I remind myself he can't possibly know how hard this is for me, to talk about the life I left behind. He wants answers, and rightfully so. But unfortunately, I don't have the ones he wants. The *whys* and *hows*.

"There are certain, um... responsibilities for the first-born child. Old-world, traditional stuff. Maintaining the family's pedigree through marriage, ensuring continued alliances, et cetera. Maybe Anthony knew I wasn't cut out for all that was expected of me. He was always saying I was too soft."

His gaze spears me. "They really are the mob, huh?"

"I don't really know. That word was never spoken, and God help you if you used it in my father's hearing." I pause, surprised by the twinge of longing for my father's gruff voice. "I think that's part of what makes them so dangerous—the idea that their power and wealth puts them above the law."

"Yeah, I've looked into their financials. The public stuff, anyway. Finance, oil, and real estate. All above-board." He scoffs. "But they're not, are they?"

Thinking of my uncle, I whisper, "No," then clear my throat. "And before you ask, I don't have some magical USB drive packed with incriminating evidence against my family. My stepmother never trusted me enough to include me in any of the family's business dealings."

"Why not?"

I should have known the question was coming, but it

still surprises me. Also surprising—the ease with which more truth spills out.

"I'm a spitting image of my mother, who died from an aneurism when I was a year old. My father loved her deeply. On her birthday every year, he'd get drunk and lock himself in his office for hours to look through old photo albums. A few times, he let me join him. Vivian put a stop to that. God, I still remember the yelling when those albums went missing."

Finn's lips part, and for a moment I expect him to offer sympathy. But then his gaze hardens.

Before he can speak, I tell him, "Behind her smiling, motherly public persona, Vivian is the worst of them all. If I hadn't been there when my father had his heart attack, I would have suspected she killed him."

"And now she wants to be a governor."

I nod, swallowing hard. "I wasn't shocked when the news broke. She's always had high aspirations. She likes to be seen and heard. And since she's head of the family now, she runs everything, can do whatever she wants."

"Your other uncles..." He trails off, but the question is clear.

"Sheep," I say, repeating what Uncle Ant told me long ago. "Raised to follow, not lead. No wives, no children. They're married to the family."

Finn broods silently. Waves crash below us—a

tumultuous suck and rush as the storm closes in. Absorbed in the ocean's song, I almost don't hear his soft question.

"Where have you been the last six years?"

Drifting. Hiding. Surviving.

I hedge, "I've lived in a lot of places."

Finn eyes me like he wants to press, but instead asks, "If you hadn't run, what would you be doing now?"

A hard question, and not a comfortable one to answer. "Sometimes I think if I'd stayed much longer, I would have become who they wanted me to be. The lifestyle is very... seductive to young women. I'd likely be married to a man of her choosing. Or maybe gone to law school, if that's what she wanted for me." I take a steadying breath. "Or, if I proved myself of no use to the family, I'd be dead for real. Probably of an accidental drug overdose. I lost a second cousin that way shortly after he came out as gay."

"Jesus," he hisses.

A sudden thought makes my stomach turn, pulling my gaze to his face. "When you hired those investigators, did you do it directly?"

He scans my wide eyes. "I'm not stupid. I did it through a dummy corporation that can't be traced back to me."

My relief mixes with appreciation for his cleverness. "Good. You're not on their radar, then."

The eerie sky makes the blue of his eyes so vivid I have to look away. They see too much but understand so little. I've given him the merest glimpse into the darkness. Enough, I hope, from deterring a nose-dive into the abyss.

Then he says, "I'm not going to quit."

I close my eyes, seeking relief from the icy wind, but also to hide my reaction to his words.

"Please," I murmur. "Don't do this."

Until now, I hadn't realized this wasn't just about what Molly wanted, but about what I want, as well. I barely know this man, but I don't want him anywhere near my murderous family. They will end him, quietly and convincingly. A freak accident. Being in the wrong place at the wrong time. An event that could never be traced back to the family.

I've seen it too many times before.

"I've tried, you know," he says, muted voice almost lost in the wind, "to forgive. Or at least to accept and move on like my mom and sisters have. But there's something inside me that can't let go. My father was the same. Mom used to call him Sir Charles as a joke, because he had this inflexible nobility to him. He was the guy who stood up—every time—in defense of the defenseless, with no care for his own safety."

A dim memory surfaces. "He was a firefighter, right? A chief?"

Finn nods. "He was a good man. The best kind of man, a hero. And look where it got him. So like I said, I'm not going to stop."

"You're not like them, Finn. This isn't what your dad would have wanted."

The second the words are out, I know I've made a mistake.

He stands, facing me with his shoulders bunched and rage pouring out of him. "You don't know shit about what he would have wanted, Callisto *Avellino*, and you don't know shit about me. But I'll let you in on a little secret."

I flinch as he leans down, then freeze as his lips graze my forehead.

"I'm no fucking hero, princess, and neither are you."

9

Finn

THE SECOND TIME I scare Callisto makes me feel no better than the first. Worse, even, because when she told me about what happened to her uncle, and I could see the old, familiar grief in her eyes, I was *still* an asshole to her.

I could blame jet lag, or the less-than-warm receptions from my mom and aunt, but the truth is more basic. And more damning.

I still want to sink my teeth into her skin and rut into her body like a caveman. I have no idea why, but if anything, I want her *more* now that I know who she is. Like she's a focal point my body and mind can finally agree on, a merging of my inner life with my physical needs.

I loathe everything she comes from and represents,

and her *I'm an innocent victim* act makes me want to throw something. Because it has to be an act. No way she grew up suckling at the Avellino teat and came out halfway decent. In fact, maybe she's a Trojan horse. A game piece on the Avellino chess board, sent to monitor my mom and make sure she doesn't make waves for Vivian's upcoming campaign.

The thought sends a chill down my spine. If it's true, then my actions today might have put my mom in danger. For the first time, I'm relieved she told me to kick rocks, because it means there's nothing for Callisto to report.

If, in fact, she's a spy.

I'm so tired, facts are starting to bleed into feelings and feelings into facts.

Regardless of whether Callisto was telling me the truth or not, I know my aunt was right to warn me away from this path. Going after the Avellinos is a million shades of Bad Idea. I'm not crazy. I know this could—probably will—end badly. But I'm resigned to the fact there's nothing anyone can say to stop me. One thing I have in common with my dad, apparently. Stubbornness. Or maybe unfailing dedication to a cause, no matter how unworthy it may be.

Please don't go to the deposition today. My mother had begged him to leave it alone. To let someone else take the risk. But he still went. Sir Charles, ready and able to fight the good fight, whether or not it put a blazing target on his back.

Sometimes, I hate my father just as much as the Avellinos. Hate him for always doing the right thing. For putting justice above his family. For ignoring all the warnings and the danger when the law demanded his testimony for the crime he'd uncovered.

I always knew this would be my path. While most of my friends are married and starting families, I remain alone.

I won't do to a family what my dad did to ours.

AFTER LEAVING Callisto at the cove, I head back to the motel. I need a shower and at least five hours of sleep. Mentally, I'm off the fucking rails.

Hot water on my stiff shoulders goes a long way to making me feel normal again—or at least more like myself. By the time I close the curtains and crawl into bed, I've decided that even though I'd love to ride the *Callisto as Trojan horse* train, I'm being paranoid.

On the off chance Vivian Avellino even *remembers* my mother, there's no way she'd orchestrate a long game like faking the death of her stepdaughter to use her as bait in a revenge plot.

Not only is it ridiculous, instinct tells me Callisto's not that good of an actress. And my gut is rarely wrong.

As a photographer, I'm essentially a highly paid voyeur, and I've been doing it a long time. It's why I'm so successful—reading people comes naturally. Even in the most resistant client, I can dig past the superficial layers and find a spark of honest emotion. Longing. Lust. Hope. Confusion. Anger...

Fear.

Callisto is afraid of her family, that much I know. It's no surprise her uncle tried to toughen her up by telling her she was too weak. In the world she comes from, goodness is a flower destined to be overcome by weeds, while traits like kindness, charity, compassion are merely tools to advance an agenda.

Vivian Avellino, on the other hand, is a stellar actress, her propaganda flawless. Last year she donated a wing to a children's hospital and funded the construction of several youth centers in underprivileged communities. Every year, she donates millions to various organizations. A pittance of the family's actual worth. A payoff to the public so they don't look harder at the *how* or *why*.

I lied to my aunt when she asked what my investigators turned up. The man who died—he found something. Something big enough to prompt his murder. His last voicemail to me was urgent, his voice thick with fear.

We've got 'em. Call me back.

I did, but it was too late.

I'll find out what he discovered no matter the cost. Because as much as the old hate burns unquenched inside me, I'm tired, too. Tired of living with this darkness. Of pretending everything's fine. Of photoshoots, screwing strangers, and partying as I travel the world like I don't have a care.

If I have to be like the Avellinos in order to destroy them, that's a price I'll pay.

I'll be the villain.

I'll be a better one.

10

Callisto

SOMETIMES THE WORLD CLEARS UP. All the way up to blinding clarity. And you realize you've been looking at life through a foggy lens. What you thought was important isn't. Actions you believed justified weren't.

I'm no hero, and neither are you.

After Finn left me at the cove, I retreated to the only other place I knew would give me the peace and quiet I needed to think.

Mud squelches beneath my sneakers, the worn trail crowded on either side by trees: pine and spruce, hemlock and fir. Ancient and tempered by the sea, they offer me a portal to a timeless world. A world in which I am right-sized. No better or worse, weaker or stronger. Here, in the pause between breaths, I'm forcibly separated from all my preconceptions and biases toward life and more profoundly, myself.

The air is still, heavier and warmer than at the coast. It seeps through my pores, into my blood and mind. Calming. Stabilizing.

And then it happens.

The hazy world clears up, allowing space for Finn's words—his rage and pain—to hit me like a flash fire and vaporize the shell of my delusion. Into the void rises doubt. Once, I believed it was better to save myself and leave my little sisters behind, than to stay and suffer. Or, God forbid, fight the family and fail, like my cousin who just wanted the freedom to love who he chose.

My uncle loved me, wanted to protect me, but he also crippled me. He convinced me I was weak. That the tide of the family was impossible to turn, their influence so vast no one person could stand against it. That my options were to either surrender or escape. But Finn is absolutely right. I'm no hero—I'm a coward.

Confusion battles clarity in a spin cycle of thoughts.

Maybe he is the only one willing to do the right thing.

He's going to get himself killed.

What's the moral price of looking the other way as Vivian widens the net of her power?

There's no stopping her.

She's not going to be satisfied until she's forming policy in Washington, DC.

How many deaths has she orchestrated? How many bribes, under-the-table transaction, and illegal dealings?

Too many.

With my blinders torn off, childhood memories lift from my subconscious, gaining substance and detail as they feed on my newfound focus. Memories I've spent years burying, that bring with them equal parts shame and shock.

And they chill me to my bones.

One evening after my father was arrested, I heard voices in his office and snuck close to listen. My uncle Franco was in the middle of telling my stepmother that the judge in my father's trial couldn't be bought. He was angry. Desperate. But what struck me most was Vivian's response. I expected her to demand he find a way, to express her own frustration... but she didn't. She didn't say anything at all, and I crept away from the open office door before any of the staff could spot me and haul me inside for punishment.

Another time, a filing cabinet in the basement had been left unlocked and ajar. Inside were hundreds of manila files with names printed neatly on them in my father's handwriting. I wasn't so lucky that time. Vivian found me as I was lifting the first file, and she slapped me so hard I had a bruise on my cheek for a week.

After the conviction and sentencing, there were more changes. Or maybe I was merely old enough to start noticing things that had been happening for years. There were midnight meetings with mean-looking men in the soundproofed basement. Ritzy cocktail parties with a slew of famous faces that my sisters and I weren't allowed to attend. Weekend pool parties with pretty young girls on my uncles' arms. Those same girls, weeping and bereft, whisked away in private cars the next morning.

I can still see my stepmother's smile, small and victorious, whenever she caught me where I wasn't supposed to be. And I remember well the resulting isolation and depravation. Long days spent locked in my bedroom—a prison of fancy dolls, ruffled curtains, and loneliness.

I was older, maybe twelve, when our longtime nanny, Adele, was fired. She begged and wept on the front stoop as her belongings were tossed into the driveway. I hid in a nearby drawing room, listening to her ramble, her voice high and thick with tears. *I won't tell a soul. I swear it, Mrs. Avellino. Please, don't take me from the children.*

For the first time since my youth, I wonder what happened to her. Whether she's alive.

My jaded inner voice answers easily enough: *You know she isn't.*

I walk for another hour, a spectator to my emotional evolution, my thoughts falling like the raindrops on the canopy above. *Drip, drip...* they hit me and are absorbed.

Feeding a new version of myself.

Changing me.

———

"YOU OKAY, GRACE?" asks my current patron, a regular whose craggy face is pinched in a frown. "You're lookin' more pale than usual."

"She's fine," Molly says, her voice so close and unexpected that my fingers spasm on the glass I'm refilling from a tap.

Molly deftly takes over the pour and murmurs, "Why don't you head home a little early. It's a slow night." She hands the pint to the customer, who nods and heads back to his friends.

"I'm sorry," I say reflexively.

Her brows lift. "For what?"

My smile wobbles but holds. "Be honest—I'm a horrible bartender."

She laughs. "You really are. I've never dealt with so much broken glass and wasted alcohol in my life. But no one here cares." She gestures behind her to the sparsely populated bar. "We love our misfits in Solstice Bay. Hell, the town was founded by outcasts who wanted a place to call their own. Besides, we've had quite a day, haven't we?"

I nod, emotion clogging my throat. "You never answered me this morning—if you knew who I was, why did you take me in? My family has caused yours so much pain. I just... I don't understand."

She squeezes my shoulder gently. "In my experience, the past is never as important as we think it is. It's what we do now that matters. Everyone needs a little help sometimes, and I'm just glad fate brought you here. And don't forget—I happen to be an excellent judge of character, and you, my dear, have a good heart. One of the best." She winks. "Plus, my customers love a pretty face."

I laugh, grateful for the humor. I was close to embarrassing myself with tears.

A quick glance around the bar tells me Molly's right —I'm really not needed. "I think I will head home," I say after a moment. "I need some time to get my head around... everything."

To find the courage I need to leave you.

"Good." She grabs a rag, then asks without looking at

me, "You'll be there when I wake up tomorrow, won't you?"

My heart jolts. "Yes, of course," I lie, glad I can't see her eyes.

"See you in the morning, then. Oh, and, Grace?"

"Yes?"

She glances over her shoulder. "You're not alone anymore. You have a home, and, if you want it, a family."

"Thank you, Molly," I whisper, then flee to the back before the first tear falls.

By the time I arrive home, my eyes are dry and my limbs buzz. The conviction I found on my walk today has blossomed, enveloping me with frenetic purpose.

The Avellinos are a tribe of moral thieves, leeching goodness from the world. I'll never be like Vivian and my uncles, or even my father. Cruel and ruthless. Ambitious to the point of tyranny.

But maybe I don't have to be.

Maybe I can be *better*.

11

Finn

I'M JOLTED from sleep by someone pounding on my motel door. Blinking groggily, I take in the light behind the curtains, which is brighter than it should be. A glance at the clock has me doing a double take.

It's seven thirty in the morning. I slept close to eighteen hours.

"Finnegan McCowen, I know you're in there!"

My aunt's voice is shrill, with an edge of panic. Throwing off the covers, I stumble to my feet.

"Coming!" I bark, wincing at the pins and needles in my feet as I lumber to the door. The chain is barely free when the door flies inward. I lurch backward to avoid being hit. "Whoa! What the hell?"

Molly storms into the dim room, then spins toward

me in a flurry of righteous rage. "What the hell did you say to her?"

I blink. My eyes hurt. My brain feels like Swiss cheese.

"What?"

"She's gone! *Gone!* Left her cell phone and most of her things. So tell me what you said to her to make her run!"

Callisto.

A heady surge of adrenaline wakes me right the fuck up.

"What do you mean, she's gone?" I demand, snatching my discarded jeans off the floor and yanking them on over my boxers. "And why do you think it's my fault? I didn't threaten her or anything."

Only, I kind of did. I was a major dick and probably spooked her into leaving town.

"She told me she'd be here in the morning," says my aunt, and alarmingly, she looks like she's about to cry. She sits heavily on the foot of the bed. "She has no one, Finn. I've never met anyone so alone in the world as that poor girl."

The gravity of the situation, and my aunt's distress, sinks in. Dropping onto the bed beside her, I lower my head into my hands.

"You're right. This is totally my fault. I basically told

her to fuck off and that I was going after her family." Turning my head, I meet Molly's red-rimmed eyes. "She won't warn them, will she?"

Her eyes widen with shock, then narrow to slits of anger. "I love you, Finn, because you're blood and I remember changing your shitty diapers and how sweet you were as a kid, but right now I don't much like the man you've become."

Neither do I.

I swallow my pride and say, "I'm sorry. I shouldn't have said that."

"Damn right, you shouldn't have. Callisto has suffered just as much, if not more, than you have at the hands of her family. And for some miraculous reason, she's managed to raise herself into a kind, compassionate young woman. Don't you forget that. She may be a gentle soul, but she has a warrior's heart."

Thinking of Callisto's dark eyes, I hesitate over my next words. "She's really scared of them, isn't she?"

"Yes."

It suddenly hits me that my chances of seeing Callisto again are slim to none. She successfully staged her own death and has been presumed dead for the last six years. Clearly, she knows how to disappear.

The thought of never seeing her enigmatic eyes again is more disturbing than I care to admit.

"Where do you think she'll go?" I finally ask.

Molly sighs. "Somewhere far away from here."

From you.

The unspoken words send a flush of shame through me. I bow my head. "I fucked up, Mol."

After a long pause, she grabs my hand and squeezes it tightly. "I know. And I also know Calli's her own woman and makes her own decisions. A part of me always knew we wouldn't be lucky enough to keep her in Solstice Bay. I'm going to miss her something fierce."

With every word, I deflate further. Thoughts of Callisto, alone on the road, nowhere to go, no friends to speak of... Fuck, it hurts. I feel responsible. Helpless. Were he alive, my dad would have some strong words for me about how I treated her.

Releasing me, Molly swipes the tears from her face and stands. "Put a damn shirt on. If we're going after the Avellinos, we need a plan."

My jaw unhinges. *"What?"*

Defiance sparks in her eyes. "Calli is the closest thing to a daughter I'll ever have, and the only way she'll be free in this world is if the Avellinos are brought to heel. So we're going to do just that."

I keep gaping.

Molly smiles, but not in humor. "Family is everything, isn't it? You need to read this."

She lifts her hand, a thick square of folded white paper between her fingers. I reach for it, gripped by sudden foreboding. I'm not sure I want to know what's inside it. From the look on Molly's face, it's something that will change me.

Change everything.

My fingers tingle, like they're waking from sleep, as I unfold the page filled with graceful, slanted handwriting.

Molly,

For years, I drifted across the country looking for something I couldn't define. That is, I couldn't define it until I found you and Solstice Bay. I was looking for a home. Thank you for giving me what money could never buy—acceptance, understanding, and love. I'm sorry I never told you how much your kindness meant to me.

You healed a part of my heart I didn't know was broken. You also gave me the courage to finally fix the rest.

When I ran, I thought I was doing the right thing. But I was young and selfish, and I sacrificed my innocent sisters to save myself. I can't do it anymore— live this half-life caught between denial and regret. I've realized that as long as I linger in the past, I'll never have a future.

I guess I have your nephew to thank for the final push. Please don't blame him. He's not at fault, just another victim of my family. And honestly, I'm grateful to him. He made me realize that sometimes, all it takes to change everything is one person.

If something happens to me, please let it go. This is my choice, and I know exactly what I'm facing.

I'm not afraid anymore. You gave me a home. That's all I ever wanted, and nothing—no one—can take that away from me.

Love,
Calli

12

Callisto

I ALMOST DON'T MAKE it. At least a hundred times, I nearly turn the car around on the sixteen-plus-hour drive to Los Angeles.

When I wrote the letter for Molly, I told the truth at the time—I wasn't afraid. Too bad bravery isn't a switch you can flip and lock in place. Instead, it's rolling waves. Courage lives at the foamy peaks; fear in every trough.

I now understand what people talk about when they describe walking toward clear and present danger. The battle of the mind over growing pulses of fear. The urgency in the body to run the other way, toward safety, and the effects of sustained adrenaline.

But I make it. A menial victory to anyone else is a monumental one for me.

I'm not running anymore.

It's late, after nine, by the time I arrive at Police Headquarters in downtown L.A.

I find a spot in the parking lot and turn off the car. *This is it.* My ass and legs are numb, and my mouth tastes like metal and stale coffee. A quick glance in the visor mirror shows my bloodshot eyes framed by half-moon shadows, and pale—too pale—skin. Even my lips are white. I look weak. Anemic.

Flipping up the visor, I stare at the dauntingly modern building ahead, and everything slams into me and it's all suddenly real. Every survival instinct I have screams at me to stop what I'm doing. Turn on the car and get the hell out of here.

My heart pounds a staccato rhythm in my ears as I open the car door and get out. Another small victory of mind over matter.

I can do this.

I am brave.

I will prove them all wrong.

The asphalt beneath my sneakers radiates heat as I walk toward the building. Winter has a different definition in Southern California, and longing for the misty cold of Solstice Bay momentarily grips me.

I wonder if I'll ever see the town—the only place that ever felt like home—again. Or have morning coffee with Molly again. Or sit on the bench overlooking the cove and doodle in my sketchbook or read a book.

Life was simpler two days ago.

I approach the wall of glass, angling for the doors. A woman is leaving, talking rapidly into her cell phone. Business attire and a briefcase. *Lawyer.* Head down, I slip past her into the lobby.

As I approach the main counter, the seated officer looks up. "Can I help you?"

His sharp gaze scans my face, a frown deepening the lines on his forehead. He's older—mid-fifties—which means he remembers well the media storm after my suspected death. He knows my face, and he's struggling to comprehend why I look like a dead girl.

"Yes." My voice comes out as a whisper. I clear my throat and try again. "Yes. I need to speak with someone about a missing person."

His gaze veers to a computer screen. "What's the name?"

The hilarity of the moment hits me, and I almost laugh. "It's me, actually. I'm the missing person. Callisto Avellino."

The name in my mouth feels displaced, like it belongs to someone else. And it does. It belongs to the person I used to be. The person I killed so she could be free of the life that was smothering her.

I haven't been her—*Callisto*—for years. Until yesterday.

Until right now.

Oddly, it feels good. Powerful. Like I'm reclaiming a part of myself I sacrificed against my will.

Recognition slowly dawns on the officer's face, draining the color from his ruddy complexion. Shooting to his feet, he lifts a beseeching hand. "Please, stay right there."

He fumbles for the phone.

Showtime.

"AND YOU DON'T REMEMBER anything else about your abduction or the following weeks in which you were held captive?"

The shrewd eyes of Detective Francis Wilson narrow on my face as she looks up from her notepad.

She's skeptical of my story. Any decent detective would be. But I spent most of the drive crafting it, repeating it, and embracing it, that when it comes out, it feels true.

Another life lesson courtesy of my family—if your lie is close to the truth, all it takes for people to believe it is for *you* to believe it.

"No, I don't," I tell her. "All I remember is waking up in a field one day with blood all over me and no idea how I got there. Or who I was."

"Tell me again why didn't you go to the police? Or a hospital?"

"I was terrified, Detective. In shock. All I knew was that someone was looking for me and I needed to run. I swear to you, I didn't remember anything until a few months ago. It started with dreams, then flashes of memories and faces. Yesterday I woke up and remembered who I was. I came straight here."

The tears welling in my eyes are real, because the last words, at least, are true.

She leans back in her chair with a sigh and closes the notepad. "Callisto—"

"Call me Calli."

"Calli, I'll be frank. I don't think you're telling me the whole truth. You've been through a harrowing experience, and I understand it might be difficult to talk about. I'd like to get you checked out by a doctor, and potentially meet with a—"

The door of the interview room rattles as someone pounds on it. Before Detective Wilson is halfway out of her chair, it opens. I stand just as a man in a custom suit strolls inside.

I recognize him immediately.

"This interview is over," snaps Hugo Barnes, long-time lawyer for my family. His flat gray eyes land on me. There's no emotion in them; not because he isn't shocked to see me, which he likely is, but because he's paid handsomely to remain stoic during all manner of crises.

Behind Hugo stands another detective. He shakes his head at Detective Wilson, whose pinched expression tells me she's gearing up for a fight.

"Calli, good to see you," croons Hugo. "I'm sorry I couldn't be here sooner to spare you this indignity. Come with me, please."

Detective Wilson stares at him with contempt. "Calli is the victim of a crime, Mr. Barnes. She walked into the building of her own accord, and it's our job to find out what happened to her so her abductor can be brought to justice. I can't do that without—"

"Yes, yes," interrupts Hugo in a bored tone. "You have my assurances that she'll be entirely forthcoming with any ongoing investigation. At this time, however, it is the wishes of my client's family that she be brought home immediately." His voice lowers, edged with ice. "Or do you want to explain to your superiors—and every news outlet in the country—why you're preventing the decade's most anticipated homecoming?"

The other detective rolls his eyes. Wilson glances at

me, her gaze probing. "Do you want to leave with this man, Calli?" she asks softly, a thread of steel in her voice.

She knows.

Somehow, this woman knows, or suspects, that the Avellinos aren't the shining example of goodness they pretend to be. Perhaps she wonders if they might have had something to do with my abduction themselves.

For a moment, I consider staying and telling her everything. The actual truth. Why I ran and what I'm afraid of. But without any real evidence to give her, I might as well tie nooses around both our necks.

"Yes, I'd like to go home," I say in the firmest tone I can manage. "I want to see my sisters and stepmom."

She scans my face for another moment.

"Are we done?" asks Hugo.

The other detective says, "You're free to go, Ms. Avellino."

Wilson tries one more time. "She needs to see a doctor. We'd like to compare past and present medical records."

Hugo waves away her words. "She'll see the family doctor, of course, and we'll disclose all necessary information."

I don't miss the subtext—they'll disclose what *they* deem necessary—and neither does Wilson, who flushes an angry red.

"Mr. Barnes, I don't think you understand the gravity of the situation. Obviously the case of Callisto's disappearance has been reopened. If I could speak with Vivian Avellino—"

"Mrs. Avellino has no comment at this time." Hugo's reptilian eyes fix on me. "All she wants is to welcome her stepdaughter home."

I'm sure she does.

I turn to Detective Wilson. "Thank you for being so kind and listening to me. I'm sorry I wasn't more help."

She extends her card. "If you remember anything else, and I mean *anything*, please give me a call." After I've taken it, she steps back, a professional mask sliding into place as she looks at Hugo. "My partner and I will be in touch. I'm sure Mrs. Avellino wants the person who abducted her stepdaughter behind bars as much as we do."

Hugo nods, ignoring the implied barb, and gestures me toward the door. A small, oily smile tilts his thin lips.

"After you."

13

Callisto

A BLACK TOWN car idles outside the department. Hugo ushers me into the backseat, then slides in beside me.

"My car—"

"Is not our priority at the moment."

The door closes and the sounds of traffic outside fade to a hum. Hugo fastens his seatbelt, waits to me to fasten mine, then nods at the driver.

As we pull away from the building, Hugo tugs at his tie, loosening it around his neck. His cologne is overpowering, his annoyance clear in the set of his narrow shoulders.

"What on earth were you thinking, walking into the damn police department?" he hisses. "Why didn't you just come to the house? And where the fuck have you been for six years? We don't like surprises, Calli."

We, but we both know he means Vivian.

"I had amnesia," I tell him indignantly. "Probably from the trauma of someone abducting me, keeping me drugged in a basement for weeks, then bashing me on the head and dumping me in a field to die."

Hugo stares at me appraisingly, one thin eyebrow raised. "My, my, someone's grown a backbone."

I snort. "Yeah, well, I spent years not knowing who I was or where I came from. I guess you could say I learned everything no one ever taught me about survival in the real world."

After a pregnant silence, Hugo coughs. "I have to ask, were you forced to... or rather, did you, you know, to earn money—"

"No," I snap, eyeing him with disgust. "I didn't prostitute myself. This conversation is over. I don't want to talk about it, and when I do, it definitely won't be with you. I'd like to see my family, take a long bath, drink a bottle of champagne, and forget the last six years."

Hugo's phone rings and he answers. "Yes, I have her —Twenty-five minutes or less—Uh-huh—Don't worry about that, Vivian—Of course, we'll spin it however we want to." He glances at me. "No—You'll see for yourself —That's fine."

He hangs up and fiddles with his cuff links. "Your stepmother is beyond excited to see you, my dear. But your timing is shit. A word of advice? Behave as you were raised to, or your homecoming won't be everything you hope it to be."

I settle back in my seat, oddly calm in the face of the veiled threat. *Be the doormat you were before. Stay in line. Behave.*

In the reflection of the window, I see my small smile. *Not gonna happen.*

IN THE HILLS of affluent Calabasas, the town car approaches iron gates and they slide open on a cobblestone driveway lined with trimmed hedges. At the end, seated like a fat monarch with his hands out, is the house my father bought Vivian in their first year of marriage.

The palatial, Spanish reconstruction glows from within. Outside, hundreds of tasteful landscape lights bathe the exterior. Above the red-tile roof, the evening sky is starless and expansive, punctuated only by the shadowed, spiked heads of palms.

The car veers in a smooth arc around a gaudy, imported marble fountain and comes to a stop before the oversized front door.

Hugo exits the car with me, leading the way toward the front door, which opens as we approach it. Light spills out, along with rosewater perfume and my smiling stepmother.

"Callisto!" she gasps, rushing down the steps in a flurry of silk, pearls, and surgically enhanced beauty to take me in her skeletal arms. "My sweet girl, God be praised, He brought you back to us at last. How I wish your father could be here!"

Her too-tight embrace makes my skin crawl. It only takes a moment for me to find the hired photographer standing behind a nearby row of bushes. No doubt he captured every moment of her graceful flight from the house to me, as well as the tears on her face, likely courtesy of eye drops.

"I'm so glad to be home," I say, then extricate myself from her grip to look toward the empty foyer. "Where are Ellie and Lizzie?"

Vivian ignores me, tucking her arm in mine and pulling me into the gilded foyer with its huge portrait of my father that, with one glance, I still don't think resembles him. Hugo follows us in, closing the door with a resounding thump. My stepmother releases me to pat the damp skin beneath her eyes.

"Eleanor will drive up from UCLA in the morning, and it's late, so Elizabeth is sleeping. She'll greet you tomorrow." Her voice has dropped its saccharine pretense, reverting to the crisp tones I remember well.

I nod, my face carefully blank.

"Your old room has been repurposed, so I had the staff make up a guest room for you. If you're hungry now, you can help yourself to whatever's in the kitchen. When you're finished, I'd like to see you in my office."

"I'm not hungry, thank you."

After a pause in which her dark green eyes scan my face, she looks pointedly at Hugo. The fine fabric of his suit whispers as he takes a step forward and clears his throat.

"The police would like a current medical exam to compare to old records."

Vivian nods. "Very well. What else?"

"Enzo is scheduling interviews with the usual morning shows for next week." His gaze slides to me. "Long enough to decide how to... present everything."

"Good. That will be all for this evening, Hugo. We'll reconvene at three sharp tomorrow afternoon."

Hugo takes the cue and leaves. As the front door shuts, a maid darts from an adjoining room to lock it.

"Come with me, Callisto. We need to talk." Expecting my compliance, she moves toward the hallway, high heels rapping sharply on tile.

"I'd like to take a shower and go to bed. We can talk in the morning."

She jerks to a stop, her head swiveling toward me, eyes narrowed to glittering slits. "Excuse me?"

"I'm sorry, but I'm exhausted. I've been driving the better part of three days." I gesture at the elegant space around us. "Honestly, I'm at my emotional max right now."

"You've changed," she states flatly.

You haven't.

Since now isn't the time to start the real game, I offer a placating smile. "I've been through a lot, and I'm overwhelmed with finally being home. I hope you understand."

Enhanced lips curve in a facsimile of a smile. "Of course. Get a good night's rest. I'll see you in my office no later than eight tomorrow."

It's not a question, but I say, "I'll be there."

Her shrewd eyes appraise me, but no matter how good an actress she is or how much Botox lives in her smooth forehead, I can tell I've rattled her. Unable to help myself, I close the distance between us and hug her like she's the mother I wanted, not the monster I loathe.

Because the goal isn't for her to see me as an opponent.

"I've missed you so much," I whisper into her soft

blond hair. Drawing away, I sniff back nonexistent tears. "I've missed everyone and everything about my life. We have so much catching up to do."

I've shocked her—that much is clear—but she recovers swiftly. "Yes, we do." For a moment, I think I see genuine feeling in her eyes. Then she blinks and steps back. "Sleep well. I'll see you in the morning."

She glides away, but pauses to turn back. Tears—real ones—shimmer in her eyes. "Welcome home."

I stare after her until soft footsteps alert me to a presence. The same maid who locked the door appears beside me. She's younger than I thought, mid-thirties, with a kind face and downcast eyes.

"I can escort you to your room now, miss," she says in a soft accent.

"Thank you. What's your name?"

Her eyes flicker up. "Selina."

"Thank you, Selina. I'm Calli."

"I know," she whispers. "Welcome back, miss. Please, follow me."

Five minutes later, with a locked door at my back and a richly appointed guest suite before me, I sink to the hardwood floor and bite my knuckle against a scream containing all the emotion I've kept locked away. Silent tears leak out, an overflow of repressed fear, doubt, and bone-deep fatigue.

Eventually I make it to the bathroom, then the bed, crawling beneath the smooth, pressed sheets fully clothed. I pass out in seconds, only to dream an old dream—an endless loop of being chased, captured, and locked in a windowless cell with fancy dolls wearing faces of the dead.

14

Finn

"TURN IT UP."

Molly jabs her finger into the remote, cranking up the volume on the television. We listen in silence as CNN relays Callisto Avellino's miraculous return to her family. We'd surmised from the letter that she was headed back to them, but hearing that she actually did it? It makes me question her sanity along with her motives.

As photographs of Vivian Avellino welcoming her stepdaughter home parade across the screen, Molly makes a soft sound of anguish. Even I flinch. It's a bit like watching a Venus flytrap close around an unsuspecting insect. As the anchor babbles on, I stare at a pale slice of Callisto's face, her chin tucked on Vivian's shoulder. She looks numb, and my mind flashes back to the same blankness I saw on her face in the courtroom all those years ago.

What was she thinking in that moment? Was a part of her happy to be there, back in the dark fold of her family? Relieved?

I can't help the doubts I still have about Callisto's motives. Despite the seeming sincerity of her letter to Molly, something inside me rebels against the idea of trusting her. I know well how deeply the threads of childhood experience root, how subtly they can guide us as adults.

It's not rocket science to assume that Callisto's childhood left its mark on her in ways she might not fully understand. Or for that matter, have control over.

"What do you think she plans to do?" I ask as a commercial takes over the screen.

Molly shakes her head. She laughs, a little shrilly. "All I can imagine is her in a burglar costume with a flashlight in her mouth, looking through desk drawers in the dark. I have no idea what her intentions are, or how she plans to expose her family. But I know she's not safe." Her wide eyes find mine. "I'm scared for her."

"I know." Propping my elbows on my knees, I scrub my face with my hands. "I haven't told you everything, Mol, about what my PI turned up."

She jerks. "Tell me."

So I fill her in, detailing the investigator's voicemail, that he found something incriminating and died for it. Molly listens with wide eyes.

"We need to tell the police," she says when I'm finished. "I know Rafael's sentence being overturned gave you a bad taste in your mouth, but there are honest people in law enforcement, Finn. We need to find one. Let them look into what the PI found."

"I wish it were that simple," I tell her, "but it's not. My PI died in a hit-and-run and there are no witnesses or leads. Did you know only eight percent of hit-and-runs were solved in Los Angeles last year? It's a dead end."

"But you can tell them—"

"What?" I snap, then sigh. "I'm sorry, but really, what can I tell them? A conspiracy theory? My gut instinct? Whatever proof he had, it was in his head and died with him."

"What if it wasn't—didn't?" she asks mutedly. "Do you know where he lived?"

This conversation has crossed into surreal territory.

The news is back on, Callisto's return left in the dust of the commercial break as the anchors eagerly focus on the next story.

"Are you suggesting we break into his house?" I ask, then shake my head. "The Avellinos are thorough. They would have searched his files and computer and destroyed whatever they found."

Molly grabs my hands. Hers are ice-cold. I meet her gaze and am surprised by the ferocity I see in her eyes.

"We have to start somewhere, and this is as good a place as any." Her lips quirk. "Besides, I wasn't always the upstanding citizen I am now. I was a teenager with a lock-picking kit back in the day."

"Wow," I deadpan, then frown. "Who are you and what did you do with my aunt?"

She smirks. "There are only so many ways to entertain yourself as a kid in Solstice Bay. Ask your mom if you don't believe me." She frowns. "On second thought, don't."

Unsmiling, I scan her face. "We're talking about breaking and entering, which is illegal. If we get caught..."

"I know," she says decisively. "That's why I'm going to do it alone."

"Aunt Mol—"

"Listen to me, Finn, and listen good. We can sit here for weeks chasing our tails, or we can take action. We're leaving for L.A. in the morning. I'm going to look into the PI, and you're going to do exactly what we both know you're going to do, but have been too much of a chicken to say out loud."

I still, unnerved. "What are you talking about? What is it you think I'm going to do?"

"Use the high-society connections you've cultivated for years to get close to the family." She pauses, gaze sharpening further. "Now that there's a daughter in the house over twenty-five."

I have the errant thought that my aunt is a witch. Or perhaps it's as I've always thought—we're so alike that despite time and distance, she knows me in a way no one else in my family does.

Because she's right.

I've been waiting years for the middle daughter, Eleanor, to hit an acceptable age. It didn't matter that she wasn't my type—blond, for starters—or that she seemed like every other airhead debutante. My plan all along has been to seduce her, make her fall in love with me, use her to get close to the family, find some hard evidence of illegal dealings, and watch them all burn.

Back when I hatched the plan, on a lonely, drunken night in college, it was supposed to be the eldest daughter. The one closest to my age. The petite, dark-haired one. The one who has repelled me and intrigued me in equal measure ever since I saw her in that stupid dress in the courtroom so many years ago.

It was always supposed to be Callisto.

"That's why you dropped your last name," muses

Molly, pulling me from my thoughts. "You've been angling for this for a long time, haven't you?"

Definitely a witch.

"Yes," I admit.

To the world of high-end fashion photography, I'm known by my first and middle names: Finn Reid. Very few people know my real last name; outside of family members, I can count them on one hand. Callisto is now included in that number, but I can't dwell on it. I have to believe she wants the same thing I do. The end of the Avellinos.

If she doesn't? whispers my inner pessimist.

I'll cross that bridge when I come to it.

"Don't hurt her, Finn," Molly says softly. "She's on our side."

"I'll try." Giving her hands a final squeeze, I stand. "I need to head to the motel and pack. I'll see you in the morning. Around seven?"

She nods. "Sounds good."

I hesitate at the front door, looking back. "We're not telling Mom, are we?"

Molly's eyes shimmer with conflict, but she shakes her head. "She won't understand."

I smile wryly. "No, she won't. Goodnight, Aunt Mol."

"Goodnight, Finn."

The air outside is frigid and still. With the lack of light pollution, the stars above show their true faces, multicolored and shimmering behind the gauze of Earth's atmosphere.

My mom loved astronomy and Greek mythology.

Although I don't know much about astronomy or mythology, I can still easily spot what I'm looking for.

Ursa Major. More commonly known as the Big Dipper. But to the Greeks, it wasn't a big-ass cup that kids imagined a giant hand wielding. It was the Great Bear. And before it was the Great Bear, it was a woman named Callisto.

A virginal nymph sworn to Artemis, Callisto caught the eye of randy Zeus. The god tricked her, seduced her, impregnated her, then wiped his hands of the crime. For her trouble, Callisto was turned into a bear. For years, she roamed alone in the wilderness, but one day her grown son came upon her while hunting. Before the son could kill his mother-turned-bear or vice versa, some benevolent deity acted and placed Callisto in the sky.

There she remains, safe from the vile deeds of men and god alike, untarnished by time or fear.

And utterly alone.

15

Callisto

I HEAR familiar voices inside the kitchen. My heart swells with the need to race inside to see my sisters, but some instinct makes me pause outside. As I listen to the conversation, nerves tickle my throat and shorten my breath.

Six years is a long time, and the kids I remember are women now, twenty-two and nineteen years old. Vivian said Ellie is at UCLA, and Lizzie would have graduated high school last year.

"It's weird, is all." Ellie's voice, drawling and dismissive.

"Who cares?" asks a higher, smoother voice. *Lizzie.* "I can't wait to see her. I wonder if she's changed. Does she look different, Mom?"

"Not especially," Vivian answers, sounding as bored as Ellie. "And given her lateness for breakfast, she hasn't changed much, either."

Back from the dead and nothing's changed. The insult is so familiar it triggers nostalgia. I've never been a morning person, and Vivian has never wasted a chance to demean me for it.

A maid leaves the kitchen, turning the corner with quick steps, and yelps when we nearly collide.

"I'm so sorry," I say quickly, stepping out of her way.

Selina, wide-eyed, whispers, "Forgive me."

Before I can tell her that's ridiculous, that it was my fault, Vivian's voice rings out, "Callisto, is that you?"

"Here goes nothing," I whisper, then call out, "Yes, coming!"

Selina mouths, "Good luck," and scurries past me.

I glance after her, bemused, and when I turn back around, a slender form barrels into me.

"Holy shit, I'm so glad you're alive," Lizzie cries with a half sob, half laugh.

"Language!" snaps Vivian.

I hug Lizzie back, pressing my face into her honey-blond hair. She smells the same—like the fruity lotion she loves. Tears prick like hot needles behind my eyelids as memories race through me. All the happy times with my siblings I've worked so hard to forget. Mud pies, skinned knees, and hide-and-go-seek. And later, staying up to all hours braiding each other's hair, painting our nails, and cutting up magazines to make dream boards.

Opening my eyes, I look over Lizzie's shoulder and meet Ellie's hard, sea-green gaze. Standing next to her mother with her arms crossed, she looks about as happy to see me as a hangnail.

As the closest in age, we've always had a complex relationship. But it changed at puberty when Ellie decided I wasn't her friend but her competition—a betrayal of our bond I never understood. She was always brighter, bolder, and more beautiful. The crown jewel of the family, while I was ever on the outside, the sister who didn't belong. While we've enjoyed periods of renewed closeness—especially when her first boyfriend broke her heart in high school—a thread of tension lives between us that doesn't exist between me and Lizzie.

Still, when Lizzie releases me, I walk to Ellie and hug her hard. Slowly, her body loses tension and her arms lift to return my embrace. It's lackluster compared to Lizzie's, but it's something.

"It's so good to see you," I tell her, leaning back to see that her eyes have somewhat thawed.

"You too," she says, then sniffs and looks at Vivian. "Like I said earlier, I can't stay. I have a paper to write."

I open my mouth to protest, but Vivian speaks first. "Very well. Will you be here for Thursday dinner?"

"I have to check my schedule—"

"*Eleanor.*"

Lizzie snorts, which earns her a sharp glance from Vivian.

Ellie rolls her eyes. "Fine, I'll be here."

"And don't forget about the garden party on Saturday."

"How could I," she mutters, then swipes her cell phone and purse from the counter, leaving her half-eaten breakfast on the table. With the barest glance in my direction and a tight smile, she rushes from the room.

As I watch her go, Lizzie slips her arm around my waist.

"She hates surprises, same as always," she murmurs.

I nod, smiling for her benefit even though there's an ache in my chest.

"Eat something, Callisto," Vivian tells me, "then come to my office, please."

I nod, and she leaves.

Lizzie giggles, her hazel eyes sparkling. "At least she said 'please,' right? She says it more nowadays. I think the whole *I want to be governor* thing has been good for her. There's this lady who comes once a week. Super posh but so nice. She's giving Mom lessons on how to be more appealing to voters."

Lizzie chatters on as she finishes her breakfast and I eat mine, filling me in on a host of mundane facts about her life, Ellie's life, and Vivian's new venture. She lets me finish my oatmeal before asking about the elephant in the room.

"So, what happened?"

I set down my spoon, acknowledging that it was only a matter of time. Lizzie has never been one to beat around the bush.

"I don't know who took me," I start, careful to keep my face neutral and my eyes guileless. "One minute I was asleep in my dorm, and the next thing I knew, I was blindfolded in the trunk of a car. After that, it's kind of a blur. They must have sedated me, because I don't remember much of the next few weeks other than being in an empty basement that was locked from the outside."

"They?" She swallows. "Was it two men?"

At the horror on her face, I say quickly, "Nothing bad happened to me—not like that, anyway. And I think it was two. Honestly, it's such a mess in my head. I heard different voices, but sometimes I thought it was one person trying to trick me."

"You must have been terrified."

Thinking of nights I spent on the street when I ran out of money the first year, and the shock of suddenly being no one with nothing, I nod.

"Then you escaped." Lizzie says it proudly, with a gleam that tells me she expected nothing less. I quell a surge of guilt.

"Not exactly. I don't know what changed, but one night they blindfolded me again and drove me somewhere. They dragged me out of the car and made me kneel, then there was nothing. Just blackness. I woke up the next day in a field with blood on the back of my head and no memory."

"Oh my God! What did you do?"

"I walked until I found a house. A shack, really. The woman who lived there didn't speak English, but she was kind to me. She patched me up and fed me, then gave me money for a bus ticket to Sacramento. That was over five years ago."

Lizzie blinks huge eyes. "That's insane."

You have no idea.

"I know. I'm still a bit in shock, honestly. The last six years seem surreal, like they happened to someone else. I can't believe I'm back."

Her mouth hangs open. "You didn't remember anything at all? Why didn't you go to the hospital? The police? Did you ever think someone might be looking for you or want you to come home?"

The rapid-fire questions are underlaid with hurt. But she wants an answer I can't give—one that could make her hate me. That I *chose* to stay away. That I abandoned her willingly.

Shifting in my seat, I look out the nearby window at the groomed backyard. "I don't really know, Lizzie," I say at length. "All I remembered was that I had to hide because people were after me."

"But... but what did you *do*? How did you live?"

I'm struck suddenly by how young she is. How young I was when I left. Raised in the lap of luxury, the notion of being homeless and penniless is as foreign to Lizzie as flying to Bora Bora in a private jet is to the general population. Echoes of my old self, the limitations of my pampered mindset, hit me anew.

"I scraped by," I tell her honestly. "Worked odd jobs for people who didn't care about taxes or valid ID. And I kept moving, every few months. Eventually I had enough saved to rent a room from a coworker near Seattle. I saved more, and a few years ago, bought a car." My lips tilt sardonically. "You'd be surprised by how much you can do as a young white woman, past or no past."

She shakes her head. "I can't imagine."

"I know." Reaching across the table, I grab her hand. "And I hope to God you'll never find out."

Lizzie shudders, a shadow crossing her face. *My* shadow. That of my presumed death, long absence, and return. For better or worse, the shadow of my choices—present, past, and future—stains us all.

16

Callisto

"YOU ALWAYS WERE one for tall tales, Callisto, but this is beyond the pale."

Vivian doesn't look at me as she speaks, her gaze trained on a sleek computer monitor. The three-carat diamond studs in her ears wink in the sunlight streaming through the windows behind her.

She looks exactly the same. Better, even, thanks to surgical magic. I'm pretty sure she used to have a few wrinkles, especially around her mouth from all the scowling she did. Now her skin is pillowy and pore-less, radiant with purchased youth.

"It's not a tall tale," I say, my exhaustion unfeigned. "Far-fetched, I'll admit that. But it's true."

Sharp green eyes avert from the screen and affix to my face. "You expect me to believe you had amnesia for

107

close to five years, then *poof*, three months ago, you started remembering your life? Then, instead of giving me a damn phone call, you stayed away because you were afraid of how your return would affect the girls?"

The less you say, the easier the lie.

I nod placidly, confirming the version of events I've tailored specifically to her. I want her to believe protecting my sisters is my highest priority—not hard, because it's true. I didn't mention Ellie or Lizzie to the detective, of course. Vivian would consider that a violation of the family's privacy.

"Suppose I do believe you... then tell me, what made you come back? And why the hell did you go to the police instead of coming here?"

I swallow a sigh. "The short answer is I missed my family. The long answer..." I pause, meeting her gaze directly. "I saw that you were running for governor and realized I could help you. That my story could. Maybe I finally remembered the last piece of myself—the legacy of my father. Ambition and service to the family."

Vivian watches me, motionless and expressionless. Expecting me to balk, maybe, or change my story. But right now, I'm not afraid of her. I have something she wants—a connection to voters she'll never have. I read the news on my phone this morning. I'm all over it, an innocent victim of tragedy risen from the ashes. A princess who forgot herself and spent years as a penniless pauper.

God, I hate the press. Especially since the family's desired spin on the story is already apparent. But if they want me to be a bridge between the classes, that's fine by me. I'm going to make Vivian jump off the highest point.

The thought crosses my mind that the game I'm playing might consume me right along with her, that I'm swimming in morally ambiguous waters, but potential victory outweighs the costs.

Maybe this is what Finn has felt for years, this single-minded focus on an end goal.

I can't think of my sisters. Won't.

Eventually Vivian relaxes in her chair, though her gaze cuts as it rakes me from head to toe. Then she reaches for her cell phone.

"You're going shopping," she tells me as she types out a text message. "Casual, accessible style, but quality. A full formal wardrobe as well." She glances up. "Please tell me you don't have tattoos or have forgotten how to walk in heels."

"I don't. And haven't."

"Good." She puts down the phone. "My stylist will be here in two hours. He'll schedule private fittings so the bloodhounds won't pick up your scent. You heard me mention a garden party?"

I nod, nerves glimmering inside me. I hadn't expected my first public appearance—and test—to be so soon.

"Saturday at two. You'll be expected to make an impression. Can you handle that?"

"Of course. Will I be briefed on the attendees prior? I'd like to be given priority targets."

Her surprise is swiftly concealed. "That can be arranged."

I nod. "Is that all?"

"Family dinner tomorrow at six sharp. I've told your uncles to give you space until then. I figured you'd want some time to reacclimate before the reunion."

Caught off guard by the unexpected thoughtfulness, I stand. "I appreciate that. And thank you, Vivian."

This time, surprise lifts her brows. "For what?"

I smile even as my insides kick with revulsion. "For being a mother to me."

She freezes, hand halfway extended to her phone. Sparing her the effort of a reply, I head for the door.

"Callisto."

Pausing, I turn. "Yes?"

With a small smile and tilt of her head, she says, "I rather like this new version of you."

In the hallway, my wide smile disintegrates, and my body ripples with disquiet.

But there's satisfaction, too.

She won't know what hits her.

SEVEN HOURS LATER, exhausted more from Vivian's hyperactive stylist than trying on a million outfits, I fall onto the guest room bed and decide I'm not moving until morning.

I'm on the edge of sleep when there's a soft knock on the door.

"Yes?" I croak.

"Miss?" comes Selina's soft voice. "There's a phone call for you."

I whip upright, my sleepy mind sloshing against my temples. "A phone call?"

"Yes, miss."

I run through a short list of who it could be—a family member or Hugo.

"Can you take a message?" I ask after a moment. "Unless it's one of my sisters. Is it?"

"No, miss. It's a woman. She, um, goes by the name Rabbit? She's called many times today. Mrs. Avellino just now gave me leave to tell you." By the tone of her last words, I know Vivian used more colorful words.

I'm already halfway to the door, a grin on my face and unexpected joy lifting my heart.

Rabbit.

I'm the only one who ever called her that. Her name is Jessica, and she's been my best friend since she moved to Los Angeles our sophomore year of high school. She was my ride or die. Almost literally, as it turned out. Missing her has been a toothache with no cure—a persistent pain, only tolerable when I accepted its permanence.

In the hallway, Selina greets me with a nod, then leads me into a small library at the back of the house. I rush to the side table with an antique rotary phone, the receiver sitting beside it.

"Jessica?" I gasp.

There's a two-second pause.

Then my best friend—and the only person who, up until a few days ago, knew I faked my death—snarls, "What the *fuck* is going on!"

"Hold on." After a quick glance at the door, thankfully closed, I whisper, "I can't talk about it."

Well versed in my paranoia about surveillance in the house, she says, "Meet me at our usual place in an hour?"

I almost agree, then realize my car is MIA. For a minute, I consider asking Vivian for a driver, but discard the idea. It's too soon for her to trust me, and more importantly, it's too soon for me to trust any of the staff.

"I, uh, might be on lockdown."

She sighs. "Okay. I guess I'll see you when I see you."

The old code makes me smile. "Sooner rather than later."

"You got it."

I gently replace the receiver. Now wide awake, I need to kill a few hours. I consider seeking out Lizzie, maybe chatting for a bit before she goes to sleep, but my guilt for abandoning her rears its head. My empty stomach eventually decides for me, and I head for the kitchen.

The house is a mausoleum, spotless and lifeless, but when I pass Vivian's office there's a sliver of light beneath the door. Her voice, low and indistinct, reaches my ears. I suppress a shiver and walk faster.

In the kitchen, I grab a bottle of water and a snack, then head back to my room and lock the door behind me. A memory surfaces of a conversation not meant for a child's ears, triggered by the sound of Vivian's sharp voice through the office door.

"Handle it."

"Are you sure?"

"Get rid of him, Enzo! With Rafael behind bars, I'm in charge of this family. Don't make me repeat myself again."

"You got it."

Would the recollection of an imaginative child hold up in court? No. Not without supporting evidence, which I don't have. I don't even know how old I was when I heard those words. Maybe fourteen? Sixteen? Like any teenager, my worldview was limited, my focus primarily on myself. What to wear to school the next day. Whether or not David would finally ask me out after months of flirting. How to navigate the minefield of high school and an increasingly hostile home life.

God, I wish I could go back in time and slap myself. Tell myself to wake the fuck up and face the nightmare that lived under the same roof. Do the right thing and go to the authorities.

But I hadn't. I'd liked my BMW convertible. My legacy acceptance to university. My spending account and personal shoppers and the envy of my classmates.

"Your family is full of crooked elitists and murderers."

Finn was right. In some ways, I'm as guilty as they are.

17

Callisto

AT A FEW MINUTES TILL MIDNIGHT, I leave the house through the side door of the garage, fingers crossed that it's still the only exit that lacks a motion-sensing floodlight. It does. With a sigh of relief, I move quickly along the side of the house, then dart across a grass lawn toward the dark thicket of trees near the wall.

I'm breathless by the time I reach my destination: an old, oxidized iron bench safe from the angled ground lights, forgotten behind the border of trees. The surrounding foliage has crept closer over the years, and the peeling surface is sprinkled with bird shit and leaves. Meager moonlight reveals the solitary figure leaning against the wall past the bench.

"Rabbit," I breathe.

She pushes away from the wall. Her arms surround

me and we hold each other tightly, our bodies speaking the words our mouths can't.

"What the fuck, Calli?" she whispers as we part.

"I can explain."

"You better." She shakes her head. "I almost had a heart attack when I saw the news. What happened? Why are you here? It's because of the governor shit, isn't it?"

"Mostly, yes."

"Damnit. I *knew* you wouldn't be able to stomach it, but I hoped you were chilling in a jungle somewhere with no TV or radio." She clasps my hands in hers. "You're not safe here. You know that. That woman hates you, your uncles are savages, and God only knows what your sisters have turned into."

"They're okay," I murmur. "Still clueless, I think."

I hope.

Rabbit stares at me hard, her face painted with moonlight, heart-shaped features older, sharper, and even more arresting than they were at nineteen.

I finger her short hair. "Orange or pink?"

She smirks. "Orange."

"I love it."

"You can't see the color in the dark."

I shrug. "I still love it."

She sighs. "You kill me, you really do. What's your

endgame, huh?"

"Vivian and my uncles behind bars."

"How?"

"Evidence."

"What evidence?"

"I don't know yet."

"Wow. Solid plan."

I smile at the familiar, acerbic tone. "You missed me."

"Like a limb I severed that suddenly grew back."

I bite my lips to keep from laughing. "What have you been up to? Tell me everything."

"Same old same old."

"Did you finish your degree?" I ask wistfully.

"Yeah," she says, voice subdued. "It sucked after you fake-died, though. I was the chick whose best friend was probably murdered."

"I thought you hated Los Angeles and were never coming back."

She shrugs. "Feelings change. After four years on the East Coast, I missed it. Things are cool now, though. I work for a boutique design agency downtown. I like it. Pay is great."

"What else? Any serious relationships? You're not married, are you?" I gasp. "Are you a mom?"

I see a flash of teeth as she grins. "No, but the idea

isn't as horrifying as it used to be. I have a boyfriend—he's a total jock. I have no idea how we started dating, but somehow it's been almost four years."

"He treats you right?"

She nods. "Like the goddess I am."

I can't resist giving her another quick hug. "I'm so happy for you. I've missed you so much. There are so many things I never got a chance to tell you, like thank you for—"

"Save it for later," she interjects softly. "Callie, what can I do to help? Time's almost up."

I glance warily at the house. At exactly twelve twenty-five, the main alarm is set and all the doors auto-locked.

"Can you get me a burner phone?"

"I'll leave it under the bench tomorrow night. What else?"

I shake my head. "Nothing." When she starts to protest, I lift a hand. "Seriously."

"Are you Lone Rangering me? For real? After everything we've been through?"

"I don't want you anywhere near this, Rabbit. I love you, and I'm so happy you're happy. I won't risk screwing up your life, too."

She pulls me in for a hard, final hug. "Be safe," she whispers. "I love you, too."

She jogs back to the stone wall, scaling it easily using the footholds we installed in high school and the muscle memory of having made the climb countless times. Draped as the wall is with vines, it looks like magic as her lithe body zigzags to the top. Then she's gone.

With two minutes to spare, I slip into the dark garage and carefully close the door. I'm halfway down the hall to my room when I hear the familiar *beep beep* of the alarm being set. Like a net has closed around me, cinching tight, I feel the air in my lungs compress. Quickening my steps, I dart into my room and lock the door, then stand panting until my heart rate slows.

When I see the Post-it on the nightstand, my pulse jumps anew. Someone was here.

Calm down, idiot. Maybe it was Lizzie.

I grab the note and read the three words.

Painting over dresser.

"What the hell?" I whisper, glancing at the framed Monet replication.

Hackles rising, I walk to the dresser. My eyes track slowly over the canvas and frame, and when I don't see anything, I look again from another angle.

And there it is.

A tiny, shiny black circle set into the baroque, gold frame near the bottom left corner.

A camera.

18

Callisto

WHEN I WALK into the formal dining room for family dinner the following night, I'm intentionally ten minutes late and armed. My weapon? The minuscule camera I dug out of the painting's frame with scissors and a steak knife. The frame is a goner, but at least I was careful with the canvas.

The first course—ceviche, which I hate—has already been served, and I'm met with a range of reactions. Vivian's mouth is pinched in disapproval; Lizzie's fork slips from her fingers and clatters on a dish; Ellie stares at me with openmouthed shock.

And finally, my dear uncles Enzo and Franco jolt to standing, their fixed smiles disappearing as I stalk forward and toss the camera on the table next to my stepmother.

"What on earth is that?" she asks with convincing surprise. She picks it up, examining it like she's never seen anything like it before.

"It's a camera I found in my room."

Lizzie gasps. "What the fuck?"

"Language," murmurs Vivian distractedly. She glances up at me, and for a moment, I think she's being genuine and didn't know about the surveillance. Then her eyes flicker behind me and narrow with accusation, and I can't believe I didn't put two and two together before now.

I turn a glare on Franco, the family's tech wizard. He offers a rueful grin, his hands lifting, palms facing me. With his slicked-back hair and narrow face, he always reminded me of a weasel. And he still does.

"Hey, can you really blame me? We aren't the trusting sort, Callie-Bear, and you've been gone a long time. Besides, it was just sound. I'm not creepy like that."

"Yes, you are," mutters Ellie, and Lizzie snorts.

Vivian ignores the girls. "Enzo, did you know about this?"

Enzo, beefier and rougher all around than his younger brother, shrugs. "Maybe."

Vivian sighs and turns her attention back to me. "Callisto, I apologize for the breach of your privacy. It was inexcusable. Franco, apologize to your niece."

"Sorry," he says, without sounding sorry at all.

"Now for the love of God, everyone sit down so we can eat like civilized people."

Just like that, it's over.

I sit in the empty spot adjacent to the head of the table and Vivian. Chairs shift, forks lift, and the rest of the meal passes like a theatrical production of normalcy, with questions like, *How did your paper come out, Eleanor?* and *Any more thought on what college you'd like to attend, Elizabeth?* When my sisters attempt to engage me, Vivian interjects and steers the conversation away.

I pick at the main course—veal, which I'm also not a big fan of—and am ignored by everyone but Lizzie, who sends me funny faces and eye-rolls. Her engagement is all that keeps me anchored in the present, reminding me I'm not a ghost.

By the time dessert is cleared, my shoulders are knotted with tension. I didn't know what to expect from confronting them about the camera, but the swift, blasé response has left me reeling and deflated, and feeling much like I did most of my life in this house—powerless.

I use a headache to excuse myself.

Vivian smiles slightly. "Get some rest, dear."

Avoiding my uncles' pointed, knowing stares, I say goodnight to everyone and retreat to my room. I don't notice Selina walking toward me until she says, "Are you all right, miss?"

I startle, then smile. "I'm fine, thank you. How are you?"

"I'm well." She pauses. "I took the liberty of cleaning your room and replacing the painting with another. I hope you don't mind."

Embarrassment flushes my face. "Oh, um, about the frame—"

"No need to explain," she says, then drops her voice to a whisper. "I'm glad you found it."

I freeze. "You left the note?"

She nods, glancing furtively behind me, then asks, "What note?"

My neck crawls with confirmation of the long-held fear. "Never mind, I was confused for a second. Thank you, Selina. I'll see you tomorrow."

"Goodnight, miss."

As we walk past each other, she touches my arm and whispers, "Phone calls in the bathroom only. Turn the shower on first."

Swallowing the lump in my throat, I nod and hurry to my room. It doesn't occur to me until much later that night, when I have the burner phone Rabbit delivered in my hand, to wonder how Selina seemed to know so much about avoiding surveillance. But by then, I'm half-asleep and it isn't the danger I'm in or the insanity of being here I'm thinking about.

Instead, I'm thinking about a pair of blue eyes and the challenge in them.

You're no hero.

Maybe tomorrow, I'll feel again the need to prove him wrong.

But tonight? I agree with him.

19

Finn

BEYOND THE SPARKLING waters of a stone-rimmed swimming pool, the elite of Los Angeles mingle in the afternoon sun. The scents of freshly mown grass and faint chlorine mix with the perfumes of entitlement.

This echelon of society has always intrigued me. From an artistic standpoint, I'd love to wash off all the makeup, hairspray, tanning lotions, and pomades, and strip off the tailored polos, slacks, dresses, and Spanx, and photograph them in this current tableau—laughing too loudly as they sip champagne and scotch, oozing sincerity while inside they're bursting with contempt. All framed by the placid Southern California weather and Vivian Avellino's so-perfect-it-looks-fake backyard.

It could win me a Pulitzer, for sure.

Too bad I'm not here for art.

"What are we doing here again?" grumbles the man beside me.

"Mingling."

Teddy Prescott III was the first person I called and the last person I expected to be the answer to my prayers. We were buddies in college—the drinking kind —and he happens to be the son of one of the city's oldest and most monied families. It was sheer luck he had an invite to this little soiree sitting on his desk when I called. It didn't take much to convince him to bring me as his guest—a bottle of thirty-year-old single malt Balvenie a client sent me for Christmas last year.

I'm regretting the sacrifice now, as we've only been here twenty minutes and he's already complaining.

"All the women here are over forty."

"This party is boring as fuck."

"At least the caterers are hot."

Then,

"Hello there," he murmurs with a lecherous grin. I follow his gaze to the French doors at the back of the house, my blood running hotter and faster in anticipation.

But it's not her. Just a couple of young, blond socialites in stylish pastel dresses. The younger Avellino sisters. They look cartoonish to me—too groomed, too pretty. I prefer women with a little character to their faces. One or two flaws. My camera prefers them as well.

Teddy whistles softly. "Well, well. America's Undead Sweetheart is looking damn fine today."

My head turns so fast my neck cracks.

Callisto has joined her sisters. The full moon between two distant stars. Her silky dark hair swallows the light, her creamy skin luminous. She's ethereal. Out of place. Remembering Solstice Bay and the first night we met, how vibrant and magnetic she was despite her shyness, I realize how different she appears now. There's something almost translucent about her, like she's been stripped of her personality.

It bothers me. A lot.

Her delicate features are impassive as she gazes around the scene, nodding at something one of her sisters has said. Standing stock-still, I wait for her eyes to land on me, both craving and slightly fearful of her reaction. *What will she say? Do?* The need for eye contact makes my back tighten, my fingers clench. If I could see her eyes, I might know if my being here is beyond stupid. If she has, indeed, come back here with an agenda similar to mine... or if she came back to take her place at her stepmother's side.

She doesn't see me, though, and as I watch her, I realize her eyes don't see much at all. Whatever's going on in her head, it's locked down. No more hint of the woman I met just a week ago, who blushed and stammered when I smiled at her.

Two men approach the trio of sisters. Young, cocky, and rich. Oozing charm from their waxed balls to their tanned foreheads. Most of their attention is directed at Callisto, which the middle sister, Eleanor, doesn't like much. The youngest, Elizabeth, watches her sisters with a grin on her face and happiness in her eyes, either not noticing or ignoring the undercurrent. Maybe she's just glad to have the family back together. To have her sister back.

Observing Elizabeth's innocent joy, I almost feel bad for what I plan to do to her family. My gaze tracks back to Callisto, noting the shift of her expressions, the superficiality of them. She's playing a role. *Willingly or unwillingly?*

"Bro, you look weird, all intense and shit. Are you crushing on the dead girl?"

I spare Teddy a derisive glance and a scoff, then, as my gaze latches on to two new arrivals to the party, a plan forms.

"See those women? Over by the bar?" I ask Teddy, who immediately perks up.

"Sure do." He rubs his hands together, eyes

undressing the tall, lithe beauties I've pointed out. "What's our strategy? Which one you want?"

Neither.

Aloud, I sigh. "Just follow my lead."

Without waiting for a reply, I head for the bar and the two women who turn, drinks in hand, as I reach them.

"Abby, good to see you."

"Finn!" she squeals, bouncing forward on five-inch heels to throw herself into my arms. We're almost the same height—she towers over most of the men here—but in her line of work it's an asset. Her back bowed against my chest, she grins at me. "This is probably the last place I'd ever expect to see you! What the heck are you doing here?"

Her sweet, Southern drawl reminds me of a few years ago and a weekend spent between the sheets after a photoshoot for *Vogue*. We've been friends since—last I heard, she's engaged to some foreign oil tycoon's son.

"I was about to ask you the same thing," I remark as she steps back to sip her fruity cocktail.

"Oh, you know. Expanding my horizons and what-not." She giggles. "To be honest, though, I'm mostly here out of curiosity. You?"

"Same," I whisper conspiratorially.

A quick glance shows me that Callisto and her

sisters have separated. It takes me a moment to find her—she's chatting with a former Democratic governor, laughing and touching his arm near the two-story pool house. He looks down on her dotingly, a gleam in his eye. He's old enough to be her grandfather, which shouldn't bother me. After all, she's clearly acting a part.

But it still bothers me.

Teddy claps me on the back, truncating my thoughts. "Are you going to introduce me to your friends, buddy?"

Abby's brows lift and she shares a knowing smirk with her friend. I make the introductions, learning the other woman's name, which I promptly forget. Teddy takes instant advantage, edging close to Abby's friend and laying on the charm.

I lean toward Abby and gesture over my shoulder to where Callisto is.

"Should we go say hi?"

Her eyes widen. "Ohh, should we? I don't want to be rude." Concern touches her brow as she looks. "She's probably a bit overwhelmed, don't you think?"

This is why I like Abby. Though her face is well-known after several successful, worldwide campaigns, she hasn't been poisoned by the well of vanity and self-absorption most young models drink from daily.

"Yeah, maybe you're right."

We turn to look at Callisto, now trading air kisses with a matronly woman overwhelmed by pearls and garish red lipstick. A stately man stands behind them, his attention on the phone in his hand rather than the women. He's the only one in the vicinity, though, who doesn't have at least one eye trained on Callisto. Her notoriety is a magnet—half the people here want to fuck her just to say they did, and the other half want to see her fall apart.

I continue, "Or maybe she'd like a little break from the sharks."

Abby nods thoughtfully as several small groups of people merge on Callisto's location. "She does seem in need of some rescuing."

I offer her my arm. "Shall we?"

She slips her arm through mine and grins. "We shall."

20

Callisto

I SAW HIM FIRST.

In fact, he was the first person my eyes landed on when I stepped outside to join my sisters. Thankfully, I was already buffered by a sneaked shot of vodka and a morning spent dedicated to projecting apathy. The shock that pulled my ribs tight to my heart? Inconsequential. The *why why why* pinging in my mind? The way my body sang a high, pure note at the sight of him? All of it, ignored.

His naturally haughty features are pulled tight, the stormy blue of his eyes visible even from across the pool. He doesn't know I've seen him—I've been careful not to look directly his way. Because he doesn't know this version of me. What she's capable of. Callisto Avellino, *heiress.*

Raised to rub elbows with the rich and powerful. Trained to compliance and grace. This is perhaps the first time I've truly plied my skills, but they come easily. A familiar skin.

Who I was in Solstice Bay, the fumbling, raw person, is locked back in the darkness she rose from. A tender sapling cut off from the light. Here, now, I am my father's daughter.

I'm unaffected by Finn McCowen.

At least on the outside.

When he finally makes his play, approaching me with a gorgeous model on his arm, I'm ready. Or as ready as I can be for his nearness. I struggle to hold the conversation with Mrs. Stapleton, wife of a big studio exec and friend of my stepmother's.

He's closing in. My skin ripples with awareness as I watch him from the corner of my eye. The way he moves draws heads, and not just the female ones. His tattoos are covered by an untucked, long-sleeved button-down, his hair combed back, but there's no mistaking his wildness. His *otherness*. He's a force of nature deigning to visit the realm of men, exuding the promise of destruction.

Mrs. Stapleton says her farewells, giving me a patronizing pat on the cheek before turning to her husband, who looks up from his phone and gives me a brief, disinterested nod. *At least there's one person here who doesn't give a shit about me.*

"Callisto?" asks a soft voice. The model. "I'm Abby Hassler, and this is my friend Finn Reid. We thought we'd keep you company for a bit so you could have a break from... everything. No questions from us. Just"— she gives a small, tinkling laugh—"a buffer, if you want it."

I'm taken aback by the gesture, by the kindness in her eyes. And even more by the word *friend.* I glance briefly at Finn, not maintaining eye contact for fear my mask will crack. When I saw them embrace with such familiarity, I assumed they were more. Casual, perhaps, but more than friends. From her tone—and the giant diamond I spy on her ring finger—they aren't.

I ignore the resulting swell of relief.

"That's very nice," I tell Abby, "but I'm quite all right. Are you enjoying the party?"

She looks surprised, a little hurt. "Uh, yes, thank you."

The conversation stalls. Finn clears his throat, and I brace for the impact of his voice. But before he can speak, Ellie appears beside me. She vibrates with excitement, and I notice at once that she's unbuttoned the top of her dress to display her creamy cleavage.

"Oh my gosh, Mr. Reid, it's so amazing you're here.

I've followed your work for years. You are the *best* photographer in the business. The way you capture such raw emotion in your subjects is incredible. I'm Elizabeth Avellino, by the way."

Finn smiles, shaking her hand even as his eyes shutter to blankness. I wonder if Ellie can pick up on his withdrawal, but from the way she's swaying toward him, I decide—rather pettily—that she can't. With her gorgeous face and figure, not to mention her bank account, I doubt it occurred to her that her prey might not immediately roll over.

Never one to miss an opportunity to befriend the famous, Ellie turns to Finn's companion. "And Abby Hassler. It's so nice to meet you. You're even more beautiful in person. Oh, and congrats on your recent engagement!"

Abby beams. "Thanks so much."

"I was just about to head to the bar. Would you two like to join me?"

"Sounds good to me," Abby says, looking in question at Finn.

He pivots to face me, stalling my retreat.

"I'm fine here, thanks." Firm, focused, final.

My pulse quickens, my eyes widening and snapping to Ellie. She's as shocked as I am, but for different reasons. *What the fuck is he thinking?* I try to apologize to my sister with my eyes, but she doesn't look at me.

With a forced smile, she says, "Well, maybe I'll see you a bit later?" It's impossible to miss the innuendo in her voice.

Finn says, "Maybe."

Visibly rattled, my sister leads Abby away.

I smile politely at Finn and hiss through my teeth, "What are you doing? You shouldn't be here."

A dark eyebrow arches. "Neither should you," he murmurs, "but here we are. Besides, I'm famous—or hadn't you heard?"

An angry flush lifts, unstoppable, to my cheeks. "Leave, now," I whisper.

Finn grins affably and shakes his head. My fingers curl—I want to punch his pretty face.

"Not a chance," he replies. "Now be a good hostess and give me a tour? I admit to being a real estate junkie."

"Show yourself." I wave toward the house. "Doors are open to guests."

"Nuh-uh, princess. Need I remind you that people are watching? You make a scene and there will be questions. I don't think you want to explain to your stepmother how we met."

Memory assails me, pushing more heat into my cheeks—this time fueled by embarrassment. But with a glance around us, I see the truth of his warning. People *are* watching, including my sister and Abby, standing with drinks in hand by the pool. Thankfully, I don't think Vivian has noticed us yet. But when I spy my uncles in a circle of men, I meet Enzo's flat stare. My stomach clenches. Of the two of them, Enzo has always scared me more.

"Damn you," I whisper, then wipe the expression off my face and say more clearly, "I'd be happy to show you the house, Mr. Reid."

He chuckles. "Call me Finn, please."

"Finn," I grind out through my smile. Spinning on a heel, I walk toward the back doors. His long stride effortlessly keeps pace with my faster one.

As we near thicker clusters of partygoers, he says, "So how's it been, being back?"

The tone is casual, one of generic small talk, but the undercurrent is unmistakable.

"Really great," I answer just as casually. "It's a little surreal, but every day I wake up grateful to be home."

"I'm sure. I can't imagine how difficult the last six years have been for you. I, along with the rest of the country, am so glad you're okay."

"Thank you," I say stiffly, nodding at several people near the doors. Once inside, I breathe more easily. Truth be told, I do need a break from the stares, whispers, and questions.

I lead Finn toward the formal rooms at the front of the house. We only have minutes before our absence is noted and the rumors start.

Making a quick decision, I open a door, grab his arm, and haul him inside. The door closes, swathing us in darkness.

"Is this a... closet?" His voice is too close, thick with humor, and the heat from his body paints a thick line on my front.

"Drop the act," I snap. "This is probably one of the few places in this house not under surveillance. What do you want?"

There's just enough ambient light to see his expression harden. "To find out what *you* want, Callisto. Why did you come back?"

"I think Vivian killed my father," I confess, then shift back in surprise, feeling the press of coats at my back. *Why did I tell him that?*

"Color me surprised," he says flatly. "Although I could technically thank her for ridding the world of that piece of shit, what are you going to do about it?"

Anger blooms, eager to be unleashed in place of what lies beneath it—fear and confusion. "None of your fucking business. We're not friends. Not confidants. I don't want you near me or my family. Can you get that through your thick skull?"

"Sure, but what makes you think I'll do what you say?" He takes a step toward me, shoulders consuming my vision. My breath goes short and choppy. "And why can't we be confidants? We want the same thing. In fact, I'd like to be closer to this family. Much closer."

Intuition blooms, making me bristle. "You're blackmailing me."

He shrugs. "Call it what you want. I think of it more as making you an offer you can't refuse."

My voice comes thick, "And what offer is that?"

"Invite me into your life, and I won't out you to Vivian."

My stomach goes leaden. "You wouldn't."

"Wouldn't I?" he sneers. "Prove to me you want what I want. Work with me toward that goal." He pauses, head tilting. "Or are you having second thoughts? Enjoying your return to power?"

"Fuck you."

His humorless grin slices me. "I almost did."

"You're disgusting," I seethe.

"What's it gonna be, princess? A new boyfriend, or a media lynching? Doesn't matter to me—either one ends Vivian's bid for governor. But can you imagine what the world will say when it comes out that you staged your own abduction? Lied to the cops? The entire nation?" He whistles softly. "You might be the one who ends up in a beige jumpsuit."

Trembling, near tears, I whisper, "I hate you."

"I don't care," he retorts. "I'll pick you up next Saturday at seven for our date, the first of many. From this point on, you're taken. By *me*. Like it or not, we're going to do this together."

"Bullshit," I growl. "They'll never buy it. I can't stand you."

Another chuckle, low and dark. "Oh, I think you can. I'm giving you a week to remember how much you liked me when we met."

He steps back, hand on the doorknob. "I'll go first. Thank you for the tour, it was enlightening."

"Suck a dick."

He snorts. "Don't worry, dick sucking won't be expected in our arrangement. Until next week, Callisto."

Then I'm alone in the closet with my thumping heart and scrambled mind.

21

Finn

EVERY MORNING, Aunt Molly watches the news from the couch in our rented apartment, a cup of tea in one hand and a small notebook in the other. Callisto and Vivian—and sometimes one or both of the sisters—appear on the usual programs. *Today Show, CBS This Morning, Good Morning America...*

The conversations are so scripted, everyone so polished and fake. And Callisto's story is the same every time. A series of soundbites to appease the curious public.

"*...very little memory of those days.*"

"*Yes, I'm beyond happy to be home.*"

And the coup d'état:

"*In the last six years, I met many homeless or otherwise at-risk young people in the United States who desperately need a voice. With my stepmother's help, I'm founding a charity called* Reach the Stars, *which will focus primarily on services for homeless teens."*

This has me chuckling every time I hear it. Not because I don't think it's an admirable idea, but because with it, Callisto has given me valuable insight into how she plans to play her stepmother.

She wants to be the very Trojan horse I once imagined her as—and the army inside will be public opinion. Even if Vivian did manage to sidestep any accusations or evidence Callisto brought to light, her political career would be over.

I'm only a little unnerved by how flawlessly she handles the limelight, the questions, the celebrity. There are more than a few clips of her being mobbed by weirdos convinced she's a vampire, as well as teenyboppers and grown women on the fame-train.

Molly's also collected an obscene number of magazines with society pages featuring Callisto at different events, toasting with flutes of champagne and mingling with the rich and famous.

I have no idea how she's handling it mentally, but all of it must be taking a toll. The lies that spill so sweetly from her lips, the constant microscope on everything from what she's wearing to whether she's getting therapy for PTSD.

She isn't the person I see on television or in print—the polished socialite. I don't examine my conviction, why I think I know her better than most. I just know it's true.

From my seat at the kitchen table, I hear Molly mutter, "Thank you," as she ends a phone call. Behind her, the TV is muted, the morning programs over.

Setting my pencil atop the crossword puzzle I'm dominating, I ask, "Well?"

She sighs. "No one will talk to me."

My aunt's career as a professional burglar ended before it started. The house in Ventura where my PI lived is now occupied by a family who has no idea what happened to the man's personal effects. They bought the house from the bank and it was empty when they moved in a month ago.

Molly continues, "And I can't pretend to be his sister or whatever because he didn't have any family. Only child of only children. No wife or kids. Dead end after dead end."

I give her a minute to soak in her thoughts, then say, "Maybe you should head back to Solstice Bay."

She gives me a sharp glance. "So I can watch from afar as this blows up in your face?"

She wasn't a fan of how I handled Callisto at the party on Sunday. I'm not especially proud of myself, either. I don't know why I keep acting like an asshole when she's around. Something inside me flips when I see her, and I start saying crazy shit.

Like I'm going to blackmail her.

The idea never even occurred to me until we were stuffed in that closet. I could smell her all around me, my skin felt two sizes too small, and I wanted to spank her for being so ornery before kissing her until she turned red all over... And since neither was an option, instead of charming her into compliance, I blurted out some bull-shit about turning her in if she didn't agree.

I rub the back of my neck. "I'll apologize on Satur-day. It was stupid, I know. I couldn't think straight."

Molly smirks. "Didn't expect to be attracted to her, did you?"

I groan. "Please don't go there."

She grins. "The spider is caught in his own web." Her smile falls, expression sobering. "I'm scared for you both, but I'm glad you'll be there to help her. You're creative thinkers. Survivors. Somehow, you'll figure out the best course of action."

I grunt in reply.

Molly finishes her tea and takes the cup to the kitchen. She rinses and dries it, then stands silently before the sink, her head bowed. I know she's disappointed and battling helplessness. I've been there a thousand times over the last decade. I feel for her, I do.

But right now, for the first time in so long, there's a spark of hope inside me. I finally have an in. An ally in the family. If I play my cards right, before the year is up, I'll have hard evidence that Vivian Avellino is a crook of the highest order.

I think Vivian killed my father.

Maybe we'll get her on murder charges, too. Wouldn't that be rich? Avenging the death of the man who murdered my father in order to put his widow in jail?

A shadow falls over me and I look up at my aunt, taking in her newly determined expression.

"I want you to find out how many people work full-time in that house, and I want their names."

"Molly—"

"You think you're the only obstinate one in this family?" she interjects. "The only one passionate about this? You may want revenge, but I want Callisto *home*, in Solstice Bay."

I shift in my chair, feeling six years old and on the wrong end of a verbal lashing. "Fine," I agree.

"Good."

She nods, satisfied, and turns away. On impulse, I

touch her arm to stall her, and when she meets my gaze, I say, "I'm glad you're here. Thank you. For everything."

Her eyes moisten. "I'm sorry for the way I reacted when you came back. But more than that, I'm sorry that you've shouldered so much over the years. You're not alone anymore, Finnegan."

Her words hit me like a sledgehammer, clogging my throat with long-buried emotion.

"Thanks," I choke out.

With a soft smile, she leaves me to stare, bleary-eyed, at empty squares in the crossword puzzle. Five letters. Clue: Where the Acheron flows.

A quick Google search later—yes, I cheat—I sit back with a humorless smile.

Oh, the irony.

Acheron is the river that flows into the Greek Underworld, *Hades.* And that's exactly where I'm going. Straight into the dark on a river of pain.

22

Callisto

"I REALLY DON'T UNDERSTAND IT." Ellie sniffs primly as she examines her nails.

"What's to understand?" asks Lizzie, smirking. "Is it so unbelievable to you that he's interested in our beautiful sister?"

"He probably just wants to photograph her and sell the prints to the highest bidder."

Lizzie slants me a worried look, but I shrug it off. It's always been like this with Ellie. That she's equating Finn with a bottom-dwelling paparazzo to appease her bruised ego is par for the course. Her digs used to hurt, but now they buzz past me like harmless flies. I have other, bigger problems to wrestle with. Like how to keep them safe and secure while I ruin their mother.

"I doubt it'll go anywhere," Ellie continues, petulant. "He seems like a total tool."

Seated beside her on the guest bed, Lizzie rolls her eyes, then mouths at me, "Jealous."

I smile sadly, wishing I could tell Ellie she has absolutely nothing to be jealous of. That Finn's interest in me only goes as far as how useful I can be to him.

The lies are stacking up, the weight on my heart growing.

"I love that outfit," Lizzie says brightly. "Do you know where he's taking you?"

I give myself a final, cursory glance. There's nothing special about what I'm wearing—jeans, a black top, and comfortable flats. But I appreciate Lizzie's effort. Frankly, I don't care what Finn thinks. I'm casual because, for a week straight, I've been stuffed into designer outfits I'd never wear by choice. A pair of jeans is luxury to me.

"He said he wanted to surprise me," I lie, padding the prior fabrication that he's been texting me on my shiny new iPhone all week.

Lizzie claps excitedly. "Ohh, so romantic."

Ellie flops onto her back. "Am I the only one who thinks maybe it's too soon for Calli to date?"

"Yes," chirps Lizzie with a gleam in her eye. "Why

are you even here, Ellie? It's Friday night. Shouldn't you be at a frat party or something?"

"I wanted to help Calli get ready, duh," she answers unconvincingly. "What time is it?"

"Time for you to get a hobby."

"Shut up, Ms. Does Nothing. Maybe we should work on some college applications for you, huh?"

"Shove it, El. I'm taking a break-year. It's a thing."

Ah, sisters.

"It's only a thing if you *do* something for a year. Like travel, have sex with hot European guys, or even just hang out with friends on a beach somewhere. But you don't have any friends, do you?"

"I have friends," snaps Lizzie. "And you're one to talk! If you weren't so far up Mom's ass, you'd see how pointless college is. We're not going to have careers. We're going to be married off to *whoever's* rich sons. What's the fucking point?"

Shocked, I almost drop the tube of mascara in my hand.

"Whatever," drawls Ellie. "You're delusional and paranoid. Keep at it and you'll end up in a padded room."

She's not crazy! I want to yell. But I keep my mouth shut as they continue to bicker, the subject thankfully

149

shifting to who borrowed whose designer shoes last month and conveniently forgot to return them.

When the doorbell rings a few minutes later, the girls have lapsed into rigid silence. Ellie hops off the bed. "I'll get it," she sings as she saunters from the room.

Lizzie sighs. "She's had a celebrity crush on him for a few years. I think she's hurt he didn't reciprocate."

We both know there's more to it than that, but I shake my head and grab my purse. "It's all good. Weirdly, her reaction is kind of comforting."

Lizzie grins. "I get it. She's not treating you any differently than before."

I nod. "Neither are you," I say softly, then pause. "You'd tell me if something were going on, right, Lizzie?"

She frowns. "Well, yeah. But what are you talking about?"

"I don't know... like stuff with the family."

Her gaze clears. "This is about my comment earlier, about being married off?" I nod and she chuckles, the sound so jaded, so different from her usual laughter that I wince. "I don't have to explain it to you, do I, Calli?"

Her gaze hits mine, direct and challenging, and for a moment I think she knows. My breath stills. Spots dance in my vision.

Then she rolls her eyes, laughing light and familiar. "Don't worry about me. I'm just having my first existential crisis. Figuring out what I want and all that shit. Ellie doesn't get it."

I choose my words carefully. "You can do whatever you set your heart and mind to, Lizzie."

She offers a slight smile. "As long as it serves the family, right?"

No, God no.

Somehow I make myself smile. "Right."

"Have fun tonight, okay? You deserve it."

"I'll try."

She stands up and gives me a quick hug, then shoos me toward the door. I'm on the threshold when she murmurs, "Why did you come back here?"

My knuckles blanch as I grip the doorframe, my heart sinking. Blinking away the sting in my eyes, I glance back to meet her gaze.

"For you and Ellie."

She nods, gaze dropping to the floor. "I figured as much."

I swallow hard. "I love you, Lizzie."

"Love you, too, big sis."

I don't want to leave her, but I do, my thoughts shifting gear to who waits for me, likely annoyed as he deflects the advances of my other sister.

Sure enough, when I get to the foyer, I find Ellie standing inappropriately close to my so-called date. In short-shorts that show off her lithe, tan legs, and lacy white tank, she's pushing the *fun-loving-SoCal-girl* angle hard. Though Finn doesn't look impressed, he doesn't look unimpressed, either, his expression engaged as Ellie chatters nonstop.

It hits me that he's used to women throwing themselves at him, used to flirting and probably sleeping with whoever he wants. *Maybe Ellie is his type.* The thought comes tinged green, which only makes me annoyed with myself.

I clear my throat. Finn's eyes snap to me, a smirk blooming on his lips like he could hear my irritation in the sound.

"Hi, Callisto," he says, that damnable smile growing, one eyebrow arching as he takes in my casual appearance. "You look beautiful. Ready to go?"

His execution is so flawless, for a moment I think he's actually complimenting me. That he thinks I'm beautiful. *Stupid, Calli.* Reminding myself what a joke this is—that I'm being blackmailed of all things—resets my equilibrium.

"Yep. Have a good night, Ellie. Thanks for answering the door."

Ignoring me, she touches Finn's arm, encased by a leather jacket. "Now you have my number, so let me know about that thing, okay?"

He nods. "Will do. See you later."

Ellie waves and flounces from the room.

Finn's brows lift, lips twitching as I stalk past him out the front door. He beats me to his car—a sleek BMW —and opens the passenger door.

"She's a feisty one, isn't she?" There's laughter and male appreciation in his voice, which makes me see red. "She wants new headshots, like every twenty-something in L.A. Like I'd waste my time."

I yank my door closed, then close my eyes and focus on breathing as he slips into the driver's seat. He doesn't speak again until we're cruising through the open gates.

"Where are your stepmother and uncles this evening? I expected an inquisition and was all geared up to charm them."

"A photographer, no matter how rich, isn't important enough to warrant an introduction unless he comes with a dynasty."

"Ouch." But he doesn't sound offended. "I will, though. Be introduced to your family. Soon."

I bristle, my gaze sliding to his profile, shadowed as night descends. "Why don't you just lay it out for me so I know what to do, huh? The terms of the blackmail."

He laughs like I'm not dead serious.

I growl, "What the fuck is wrong with you? This is my life we're talking about! How is this funny?"

His mirth dies, eyes slicing to me and away. I'm glad the darkness disguises their beautiful blue color. "I don't think any of this is *funny*, princess. And it's not just your life on the line. I'm well aware I could see the inside of a coffin for this."

"Then why are you here?" I cry, my voice shrill in the confines of the car.

The following silence is thick, the only sound the hum of the road beneath us. At length he answers, "My aunt considers you family, and there's nothing more important than family. Isn't that what you were taught, too?"

Sinking into my seat, I cross my arms defensively over my chest. Everything hurts—my heart, head, and body.

"I don't want my sisters to get hurt," I say finally.

"I'm not sure there's a way around that," he answers with surprising compassion. "No matter what, if we put their mother behind bars, their lives are going to drastically change."

Not for the first time, doubt rears its head, sharp teeth dripping venomous confusion and fear. "Lizzie asked me earlier why I came back, and then said if she were in my shoes, she probably wouldn't have." I'm not sure why I'm telling him this, but it feels necessary. "I told her I came back for them—my sisters—but that's not the truth."

"Then why?"

I look out the window, noticing we're on the freeway headed east and not caring. "I've been trying to convince myself it's for them, or for Uncle Ant, or for your father and everyone else who's suffered because of my family, or because I want to do the right thing..."

"But?"

"What if the only reason I'm here is to rub Vivian's face in how she treated me as a child? To gloat as everything is stripped from her, no matter the collateral damage to my sisters?"

"Why can't it be a little bit of all those things?" he asks softly. "I don't know details about what you went through, but I'm pretty confident you've earned the right to resent Vivian."

"If that's true, then I'm no different than her. Motivated by hatred, greed, and pride."

From the corner of my eye, I see his fingers clench on the steering wheel. "You're nothing like her, Callisto. Trust me."

The conviction in his voice barely reaches me, my thoughts haunted by Lizzie's sad smile, the defeat in her young eyes.

I don't have to explain it to you, do I?

Why did you come back here?

"You're not doing this alone." Finn's voice wraps around me, deep and smooth.

"Not by choice," I mutter.

He sighs. "Forget the blackmail for a minute and the fact you can't stand me. I'm a pretty smart, capable guy, and I've been on this track for a long fucking time. Somewhere in that house, on a computer or in a file, is the information we need. And if not, then there's someone out there who has it."

"And if we fail?"

He shakes his head. "Failure isn't an option."

23

Finn

LESS THAN A WEEK. Callisto has been in that house less than a week and she's already changed. Shadows ring her eyes despite tasteful makeup to conceal them. She's thinner, too. Edgy and withdrawn. Her love for her sisters is a seeping wound in her confidence, and there's not a damn thing I can do about it.

When I park the car outside the generic apartment complex, she doesn't question why I've brought her here, just gets out of the car and waits listlessly for me to come around. My need to comfort her is irrational but ever-present. I want to say something—anything—to put the light back in her eyes, but the best I can do is to take her to someone who might be able to.

When we reach the second-story apartment, the door opens before I can knock. The two women stare at each other for a beat—one smiling and one shocked—before Callisto sobs out, "Molly?"

"Come here, sweetheart," coos my aunt, and Callisto collapses into her arms.

I busy myself in the kitchen as soft words are exchanged on the couch, Molly's arms staying securely around the younger woman. A rare pang of loneliness hits me—no one has ever taken comfort in me like that.

Has anyone ever needed me?

Scoffing at my thoughts, I decide Callisto's mood must be affecting mine and do my best to ignore their voices as I finish layering various cheeses, olives, prosciutto, and crackers on the big serving plate. I tear off a few paper towels, then head for the couch.

Molly smiles as I lower the plate to the coffee table. "Thank you, Finn. This looks delicious."

"It does," agrees a wavering voice, "thank you."

"You're welcome." Avoiding Callisto's eyes, I snag a few olives and drop into the adjacent armchair. "We can talk business while we eat."

Molly makes a disgruntled sound, but says, "Calli was just telling me about the employees at the house, specifically a maid named Selina who warned her about a camera in her bedroom."

My chewing slows and my gaze veers to Callisto. "You weren't kidding about the surveillance, were you?"

She shakes her head. "It's always been that way. I think it's mostly sound. When we were kids, we thought our dad had magical powers because he always seemed to know stuff we said when he wasn't around."

"Like what?"

Her focus turns inward, her eyes glazing with memory. "When we were small, it was stuff like sneaking out of our rooms for cookies in the middle of the night. When we were older... well, imagine three teenage girls planning to sneak out to a party." A wry smile briefly appears. "It didn't happen."

Molly muses, "So we know somewhere in the house, there's access to all the audio."

Callisto nods. "Probably on Vivian's computer, in her office. There aren't too many rooms that stay locked, but that's one of them."

"What are the others?" I ask quickly.

She gives me a knowing look. "The basement and the master bedroom." Before I can ask, she continues, "My dad was mistrusting of technology and didn't like storing information on his computer. The basement used to have big filing cabinets and a standing safe. I have no idea if they're still there."

"You haven't checked?" Even I can hear the accusation in my voice.

Molly bristles. "Finn—"

159

"It's okay," says Callisto, laying a hand on Molly's arm before turning her dark eyes on me. "I spent the last six days traveling at Vivian's behest, smiling and lying. My focus right now is on gaining her trust. If she catches me snooping in the basement, or anywhere, it will all be for nothing."

I sit back with a brie-smeared cracker. "You really think if you're nice to her long enough, she'll suddenly reveal all her secrets? Don't be naïve. That could take years if it happened at all."

Ire glows in her eyes. "Not every problem can be solved with a bulldozer, Finn."

My name in her throaty voice, combined with the spark of passion in her eyes, trails up my spine like a touch. I imagine her saying my name in drastically different circumstances. Moaning it. Screaming it. Whimpering it as I take her from behind.

Like she can hear my thoughts—or see them in my face—Callisto's eyes widen and a blush blooms on her pale cheeks. She looks down quickly.

Molly clears her throat. "Let's focus on the positive. We have different approaches, which we can use to our advantage. I'll see what I can learn about the staff, especially Selina, while you two figure out where Vivian stores her files and surveillance footage."

"Assuming either exists," I mutter, then sigh. "If I

were her, I would destroy everything. Especially a paper trail. Why keep evidence of past crimes? It doesn't make sense."

Callisto murmurs, "You're probably right. Vivian wouldn't be sentimental about my father's old files. And with her run for governor coming up, I'm sure the computers in the house are squeaky clean."

Molly slumps. "Then what? Maybe there's something in the safe?"

"Like a written confession?" I grouse. "Besides, I'm not sure your amateur lock-picking skills are up for the job."

"Smartass."

"Takes one to know one."

Callisto cracks a smile—a small one, but it stirs something unfamiliar inside me. When she notices me watching her, she doesn't look away. Not this time. Instead, she holds the contact, the echoes of her smile still there, and for a moment I forget it all. My mission, my hatred, my rage... like shedding the armor I've worn for years, I feel lighter and free.

Then I open my stupid mouth.

"When can you introduce me to Vivian?"

Her eyes empty of emotion. "I, uh... I'll ask her about inviting you to dinner on Thursday. My uncles will be there."

"They're there every Thursday?"

She nods. "After dinner they usually have a meeting in Vivian's office."

I groan. "What are the chances *that* room is wired?"

She shakes her head. "Highly doubtful. And knowing my uncle Franco, it's probably got all sorts of tech to prevent anyone outside the house from listening in."

Struck with an idea, I lurch forward in my chair. "But if they're all in the office, then the rest of the house is free game."

She frowns. "You can't wander around the house alone."

"What if I get lost looking for the bathroom?"

"Then you might as well give up trying to impress my family."

I smile in spite of myself. "Good point."

Molly stirs. "What if you want to show your date around? Or"—she flushes in embarrassment—"maybe find a private place to, you know..."

Callisto turns beet red and doesn't look at me. "I'm not sure I'd take a date to the basement, but we could walk around a bit. But first I have to convince Vivian to let Finn come to dinner. Guests aren't normally allowed."

"Convince her I'm a special case."

Molly snorts. "Oh, you're a special case, all right."

I roll my eyes.

Then Callisto laughs, the soft, melodic sound surprisingly sultry, and I decide being the butt of my aunt's jokes might not be so bad.

24

Callisto

AFTER THE ROCKY start to our fake date, it ended up being one of the best nights I've had in a while. The three of us played a raucous game of Scrabble, ate too many Oreos, and Finn even disappeared for a while so Molly and I could talk. Then he drove me home, requested my phone number, and walked me to the front door with assurances he'd call tomorrow. The awkwardness of *should we hug or something?* was thankfully dispelled by Lizzie yanking open the door, hoping to catch us doing anything but what we were doing... shuffling like teenagers who don't know how to use their limbs.

At Lizzie's arrival, Finn merely grinned and waved goodbye before retreating to his car.

I don't understand him. How can a person be so hot

and cold? How can his hard gaze turn my stomach inside out, then melt it through my feet with a different look? How can the asshole who threatened me in a closet be the same person who fist-bumped me when I won Scrabble?

He makes my head spin.

After disappointing Lizzie with only the vaguest description of *the best date ever*, I say goodnight. Halfway to my room, I change my mind and head for the kitchen for a cup of tea. I'm too wired to think about sleep yet, but I need to be alone for a bit to decompress from the night.

Seeing Molly was both a joy and shock. And as much as my heart feels fuller with her near, her involvement adds one more worry to my bucket. A bucket that was already overflowing.

As the kettle heats, I take a seat at the marble-topped counter, absentmindedly tracing the veins of gold with my finger. Molly and Finn both stressed that we're a team, that none of us have to face this alone, and though I'd like to believe them, my instinct tells me they're wrong.

"Why wouldn't you want them to find me?"

Uncle Ant tapped his temple. "Because of what's in your head."

It's hard to believe Uncle Anthony wanted to take me away because I held the key to exposing the family's secrets. Not for the first time, I wonder about his endgame. Was he working with someone? A government agency? Why did he think I had something in my head that could threaten the family?

I listen to the hiss of the stove burner and rack my memory for something, *anything*, that might be what he referred to.

There's nothing. Just a jumble of memories blurred with emotion. My tenth birthday party, sabotaged by Vivian, who forgot to send the invitations and blamed it on a maid. Waking from nightmares after my father went to prison and sneaking into his office to sleep beneath his desk.

Is it possible to both love and hate someone? It must be. Thoughts of my father cycle between the two; he was all I had. The only parent in whose eyes I saw affection. But there was also anger, disappointment, and scorn. Especially after he was released from prison. He was like a different person. Hardened and cold. Snapping at everyone—Vivian most of all. There was no more gruff affection from him. Not for any of us. There was only an angry, bitter man where our father had been.

"What are you doing up?"

I startle at Vivian's voice, spinning on the barstool to

see her in the kitchen doorway. She's still in the day's clothes, a smart business suit tailored to her curves. My heart thumps, audible in my ears, as I nod to the stove.

"Having some tea."

Like magic, the kettle begins to whine. Grateful for the distraction, I hop off the stool to fetch a mug and teabag.

"May I join you?"

No. I'm flayed open by memories. Too vulnerable to play the game.

But I don't really have a choice.

"Of course. Chamomile?"

"That sounds lovely."

As I prepare our mugs, Vivian slips onto the stool next to the one I occupied.

Pull it together, I tell myself, taking slow, deep breaths. *You had a great first date with Finn. You're an ally. An asset. Act like it.*

"Here you go." I set her mug on the counter before her, then settle back onto my stool. Cradling my mug, I blow off the steam and ask, "How was your day?"

"Interesting." She pauses and I feel her eyes on me. "Whatever you said to Fred Walters at the garden party made a lasting impression. He offered a substantial contribution to my campaign today."

I vaguely remember talking to the man. Older,

white-haired, quick to laugh, with a twinkle in his eye for me. He didn't treat me like a leper or a sideshow, which made it easy to charm him.

"That's great news," I say, smiling. "He was a peach."

She chuckles. "A peach with more money than Midas."

My smile grows. "Even better."

Vivian sips her tea, sighing in pleasure. "I'm actually glad I caught you, Callisto. Now that you've had time to get used to being back, there's something I want to talk to you about."

Nerves shimmer down my arms. I keep my fingers loose on my mug as my senses sharpen in apprehension.

"What's that?"

Her eyes meet mine, her expression open and soft. Even though I know it's not real, the echoes of the small girl I used to be, who just wanted a mother, perk up.

"It's about your uncle Anthony."

It's a miracle I don't choke on my mouthful of tea. Still, there's no way Vivian missed the way my shoulders tightened.

"I want to apologize for what happened after he died. When I picked you up from school."

She looks down, a manicured fingernail sliding along

a golden vein on the counter, a disquieting reflection of my own action. *Had she been watching me?*

"Rafael told me to give you that envelope. I didn't realize what was in it—I thought it was a letter from your uncle to you or... something. I didn't know."

I say the first thing that comes into my mind, "He told you from prison?"

She nods. "He called the night before Anthony died. Enzo brought me the envelope the following morning."

"And you didn't look inside?"

Her eyes flicker up, filled with hurt. "In retrospect, I should have. I never would have given it to you. Of course, I was stunned that they were plane tickets. Did you know he was going to take you away from us?"

"No," I lie. "I was eight. All I knew was that Uncle Ant had been acting odd for months, but nothing that far out of the norm. He was always eccentric."

"That he was," she says wryly.

"You're telling me that Dad had Anthony killed?" My voice is even, my tone mild.

Vivian arches an eyebrow, gaze sharpening with something I've never seen her direct toward me. Respect.

"There was a time a conversation such as this would have put you in tears." She shakes her head. "Obviously I'm not glad you went through what you did, but at the same time, it's a joy to finally see your potential come to fruition."

You never thought I had potential.

"Thank you. Are you avoiding answering the question?"

She laughs, throaty and sincere. "Touché." Sobering, she answers, "Yes, your father was responsible for Anthony's death." Before the words—the confirmation of one of my worst fears—can sink in, she adds, "And I want you to help me find out why."

Reeling, I ask, "What do you mean? Didn't you just imply it was because he wanted to take me away?" I can't keep the resentment from my voice. "Even at eight, I understood what those tickets—and their delivery —meant."

"Again, I'm so sorry. No young girl should have to face a truth like that, and I know Anthony's death affected you deeply."

"Yes, it did. It was difficult to understand at the time."

She cocks her head, blond tresses swinging gently over her shoulder. "But you understand now?"

Tucking away my horror and grief, I nod. "Am I shocked to hear you admit it was Dad who had him killed? Yes, but only because we've never had this kind of honest conversation before. I appreciate the truth, Vivian. I'd like more of it."

She smiles wistfully. "So would I, which is why I'm asking for your help. I think there's more to why Anthony wanted to disappear with you."

My heart rate spikes. "Like what, exactly?"

"You spent a lot of time at his ranch," she says casually, then shrugs. "Maybe there's something there that might trigger a memory for you. I don't know... was there a place he used to hide things?"

My scalp tingles. Looking down, I fight to keep my reaction from my face. I don't believe in serendipity, but the fact our conversation so closely mirrors my earlier thoughts is eerie. And it means I'm on the right track.

Uncle Ant knew something. Maybe kept something. A file. A USB drive. A photograph. And Vivian wants me to find it. Whatever it is, it's damaging enough to warrant her request.

I'm not stupid enough to think she trusts me. This is a test of my loyalty, a chance to prove to her that I'm an Avellino through and through. Or, just as likely, an invitation for me to fail and confirm that I'm a stain on the family's honor.

"Not that I can recall," I say, looking up with a frown. "Wasn't the ranch searched after his death?"

"Yes, several times. But I'd like you to take a look. We've kept the property unchanged."

My frown deepens. "For seventeen years?"

"Your father's request." She sighs, head shaking. "I always marveled at what a brilliant, complex man your father was, but those same traits made him hard to understand." She touches my arm, her fingers cool on my skin. "It might be nothing. Just your father's regret and deep pain over what he had to do. But there's a reason he didn't want the ranch touched. Will you try to find that reason?"

I cover her hand with mine. "Of course, Vivian."

BACK IN MY ROOM, I take the burner phone from its hiding place behind an air vent and text Rabbit. She threatened to shave my head in my sleep if I didn't keep her updated, but we both know it's so she can tell the police if something goes wrong. Then I send the same text to Finn, whose number I have newly stored in my iPhone.

Something at my uncle's ranch Vivian wants me to look for. Will keep u posted.

Seconds later the phone vibrates with an incoming call. When I see who it is, I momentarily teeter on the cusp of declining, then rush into the bathroom and start the shower. Nervous to hear his voice and preemptively annoyed at what he'll say, I answer.

"Hello?"

"What uncle? What ranch?"

"I'm fine, thank you. How are you?"

He huffs. "I think we're past that, princess. What happened?"

Too tired for verbal sparring, I fill him in on my conversation with Vivian.

"The crazy thing is I was thinking about Uncle Ant just before then, about something he said to me a long time ago. He told me he needed to keep me safe from my parents because of what was in my head."

Finn is quiet for a moment. "Why haven't you told me this?" he growls.

Apparently I'm not tired anymore, because I lash back, "I didn't realize I had to report every thought in my head to you. Besides, when was I supposed to tell you? I didn't have your damn number until tonight."

He sighs in exasperation. "Arguing is pointless. You're taking me with you to the ranch."

"Are you nuts? No way. I haven't even asked Vivian about dinner on Thursday. Visiting my dead uncle's ranch is private family business. I'd be insane to ask to bring you."

"Private family business," he snarls. "You know who you sound like?"

In lieu of shrieking obscenities, I hiss, "You're impossible!"

He pauses. "Are you in the *shower*?"

Registering the teasing tone, I demand, "Are you bipolar? You have more mood swings than a teen on her period."

His laughter douses my anger, until eventually my own lips tilt.

"You're certifiable," I tell him, holding in my own mirth. "The shower is on so no one can hear me talking."

"But *were* you going to shower? Inquiring minds and all that."

"Are you serious?" I bleat, then wince at the volume of my voice. "First of all, it's none of your business. Second of all, jury's out on whether or not you're a psychopath. And third, what are we even talking about anymore? I'm hanging up."

"Wait. I'm sorry. Don't go."

He sounds contrite enough that I ask, "What do you want, Finn?"

"Among other things, a Scrabble rematch."

My head shakes in consternation, but my stupid lips quirk again. "You have to be the strangest person alive."

"I think you take the cake on that one, princess."

"I hate that nickname, by the way."

"Sorry, I didn't catch that. The shower scene playing out in my head is pretty loud."

I make a noise of disgust, but I'm feeling the opposite. My stomach drops, triggering pulsing need between my legs. No matter how hard I try, my body won't forget his.

"You're remembering that night," he murmurs. "Your breathing just picked up."

I yank the phone away from my mouth, but it's too late. He chuckles knowingly.

"I've tried to forget, too, but you left me a souvenir that's made it impossible."

My missing panties.

Mortified, I sink to the closed toilet seat and drop my head forward. My voice is shaky. "That's creepy and gross. Why didn't you throw them away?"

"I'm probably going to regret this in the morning, just like I regret most of what I say to you..." He sighs, and I imagine the warmth of his breath on my neck. "I kept them because I wanted a reminder."

My heart in my throat, I whisper, "Of the mistake you made?"

"No, princess." The gravelly words make my thighs clench. "Of the best almost-sex of my life, and how badly I want to do it again."

Like your average mature, level-headed woman, I gasp and hang up.

25

Callisto

TAP. Tap. Tap.

"Miss?"

Tap. Tap. Tap.

"I'm so sorry to wake you, but there's someone here demanding to see you."

I blink groggily at my bedroom door—the direction Selina's voice is coming from. "What? Who?"

"Mr. Reid."

The name might as well be a bucket of cold water. Jerking upright, I swing my feet to the floor and pad to the door. Unlocking it, I squint at Selina. From her fresh face and the light behind the curtains at my back, it's morning. But it feels like I just went to bed.

"What time is it?" I croak.

She checks her watch. "Just after nine o'clock."

I groan. "What is he doing here? Did he say?"

She shakes her head. "Would you like me to call security? I would have already, but Lizzie told me you had a successful date last night, and I didn't want to—"

"No, no, it's okay. Thank you, Selina. You did the right thing. Tell him I'll be right down. But you can leave him outside."

Her eyes twinkle as she nods. "Very well."

When she's gone, I open the closet and grab the first thing I see—a deep blue maxi dress and flip-flops—and hustle into the bathroom to brush my teeth, slap on some lip gloss, and throw my hair into a bun, all the while castigating myself for caring what I look like. For caring what he thinks, or sees, or wants. For still feeling the aftershocks from not only what he said last night, but from the intense orgasm I had later in bed courtesy of my own hand.

My breath sits high and short in my chest as I make my way to the front door, and my face feels like plastic about to crack. Thankfully, no one's around to notice my mostly mental walk of shame.

Who shows up the morning after a date like this? Let alone a fake one. What the hell is he playing at?

By the time I open the door, I'm as irritated as I am nervous. I don't wait for him to turn around before whisper-hissing, "What the hell, Finn?"

Spinning on a heel, he gives me a lazy smile as those shockingly blue eyes scan me from head to feet. After a perusal that feels more than skin-deep, he shakes his head. "Cute. Very L.A. But that dress won't work at all."

I finally tear my gaze from his face to what he's wearing. Athletic shorts, sneakers, and a faded T-shirt. He makes casual look sinful, all lean muscles, sun-kissed tattoos, and tousled hair.

God help me, it's really not fair he's so gorgeous.

"What are you talking about? I don't like surprises, and I definitely don't like being woken up before ten on a Sunday morning."

His smile only grows. "I'm being spontaneous. You said you weren't doing anything today. I didn't have plans, and I wanted to see you, so here I am." Spreading his arms, he grins through the lies, like he knows exactly how irate I am and exactly how much I don't want to be anywhere near him.

But then there's the small matter of blackmail. While I don't honestly think he'll go through with it— Molly would castrate him—it still speaks to a side of him I need to be wary of. I can't forget his rage when he realized who I was, the hatred that seeped from him at the cove that day.

He'll do anything to put a stop to Vivian's political career, to bring down the family once and for all. If it ended up being the only way for him to get revenge, I'm positive he'd feed me to the wolves without a second thought.

I need to be careful. Not push him. Let him think he's in charge.

Which means I can't tell him to fuck off.

"All right," I concede. "Where are we going?"

"It's a secret."

I don't bother repeating my stance on surprises. From the glint in his eye, he obviously doesn't care.

A headache taps hello behind my right eye. I have no idea how I'm going to survive his company. I can only hope that maybe, just maybe, he'll bring me to Molly and leave us alone.

"I'll be back in fifteen."

I retreat inside. Finn takes a step to follow me, but I slam the door in his wide-eyed face, then gloat all the way to my room. Serves him right for showing up like this.

It takes me less than ten minutes to change into shorts and a tank, apply sunblock, and find the brand-new sneakers in my closet. I stop by the kitchen for a granola bar and bottle of water, waving bye to Lizzie in the process. She smirks and makes kissy noises at my back. At least Vivian isn't around—her routine is the same as it's always been. On Sundays she golfs in the morning and spends the afternoon at the spa.

Outside, Finn waits in the car for me, engine idling and music crooning through open windows. He doesn't bother looking my way when I yank open the passenger door. I'm barely buckled in when he accelerates toward the gates.

"I didn't realize we were in a hurry," I mutter.

His eyes cut to me. "Are you always this cheery in the morning? What's wrong with a little adventure?"

"Do you always shame women for perfectly normal responses to idiocy?"

"Ha! Good one. You sound just like my sisters." He shakes his head, lips twisted wryly. "I have to say, I'm kind of amazed you have a backbone at all. No offense, but I didn't think the Avellinos were in the habit of raising feminists."

"They aren't," I snap.

For the briefest moments, I'd been enjoying our banter. Not anymore. The world dims a bit with the reminder of the only reason we're together in the first place. We're not friends. Not lovers. Barely allies, despite the weird pseudo-intimacy we've shared. And the phone call last night.

"I brought you coffee," he says, nodding toward the

center console. "Yours is the front one. Molly told me how you take it."

"Thanks," I say stiffly. "Are we seeing Molly?"

Finn shakes his head, and my stomach sinks. "Come on, princess, did you really think we wouldn't have to spend any time together? We're supposed to be diving headfirst into a serious relationship. That means we need to get used to each other. Trade information."

I sip my coffee in silence, which is the only meaningful response I can give. *Trade information.* What a perfect way to describe what we're doing—offering up pieces of our lives to build a fabricated bond.

I've spent six years—a lifetime, really—lying about my past to anyone who cared to ask about it. But now that I can tell the truth, I don't feel any relief.

Because the truth is still entwined with lies.

"I have three sisters," he says in the tense silence. "The youngest is three years older than me. That's Michelle. Then Sydney, who's two years older than Michelle. Abby is the oldest. Not to say she's old or anything. She's forty this year."

He pauses, and I know it's so I can say something. Ask a question. Pretend any of it matters, that I actually care. I don't have it in me, though, so I only nod.

"All right, then. Let's see... Abby and Michelle are nurses. Pediatric and ICU. Sydney is an elementary school teacher, like my mom was. All three are married with kids. I have seven nieces and nephews. The oldest is ten, the youngest a year and a half."

"Seven?" I echo in spite of myself. I've never been around kids and wouldn't know the first thing about handling one, let alone multiples.

He grins. "My sisters are rock stars. I don't know how they do it. Kids kinda freak me out."

"Me too," I admit.

"Yeah? Well, there you go. We have one thing in common. We're afraid of children. I blame too many horror movies when I was a kid."

I nod. *"The Omen."*

"Exorcist."

"Children of the Corn."

Finn's whole body shudders. *"Pet Cemetery."*

Laughter bubbles out of me. "Okay, we can stop now."

He grins. "Another thing in common—not a fan of horror movies?"

"At least ones with evil kids." I pause. "How did you know you wanted to be a photographer?"

Surprised eyes flicker my way. Hell, I'm surprised, too. *Why did I ask that? Who cares?*

"It was an accident, actually. I was a sophomore at UC Berkeley, majoring in journalism, when one night at a party a friend asked me to take some photos. It was the first time I held a Nikon."

"Love at first touch?"

"And sight. I was hooked. When I looked at the world through a lens, it made sense in a way it hadn't before. It was like magic."

"And now?"

He shrugs. "What matters is that now I have the financial freedom to live how I want."

"Wow. That's sad."

He stiffens. "Why?"

"Besides the fact you just reduced the value of art to a dollar bill?" I laugh bitterly. "Who am I to judge, though. Good for you. Now you have the financial freedom to pursue other lifelong goals like blackmail and entrapment. And who cares about collateral damage, right?"

The air in the car turns frosty.

"Molly says I should trust you, Callisto, but it's hard when you make me wonder what your motives are. Do you want the same things I do? Or do you want to stand in my way?"

26

Callisto

THE REST of the drive is tense and silent. It's not a short trip, either, at just over an hour, and for the last twenty minutes we've been driving through L.A.'s version of the middle of nowhere—the Angeles National Forest. Contrary to the name, so far I've seen more tumbleweeds than trees.

Every time I have the urge to ask him what we're doing, I bite my cheek until it passes.

By the time Finn pulls off the road into a small parking lot, I've consumed my coffee, water, and granola bar. Any curiosity about our destination takes a backseat to my screaming bladder. Thankfully there's a standard-looking campground attached to the parking lot. With bathrooms—rudimentary but clean.

Agony gone, I slip my sunglasses on and step into the sun, finally able to take in details of my surroundings. Lo and behold, craggy trees dot the area, thickening to a forest behind the campground and rising in the distance to low mountains. I take a deep breath, greedily sucking the smog-less air and fading coolness of the morning.

Footsteps approach me, crunching over gravel. I don't have to look to know it's him. The way he moves is familiar. Like a song I hate to love and would never admit listening to.

"Have you been out here before?" Finn asks, handing me a baseball hat and a bandana. At my questioning look, he says, "To keep the sun off the back of your neck."

"No, I haven't been here," I concede, pulling on the hat and trying unsuccessfully to attach the bandana.

Finn takes over, fingers gentle in my hair as he adjusts my ponytail and tucks the fabric under the band of the hat. "I used to come here a lot, years ago, when I lived in the city."

I frown, turning to look up at him. "Where *do* you live?"

He smiles, but even though I can't see his eyes behind dark lenses, I can tell it doesn't reach them. "I like to think of myself as a nomadic artist. Versatile. Open to opportunities."

"You don't have a home?" I blurt, then realize the ridiculousness of me making the statement. "Never mind. I've lived out of a duffel bag for years."

"We're a pair, aren't we?"

I sniff out a noncommittal, "Hmph."

His smile grows a touch. "We'll hit shade about a half-mile in, but this trail gets a little technical. You up for it?"

"I'm not afraid of technical." I nod toward his backpack. "I'm assuming you have water and food?"

"Of course not," he deadpans, "but I did pack crayons and a kite."

My lips betray me, tilting at the corners. "What on earth made you want to bring me out here?"

I'm hoping for the quick, rational explanation that Molly told him he should. But in true Finn form, he doesn't do what I want him to.

"I wanted to take you somewhere that would remind you of Oregon. Molly mentioned you did a lot of hiking in the forest up there, so I figured you'd enjoy this. It's the closest I could get you to Solstice Bay."

I have no words. Nothing that doesn't involve admitting what I don't want to admit—that I'm floored. Touched. That were I a different woman and he a different man, I might swoon.

Instead, I say, "Thanks," and set off for the nearby trailhead.

FINN WASN'T KIDDING—THE trail is a bitch. But she's as beautiful as she is sassy, thick with old growth trees, sloped and spiked from centuries of quakes and storms. She's not my beloved, rain-and-wind swept Oregon forest, but she's appreciated nonetheless. It doesn't hurt that the jewel at her heart is a forty-foot waterfall.

By some stroke of luck, the trail isn't too crowded, and when we reach the falls three miles in, there's only a small group of hikers down by the pool.

"Hungry?"

My gaze veers from the water to Finn, standing on a flat rock-shelf some ten feet away with the backpack at his feet. His hat is turned backward, face flushed, eyes bright, sunglasses dangling from one hand. Sweat darkens his gray T-shirt, which clings to his shoulders and stomach. He looks like the center spread of an athletics magazine geared toward drooling women. He's unnaturally, messily perfect. Knowing what he smells like, what his smooth, hot skin feels like only makes things worse.

My want is visceral, twisting my stomach into knots.

A dangerous thought wraps silken chords around my mind. *What if I embrace the farce of being his girlfriend? Why shouldn't I get to touch him? We're obviously physically compatible, and he did say he wanted to—*

"I'm asking if you're hungry for food, princess. Not man-meat. But I'm glad you like what you see."

Thank God my face is already flushed from the hike.

"Har har, asshole." I make my way toward him. "Please tell me Molly made those sandwiches."

"Pfft. I'll have you know I make a mean sandwich. But yes, Molly made them. She said this was your favorite."

I grab Molly's signature chicken-salad on multigrain bread. "No more talking. Just eating."

"Yes, ma'am."

I devour the sandwich and tank a bottle of water, then lower to my back and close my eyes. The waterfall churns nearby, dappled sunlight teases my face, and peace soaks into my body from the sun-warmed rock.

"Can I ask you a question?"

There goes my peace.

Shading my eyes, I frown at Finn. "I'm not going to like it, am I?"

"Probably not."

"Whatever. Go ahead."

"Why'd you do it? Fake your own abduction, allow your family and the world to think you were dead. It was so..."

"Elaborate? Extreme?"

"Yeah."

My mood darkening, I sit up and shove my sunglasses back on my face so he can't see my eyes. Pulling my knees to my chest, I stare at the waterfall.

"I told you about my second cousin, who was killed for being gay? Well, I had another cousin from that side of the family—this is my great-uncle's branch, back east in Chicago. I've never met any of them. There was some old beef between my grandfather and his brother and the families barely speak. Anyway, my cousin wanted out. She was twenty-one and about to be forced into an arranged marriage. So she ran away with her boyfriend."

"And it didn't end well."

"To put it lightly. She wasn't stupid about it, either. No credit cards, nondescript car, left her cell phone and jewelry. Even cut off all her hair and dyed it. She could have been home free if she hadn't called her mom a week later to tell her she was okay."

"Her mom gave her up?" He's incredulous, which only proves how differently we were raised. When I don't answer, he asks more mutedly, "What happened?"

"According to the police report, black ice. Their car went off the road in Colorado."

"How do you know it wasn't an accident?"

"My father called me before the car was found. I remember it vividly. I was in my dorm room at Brown, and my roommate Jessica was bleaching her hair. It smelled so foul I had the window open even though it was freezing outside. He said he'd already spoken to Ellie and Lizzie and that I needed to listen carefully. My cousin had betrayed the family and no matter what I heard, I needed to know that what happened was because of that betrayal. When I hung up the phone, I just... couldn't do it anymore. So I told Jessica I was going to fake my death. She knew enough at that point to know I was serious. It took a year of research and planning. Plus, I'm sure there's a hole in my heart from all the stress."

Finn whistles softly. "You have guts, princess. I'm not sure I would have had the same reaction. Or been able to pull it off."

I stand and stretch a bit. Brush dust from my shorts. Finish my water. Retie my shoelaces. Watch two hikers strip down to their underwear and jump screaming into the pool. And I laugh and clap with the other bystanders, pretending my heart wasn't just shoved through a meat grinder by admitting all that to Finn.

At eighteen, I didn't consider the damage my plan would inflict on my sisters or friends. Not that I had many friends. Or any besides Rabbit. But I still thought only of myself, of the life I felt I deserved and the one I didn't want.

"You ready to head back?" I ask over my shoulder, even though *back* is the last place I want to go.

"Hey, what you did was amazing." His low, earnest voice comes from close behind me. "It took incredible courage and commitment."

I shake my head. "Only vast self-centeredness."

Finn's hand on my arm is a shock. Before I can react, he tugs me gently around to face him. I stare blankly at his fingers, still wrapped around my bicep.

"Let go of me," I say hoarsely.

"Stop doing that." His face bends toward mine, so close I can see the ring of darker blue around his pupils. "Stop undermining your own success. You got *out*, Callisto. You did what your cousins couldn't. You should be proud of that."

My chest shakes with silent laughter. "If what I did was so amazing, why did I throw it away to come back? I'll tell you why. Because I never learned the lesson Jessica's been trying to teach me for years."

He frowns, hand finally falling. "What lesson?"

"Never kiss the pretty boys."

I don't know why I say it. It's not the whole truth, obviously. But it *is* true. If I hadn't met and kissed Finn McCowen, chances are I'd still be in Solstice Bay. Home. Not a whole woman, maybe, shrouded in secrets, chased by nightmares.

But I'd be free.

Tugging my hat down, I head for the trail.

27

Callisto

FINN and I barely speak on the hike back to the car, and on the drive home he keeps the music too loud for conversation. All of which is fine by me. I have enough complications in my head and heart without him in the mix. Confusing, temperamental, annoyingly attractive man.

When he drops me off, in lieu of a goodbye he reminds me to secure him the coveted invite to family dinner. *To, you know, move things along.* He won't look me in the eye when he says it, and speeds away before I can tell him about the text message Vivian sent to the family twenty minutes ago. Too bad for him, I'm feeling petty enough to leave him in the dark as to its contents.

The following morning, I'm still not feeling charitable toward Finn, so I don't text or call him after saying goodbye to Vivian.

She's leaving for two weeks of campaigning. In other words, greasing hands and pulling fingernails. While the former is all too likely, the latter is figurative. Hopefully. Then again, she is taking Enzo. Like Vivian confirming that my father had Anthony killed, I wouldn't be the least surprised if it were revealed Enzo pulled the trigger.

There's no spirit in his eyes. No kindness or any form of humanity I recognize. He's always been that way, too. I don't know what happened to make him so cold and hard, whether it was through personal tragedy or choice. I'm not sure I care, as long as he stays away from me and my sisters.

Lizzie and I are to remain in the house with a reduced staff, though Vivian said Franco would be coming and going. A clear warning that we shouldn't be entertaining any guests or otherwise doing anything we're not supposed to. We're also not allowed to leave the premises without approval. If we do leave, we're restricted to a driving service. Both edicts are familiar. Standard practice for our ultra-paranoid family.

Before they left, I asked Vivian about visiting the ranch. Her answer was dismissive. "We'll talk when I get back."

"I can go alone," I suggested.

Enzo scowled, answering before Vivian could, "Paint your nails or get a tan or something. Leave the business to the adults."

And that was that.

Vivian's parting words for me were that her concierge doctor would be stopping by this morning to give me a physical.

So here I sit, waiting for the doctor on an embroidered bench in the foyer, frowning up at the painting of my father.

As frustrated as Finn will be when he finds out he has to wait another two weeks for introductions to the family, I'm just as frustrated I have to wait to visit my uncle's ranch.

Maybe Vivian lied and there's nothing there. Maybe she just wanted to see my reaction. Maybe she knows exactly why I came back.

Paranoia apples don't fall far from the tree.

I'm also thinking about Detective Wilson. Her card lives in the same vent as my burner phone. The edges are bent, the text nearly blurred from running my thumb over it. I've read the handwritten cell number on the back so many times that it's a permanent mental fixture.

I spent most of yesterday coming to a conclusion— when I get to the ranch and find whatever it is Vivian wants, I'm going to call Detective Wilson and hand it over, come what may.

Friday night with Molly and Finn—and even parts of the hike yesterday—brought into sharp relief how poisonous my brief time home has been. Though neither said it outright, I could see the worry in Molly's eyes and knew it was for good reason. My appetite is gone, the clothes purchased recently already loose. I sleep fitfully and little, the dark circles under my eyes a daily reminder.

Every day I feel closer to a meltdown. Too many lies, secrets, and fears. I'm choking on the bread and butter of my family. The fresh air and space yesterday was nice, but not enough. Like a Band-Aid on a severed finger.

Looking up at my father's jovial expression—one he never wore in my lifetime—I whisper, "Maybe I'm too much like my mother. She couldn't survive in this family, either."

"Are you all right, miss?"

I yelp, my hands flinging to my chest. My gaze jerks across the foyer to Selina. "Jesus, you scared me."

She smiles an apology. "It's my sneakers. Miss Vivian bought them for me because my old ones squeaked. Silent as a mouse now."

I smile wanly. "Yes, you are."

She gestures to the bench. "May I?"

"Of course."

She sits beside me, smelling faintly of the lavender and vinegar cleaning solution Vivian likes. Glancing at me, she murmurs conspiratorially, "I rather like it when Miss Vivian is gone. Not that I slack on my duties, but we're normally not allowed to sit during our shift."

I blink in surprise. "That's ludicrous."

She shrugs. "I'm a thirty-eight-year-old woman with no college experience and a family to care for. This job pays the bills and then some. I'm very lucky."

The words don't ring false, exactly, but there's a dissonance to them. They definitely don't sound like something she would say—not the woman who warned me about the bug in my room and told me how to keep phone calls private.

Not sure how to respond, I nod.

"I've been here almost five years," she continues idly. "Long enough to know how hard it was for the girls when you were gone. I know they're very glad you're back. Your uncles missed you as well. They spoke of you often."

"They did?" My voice is dry.

"Of course." Her brows lift. "They're your family."

I'm beginning to feel like I'm missing an entire subtext of the conversation.

The doorbell rings.

Selina smiles and stands. "That must be the doctor. I'll let her in."

"Thank you."

I sit a moment more, unsettled, then stand. A folded piece of paper flutters to the floor.

"Miss Calli," says Selina sweetly, "it looks like something fell from your pocket."

My ears ring with adrenaline. "Oh, thank you."

I snatch the paper up and tuck it quickly into my pocket. When I straighten, Selina watches me placidly while the doctor—a slender, WASPish woman—regards me with blatant curiosity.

"It's, ah, my grocery list for the cook." I flash a smile. "Gotta watch those carbs."

Selina ducks away, silent as usual, while the doctor smiles and nods. "Absolutely."

28

Finn

THANKS TO CNN, Monday morning I learn that Vivian is campaigning out of town the next two weeks. No family dinners for me. And no heads-up from Callisto.

I want to be angry, but I can't be. Not when, were the situation reversed, I'd probably give myself the silent treatment, too. And that's exactly what she does for most of the first week.

She doesn't answer the phone—either one—when I call, and I'm lucky to get a text back for every five I send. I have no idea what she's doing, if she's okay. The only evidence I have that she's alive are a few live phone interviews on morning radio programs.

As the days pass, Molly becomes increasingly frantic. I hide my own worry behind my camera, taking action the only way I know how. Thanks to a few amateur stakeouts, I know the Avellino maid, Selina Hernandez, arrives promptly at the house at 7:00 a.m. and leaves at 8:00 p.m. She drives a well-kept 2000 Nissan Pathfinder with a booster seat in back, and lives in a condo complex in Encino, about thirty minutes away. Wednesday is her day off. Cramped from dozing in my car and with a pressing need to piss, I stick around only long enough to see her leave midmorning with a man and a kid maybe six or seven years old.

If it weren't for Selina warning Callisto about the house surveillance, I'd say there was nothing interesting about the woman. But it's somewhat of a relief to relay the information to Molly, who attacks it like a problem she's waited her whole life to solve.

I don't get in her way, even when she leaves Thursday evening to intercept Selina outside her condo. I trust my aunt. She's smart, and she's a people person. Whatever her angle she pursues, the worst thing that could happen is it's another dead end.

Alone in the apartment, I take a shower, eat some dinner, and stare at the wall for twenty minutes before breaking down and calling Callisto's iPhone for what feels like the eight millionth time. She doesn't answer. I try her burner phone next, and the call is declined after the second ring.

It might be the first time a woman has declined my call—repeatedly, no less. It's almost refreshing. If I weren't so irritated, I might be impressed by how stubborn she is.

But what Callisto doesn't know about me, and is about to learn, is that I'm not just a prickly asshole. I'm a *tenacious,* prickly asshole.

Mind made up, I grab my keys.

I'm done waiting. If she won't answer the phone, even to give me a simple *Stop calling, dickhead,* then I'm going to her.

When I reach the estate, I park a half block away, then pull my beanie down low and jog to the vine-covered wall. My gaze ricochets around the dark, silent street like a certified creeper, and if someone sees me it's a call to the cops for sure. But the threat of handcuffs isn't enough to make me turn back. Now that I'm here, the need to see Callisto drives everything else from my mind.

Ducking behind some bushes, I pull out my phone and text her.

Don't make me climb this wall, princess.

It takes close to a minute, but she finally responds.

What?! What are you doing? Where are you?

Outside your house. Obviously.

The phone rings in my hand. All my anger vanishes, and I fight to hold back a grin.

"Why, hello."

"Dammit, Finn," she hisses. "This is the worst possible time."

"You're avoiding me and I don't like it." Just to throw gas on the fire, I add, "Have you forgotten our agreement already?"

She growls at me, and it's so cute my dick twitches. I have no idea why I want this woman so much. She clearly hates me. But my body doesn't care, and increasingly, neither does my mind.

"How could I?" she snarls. "Did it occur to you I might be making progress on my own? I don't need your help!"

"Too bad," I retort. "We can fight each other, Callisto, or we can fight together. Your choice."

After a small pause—in which I imagine her grinding her teeth and shaking a fist at the sky—she heaves a loud, groaning sigh.

"Fine. I was leaving anyway. Meet me by the pine tree."

She hangs up before I can ask what fucking pine tree. I'm standing next to one—I considered climbing it because it's close to the wall—but there are no street-lights in the neighborhood and with a cloudy sky over-head, minimal ambient light. This particular pine tree could have buddies all over the estate.

Newly annoyed, I retrace my steps to the street, hoping for a better view. I'm seconds from trekking around to the other side of the property when there's a rustle and *thump* near the wall. A Callisto-shaped shadow rises from the ground beside the pine's trunk.

Feeling smug, I remark, "I chose the right tree."

The shadow whispers angrily, "It's the only pine tree."

Three steps and I'm right before her, close enough to see her features, her pretty scowl. Before I can stop myself, my fingers find her soft cheek.

She jerks back. "What are you doing?"

"Wanted to make sure you were real. I thought maybe you'd been discovered and locked in a cage in the basement all week."

Even in the darkness, I can see her eyes roll. "I've been busy."

I take stock of her black clothing and sweatshirt with the hood up. "Planning a robbery?" I'm only half joking.

"Kind of." She takes a deep breath. "I'm going to my uncle's ranch tonight, and I guess you're coming too."

29

Callisto

GLANCING ACROSS THE CAR, I study Finn's face. Determined expression, furrowed brows. His stubble has filled in and thickened. I want to scratch my fingers through it. Feel it on my body. His scent—unavoidable in the small space—triggers a visceral memory of my lips on his neck, of breathing him in, feeling wanted and seen.

Sadly, admitting my physical attraction to him is easier than admitting I'm glad he's here. That I feel safer with him by my side. That I want to crawl inside him and... *rest*. Let go of the weight of the future. Or at the least, share it with someone else.

Annoyed by my thoughts, I shift my gaze out the passenger window as we head east toward the edge of the San Fernando Valley.

"So this note from Selina you've referenced—that made you hatch this crazy plan *without telling me*—what did it say exactly?"

He's so much easier to be around when he doesn't talk. Not that I missed being around him. Or thought about him at all in the last ten days.

I'm so good at lying now, I even believe the ones I tell myself.

"Not much," I answer, forcing myself to focus. "*Ants in the stables.* Since we don't have stables, and I called my Uncle Anthony 'Ant'..." I trail off.

He nods decisively. "She's gotta be a cop."

We've been over this three times since leaving Calabasas.

"I don't know what her motive is, but she's not a cop. She's been with the family for five years, for Christ's sake." I frown. "I've barely seen her since she gave it to me. She must be avoiding me."

"No shit. But hear me out—if she's not a cop, why the hell does she know so much? Like that what we want is in the stables at your uncle's ranch. That's pretty damn specific. More importantly, how do we even know we can trust her?"

"I don't know," I sigh out. "I thought she might be the daughter of a disgruntled employee or related to a victim of my family, so I Googled her name linked to Avellino. Nothing came up. I also asked Lizzie and Ellie what they knew about Selina's history, but they looked at me like I was nuts. I can't ask Uncle Franco without making him suspicious, and I definitely don't want him monitoring Selina if she's trying to help me."

"Help *us*. Say it with me, princess. U-S spells *us*."

I glare. "Really?"

He laughs softly. "Anyway, an undercover cop would be using a fake identity."

"Ugh, will you get off that?"

Finn pauses. "How are your sisters doing?"

"Do you care?"

His gaze cuts to me. "Yes, actually. I'm not heartless."

I bite my tongue on a retort. "They're fine. Lizzie spends most of her time on her laptop. She says she's trying to find what to do with her life, but I think she's chatting with a secret boyfriend she's afraid to tell me about."

I hate that my relationship with Lizzie is being affected, that she might not trust me anymore since I've been spending more time with Vivian, playing the part of dutiful subject. And the worst fact is, the fracture between us might never be repaired. Only blown impossibly wide by what I'm trying to accomplish.

"What about the other one?" Finn asks with a little smile.

I roll my eyes. "Your number one fan is busy with school, so I don't see her at the house much. Maybe she knows these four years are her last taste of freedom." I stare morosely at my lap. "Some days it's like I never left, but other times I get the sense my sisters wish I'd stayed dead."

"Jesus, why would you say that?"

I think of the isolated moments with Lizzie, her eerie maturity and honesty. Ellie's avoidance and denial.

"Maybe they're not as oblivious as I thought."

"You're talking about Lizzie asking you why you came back?"

I nod. "She's made other remarks. Nothing as serious as that. Mainly in reference to Vivian wanting to marry her off." A sudden thought makes my stomach lurch. "Shit, maybe that's what she's been hinting at, and why she's not in college. What if that's the plan and Lizzie found out?"

"Explain."

"Okay, this is going to sound archaic. You've been warned. But the family's been this way for generations."

"Just tell me, princess."

"The eldest child is groomed to take over leadership of the family, while the younger children are prepared for supporting roles. As far as I know, we're the first generation of all daughters. Normally... well, I already told you what happens to girls."

"But you're the eldest and you said you weren't—"

"I know what I said, okay?" I interject. "Taking over for my father was never the plan for me. Maybe it was once, when I was born, but since Vivian came into the picture, no. Can you imagine her allowing some other woman's child to take her husband's place? Besides, from early on it was clear I wasn't cut out for it."

"Is this more bullshit about you being too soft? You're not soft or weak, Callisto. You're the opposite. Like... titanium."

I smirk. "Titanium, really?"

"Deceptively lightweight. Strong as fuck. And if I remember correctly, you don't weigh a whole lot."

Despite myself, I laugh. "Gee, thanks."

His smile curves, sending warmth to my belly. "I want to feed you. Plump you up."

Just as swiftly as it appeared, my laughter evaporates. "You're a chauvinistic dick."

"Why? Because I'm not afraid to point out that you've lost weight you didn't need to lose? Because I felt the curves you had in Solstice Bay and I want to feel them again?"

I splutter. He grins wickedly, eyes on the road as the car slows. We pull to a stop outside a chained-off dirt road with a faded No Trespassing sign.

We're in the middle of nowhere—or as close as you can be while still inside Los Angeles County lines. Uncle Anthony liked being isolated. He even bought the adjacent properties to avoid having neighbors.

A heady pang of loss and nostalgia hits me.

I unbuckle my seat belt. "I'll get the chain," I say, then flee the car.

When the chain is down and dragged to one side, I reluctantly climb back into the car.

Finn leans over the steering wheel, squinting out the windshield. "I can't see shit past the headlights. Where are the stables?"

"Just drive. There's a fork about a quarter mile up. Stables are to the right."

"Got it."

He drives slowly down the pitted, unpaved driveway, focused on the road.

Back to business.

I'm relieved. I don't like him flirting with me. Being charming and attentive. Reminding me about our status as almost-lovers. It's confusing. It makes me forget the direness of my situation. The high stakes.

When he's not being a complete asshole, he makes me want what I can't have. A dream I gave up in high school after the death of my first boyfriend.

It makes me want *him*.

30

Finn

THE LAST TIME horses saw the inside of this stable had to be when Reagan was president. The structure was clearly beautiful once. Constructed to last, most of the support beams and walls are in place. The roof, not so much.

But the skeleton is elegant. With the vaulted ceiling and torn-out stalls, there's a bit of a feel of walking through a church in disrepair. I have photographer buddies who would die to shoot in here. They'd capture fractured windows and peeling paint. The shafts of moonlight sliding through holes in the roof. Decaying benches, dingy sheets over lumps of what could be furniture—or treasure...

I yank off a sheet and get a face-full of dust and the stench of mold.

"What are you doing?" demands Callisto.

"Trying to find whatever it is we're looking for."

"It's not under there."

I shine my phone's flashlight at the pile of firewood. "Yeah, probably not." I toss the sheet down, then sneeze. "Did your uncle even use this place?"

Callisto doesn't answer, her gaze traveling around the interior. I don't know what she sees, but from her pressed lips it doesn't look like happy memories.

At length, she says, "This used to be his workshop. He loved woodworking. Carving, making small furniture. But everything is gone. There used to be tables, tools, workbenches, saws..."

The urge to touch her presses close, so I tuck my hands in my pockets. As much as I'd like to push her boundaries a little, this isn't the time or place. Plus, she might punch me.

"Do you have any clue what we might be looking for? Something your uncle might have hidden here?"

"No." Her shoulders sag. I can't be sure, but I think her lower lip trembles.

Fuck it.

I cross to her and pull her into my arms. She stands against me like a cement pole, her hands trapped between us. It has to be the most awkward hug of all time, but I'm not deterred. Plucking her hands out one by one, I guide them around my waist.

"Stop thinking for a second and hug me back. I promise it won't hurt."

She fights the inevitable for another few moments before succumbing—like I already have—to the way our bodies fit. We sigh together, our arms tightening, pulling the other closer. Like a constellation, our bones are the stars of a design bigger than the two of us. More beautiful together than apart.

For minutes on end, we stand unmoving in the midst of ruin. And for the first time in decades, the pain of the past is an echo instead of a roar inside me. A flicker of hope ignites, sucking oxygen like a newborn.

Maybe *she* is the answer I've been looking for.

And then I see it, illumined by moonlight on the earthen floor.

"Callisto," I whisper into her hair.

"Mmm?" she murmurs back, rubbing her cheek against my chest like a cat. The motion goes straight south, and while the brain in my pants wants me to ignore what I see, the rest of me can't.

"What's that?" I ask, gently turning her sideways and pointing. "Right there, in the moonlight by the wall."

She frowns. "I don't know. Could be a strip of tarp that was buried?"

I hear the doubt, recognize the search for an answer that doesn't hurt. But as we walk toward the delicate curve of white, there's no way around it.

We're looking at a bone.

"Oh my God," she gasps, whirling toward me with wide eyes. "Tell me that's not what I think it is."

I don't want *anything* to do with digging up a corpse, but I make myself say, "Only one way to find out."

Grabbing a sliver of wood from the ground, I crouch before the bone and dig lightly around it. I'm not squeamish by nature, but as the dirt loosens and is swept away by my fingers, my gorge rises. I was really, really hoping it was a squirrel or rabbit. Maybe even a coyote.

Callisto steps closer. Before I can tell her not to look, she makes a wounded noise.

"That's a human skull." Her voice is steady, if reedy.

"Looks like it." I point to the space directly beside the empty eye socket. "And I'm no detective, but I'm pretty sure that's—"

"A bullet hole," she finishes.

I wipe my hands on my jeans and pull out my phone to snap some photos of the skull. Weeks ago—even days ago—this would have made me shout in victory.

Now all I see is the deep sadness on Callisto's face.

"If there's one body, there's more," she says softly, then meets my gaze. "This is what you wanted, isn't it? This will ruin the family."

I stand, tucking my phone in my back pocket. "I can't fucking believe I'm saying this, but I'm not so sure anymore."

Her brows lift in surprise, though her expression doesn't change, soft with shock and misery. "What are you saying?"

"I'm saying I don't want to be a part of something that ruins you and your sisters, too."

She laughs—sharp and dry. "Don't go soft on me now."

"I'm never soft when I'm around you, but that's beside the point. I'm just saying we need to think about this. We have options."

Like I knew she would, she ignores my poor attempt at humor. "You mean leverage."

I nod. "What are the chances these bones were here *before* your uncle made it his workshop?"

"None," she answers decisively. "Sometimes when he was working, he gave me a garden shovel to dig in here. He said"—she shakes her head, eyes welling—"that maybe I'd find dinosaur fossils. It was just a way to keep me occupied."

"And he wouldn't have told you that if he thought

you might find a body."

"Yeah, no," she answers dryly.

I heave a breath. "Okay, here's what I'm thinking. The family kept the ranch for a dumping site, and these bodies can't be blamed on Anthony. That means Vivian is screwed."

"Right, but even if this comes out, she could easily blame this on my father. Or throw Enzo or Franco under the bus. Or she could just pretend she never knew about it." The volume of her voice increases steadily.

"We're getting ahead of ourselves," I say, grabbing her quaking shoulder. "One thing at a time. I don't know about you, but I'm skeeved the fuck out. Let's get out of here, then we can hash this out."

She nods jerkily. "Good idea. Should we, uh..." She nods at the skull.

"I've got it."

As I cover the skull with dirt and pack it down, doing my best to make it look undisturbed, I muse that of all the things I've considered doing to impress a woman, this never made the list.

Callisto is the enemy of my enemy, but more dangerous than I ever imagined. I'm starting to think there's nothing I wouldn't do for her.

31

Callisto

THE DRIVE BEGINS SILENTLY, each of us lost in dark thoughts, but when we reach the interchange for the 101, I blurt, "Can you take me to the apartment instead?"

"Sure." He pauses. "I don't know if Molly's there. She was going to see if Selina would talk to her tonight. I can call her, if you want?"

I shake my head. "It's okay. I just don't want to go back there. Not tonight."

"I don't blame you."

Silence descends once more. Every time I close my eyes, I see the bullet hole in the skull. Single shot, close range. An execution. Whoever the shooter was, they wanted their victim to see them and know what was coming.

I think about Enzo's cold smile. Franco's shifting eyes. Vivian's perfect mask. Which one of them pulled the trigger? Maybe it was my father. Without knowing how old that skull is, I can't remove him from the equation.

Still, there's a lot that doesn't make sense. Why would Vivian bring up the ranch in the first place? What is it she wanted me to find? I can't believe she'd want me to find a body.

"You okay?"

The question makes me aware that I'm trembling. My teeth chatter softly. Finn reaches across the divide to grab my hand. Warm, sold fingers curl around my palm. Anchoring me.

"That was a pretty big shock, huh?"

I wish I could summon sarcasm. A pithy response. Something to make him remove his hand, shift our dynamic back to familiar ground. But I can't. I cling to his fingers like a life preserver, remembering our embrace in the stable. How right it felt to be in his arms.

Before the skull. Before I saw final, irrefutable confirmation that someone in my family is a cold-blooded killer.

"Thank you for coming with me," I whisper. "I can't image if..." I shake my head.

"Neither can I. I'm really glad you didn't go alone."

His voice—so solid, deep, and comforting—cocoons me and sinks beneath my skin. I stop shaking, my thoughts clearing. But I don't let go of his hand.

"Tell me again why we shouldn't call the police?" I ask.

"I'm not saying we shouldn't," he says, picking words carefully. "It would be the right thing to do."

"It would. But like you said, it would drag the entire family into hell. Lizzie and Ellie, too."

"No doubt. But on the other hand, we have to consider the victim we found. What about their family? They deserve justice."

"I know," I murmur, then huff a humorless laugh. "I'm so stupid. I actually thought the evidence I'd eventually find would be something innocuous. A USB drive. Crooked financial records. Blackmail on recorded phone calls. I guess a part of me wanted to believe that despite my intuition, they wouldn't stoop to murder."

Finn is quiet for long minutes, then says, "I was there. When your father killed mine."

My fingers spasm, reflexively releasing his hand. Horror swamps me. "Oh my God. I didn't know."

He shrugs. "No one does. Because of the high-profile nature of the case, the threat of retribution, and because I was underaged, the judge ruled that my identity should be concealed. I testified in closed chambers, just me, my mom, and the judge." He clears his throat. "That's why I'm pretty sure your father didn't kill whoever we unearthed back there. He said something before he made my father get on his knees then put a gun to the back of his head. My dad called him a coward for not being able to look him in the eye."

My stomach roils. I clench my hands so hard I feel my nails pierce skin on my palms. "You don't have to—"

"It's okay, I want to. Rafael said, *'I've never killed anyone who was my equal. You don't deserve to see my face.'* Then he pulled the trigger."

Thick tears slide down my cheeks, dripping off my chin. "I'm sorry, Finn. So, so sorry. He was a monster. They're all monsters."

"Hey." He takes my hand again, squeezing it tightly. "I'm sorry. I shouldn't have told you that, not after what we just saw."

Wiping my face with my free hand, I say, "No, I'm glad you did. I just can't believe you saw your father die."

I think of witnessing the heart attack that took my own father's life. The panic and fear in his eyes fading to nothingness. What I felt in that moment was an emptiness so vast I feared it would swallow me. Not the emptiness of shock or grief, but of indifference. How would I have felt if Rafael Avellino had been a good man, a good father? I can't imagine it.

"I knew something was wrong when he was getting ready to leave that night," Finn says at length. "He looked scared. I heard him tell my mom that he had to attend a meeting about the fire that killed twenty people in an apartment building earlier that month. Do you remember that?"

I duck my head, my neck hot with shame. "Not really."

He doesn't seem surprised. "The apartment building was your family's, and the fire was due to faulty wiring. Cutting corners during construction. My dad was the one who did the investigation and found the proof. Rafael tried to blackmail him. My father refused."

"I guess I never learned about the trail because I didn't want to know. It was easier to cling to ignorance."

He squeezes my hand again. "You were a kid."

"So were you," I mumble.

"I was an impulsive hothead who snuck into the trunk of my dad's SUV and became a witness to his murder."

A silent sob seizes my chest. Lifting his hand, I kiss the back of it. "I'm sorry. For everything. For what my father did to your family."

I don't realize the car is parked outside the apartment complex until his other hand frames my face.

"Look at me, princess."

Blinking away tears, I meet his steady gaze.

"It is not your fault. Do you understand? Not. Your. Fault. I don't blame you. No one will blame you. There's nothing you could have done to change any of it."

"I could have stayed," I babble. "Tried to stop them six years ago. But I didn't, and now it's too late. My poor sisters, when they find out... God, this is a nightmare."

Finn scoots forward until his forehead drops against mine. "I think your sisters are stronger than you give them credit, just like you're stronger and braver than you think you are. What kind of woman does what you did—escapes that life—then gives it all up to come back and make a difference?"

"A nut job," I say weakly.

"If you're a nut job, I'm certifiable, too. Maybe we can share a padded room."

His lips are curved, the sensuous slope of them teasing a new awareness from inside me. A vast, gnawing need to erase the last few hours from my skin. And the conviction that he's my perfect remedy.

"Can we go inside now?" I'm breathless. Squirming in my seat.

He moves back an inch, his eyes searching mine. There's no doubt he picked up on the shift in my tone.

"Of course we can, but, uh, maybe now isn't the time—"

"Finn," I interject. "I want you. Now."

I've never seen a man move so fast.

32

Finn

THANK God Molly isn't at the apartment, because Callisto is on me the second the door closes behind us. Taking full advantage of my male brain, I gladly shut off everything but what's happening. The fascinating, gorgeous, courageous woman dangling from my arms. The tantalizing, creamy scent of her arousal. Soft, full breasts against my chest and small fingers clenching in my hair.

Her kisses are urgent and deliciously artless as I carry her into my bedroom. The only light comes from a streetlamp outside, a golden hue that stretches across the bed in stripes from the half-closed blinds.

When I lay her down, she whimpers in protest, but I'm only apart from her long enough to drag my shirt over my head and kick off my shoes. What she doesn't realize—can't possibly realize—is how long I've waited for this. Even when I didn't know I wanted her, I wanted her. And I plan on taking my sweet time.

But then her hand cups the bulge in my pants and squeezes, and once more, I forget everything but the moment. My intentions—*honorable, dammit*—fade like smoke.

In minutes we're naked, panting, rubbing against each other like beasts in heat. She bites my thumb as I devour her throat, breasts, the soft canvas of her belly. Down, down I go.

"Yes, yes."

My first taste of her is a kick to the heart. *Perfect.* She's perfect. I'd happily spend the rest of my life with my face between her legs, breathing in the ambrosia of her scent, her flavor on my tongue.

Mine.

I'm already in too deep, never having felt this way in bed with a woman. I pulse with a raw, primitive need to stamp her, claim her, bind her to me. It's jarring. Scary as fuck.

But then again, I've always been a risk-taker.

She comes on a broken, gasping cry, her thighs trembling against my ears. Triumphant and oddly sated myself, I treat her to languorous licks until she yanks my head up by my hair.

"Inside me. *Now.*"

I reach for the condom on the nightstand, rolling it on with the last of my sanity. I'm witless, enslaved to her. In this moment, if she asked me to fuck her ear, I'd try.

Poised above her, I stare into her dark eyes. "You have no idea what you do to me."

"I do," she counters softly, "because you do the same to me."

My lips find hers as I rock forward. She's slick from her orgasm but tight, so tight, as I ease inside her. *Don't hurt her. Go slowly.*

"More," she groans, nails scraping down my back. "Harder."

The tenuous hold of brain over body snaps. I drive into her like a madman, savage and unstoppable. But as I fill her, over and over again, she fills me too—with her cries, her sweat, her lips, and the primal undulation of her body in sync with mine.

My orgasm begins as a tickle, a teasing pressure that narrows as it builds in intensity. Callisto bucks against me with a ragged cry, her pussy clamping on my cock, and suddenly nothing on earth can stop me from coming right along with her.

"Jesus, fuck, holy shit," I groan, my head hanging listlessly beside her face.

"Same," she pants. "That was..."

"If you say *good*, I'm going to spank you."

She laughs soundlessly, nudging me onto my side. My poor, spent dick whimpers as he's forced to leave her, while my brain kicks on and worries that she thinks this was a mistake.

But she merely snuggles up against me, her head nestled beneath my chin. And I feel... content. Insulated. Fucking ecstatic.

"Thank you," she murmurs.

"Anytime, princess. And I mean that literally. I'm one hundred percent available to do that again whenever, wherever you want."

She kisses my neck. "Shut up."

I smile into her hair, and I'm still smiling when I pass out. Minutes or hours later, I wake to the sensation of fingers trailing down my stomach. *Her* fingers. *Her* hair tickling my shoulder. *Her* soft breath on my chest.

I'm immediately so hard it hurts.

"Finn," she whispers.

My body responds for me, my arms eagerly pulling her above me. She gasps when her breasts flatten against my chest, her smooth belly against my harder one. Or maybe her stuttering breath can be blamed on my hips, which lift into her so she can feel what she does to me with a mere touch.

Safe in our small, dark world, the truth overrides all the lies we've told.

"I want you," she says, fingers wrapping around the base of my cock. She squeezes me, and still her fingers barely touch. "I want this."

"And I want this." I grab her ass, squeezing the globes until her breath turns to pants, then parting them. My fingers sink and find her pussy. She's blazing hot. Dripping wet. "Ah, fuck, my sweet Callisto. How am I going to survive you?"

Her hand spasms on my cock. "I'm not sure I'll survive *this* again." Her voice is dark. Raspy with lust. "But I'm willing to find out."

That's all I can take.

Flipping her onto her back, I settle atop her. Her legs instantly wrap around my hips. She bucks against me, marking me with her slick center, her breasts bobbing for attention. I've seen Heaven, and it's in front of me.

I lick, suck, bite, *devour* her breasts until she's whimpering, needy and impatient, then let her roll the condom on with her greedy hands.

"Don't hold back," she says, her hot mouth against mine.

"You want me to fuck you hard, princess?" I whisper.

Notched at her core, I'm held by only the merest

thread of restraint. She nips my lower lip, dark eyes luminous and pleading, half-mad with desperation.

"Make me forget."

So I do.

We forget everything but each other.

33

Callisto

FOR THOSE FEW, fragile moments upon waking, I don't remember the ranch. Just Finn, whose body is curled protectively around mine. I don't want to wake up. Don't want to let go of how safe I feel with this maddening, mystifying man behind me. But stubborn daylight barges through the gaps in the plastic blinds, tickling my eyelids and waking my mind. Inviting memories I'd rather live without.

Bodies in the ground.

My eyes open at a muted sound from outside the bedroom. Clinking glasses. A cupboard closing softly.

Shit. *Molly.*

Finn barely stirs as I extricate myself from his arms and find my clothes. Dressed, I give him one last, lingering look—wild hair, kiss-swollen lips, intricate tattoos—before slipping from the room. I find the bathroom first, splashing cold water on my face and fixing the disaster that is my hair. There's nothing to be done about the freshly fucked glow in my cheeks. I know Molly won't judge, but I still feel ten kinds of awkward.

As I enter the kitchen, she turns, eyebrows lifting as she takes me in. I register her smirk a second before she says, "I was in my room when you two came in last night."

Is it possible to die of mortification? We definitely weren't quiet. My raw throat is testament to my lack of restraint.

I cover my face. "God, I'm so sorry."

She chuckles knowingly. "Good thing I had headphones and a movie cued up on my laptop. Coffee?"

"Molly, I—"

"Don't you dare say you're sorry again," she says, eyes twinkling, "because that would be tragic. I hope you're *not* sorry. And to be honest, I saw this coming from a mile away. Finn has always had a thing for you."

A footstep behind me precedes Finn's sardonic words, "Way to have my back, Aunt Mol."

She waves off his comment, grinning. "Callisto isn't exempt." She points a spoon at me. "I've seen the way you look at him."

My face is hot as I turn around. Even dressed in

sweatpants and a T-shirt, Finn causes a quantifiable reaction in my body. My pulse kicks up a notch. A needy ache yawns between my legs. I want more of last night. A *lot* more.

Meeting his glittering blue gaze with effort, I whisper, "She was here last night. In her room."

The horror on his face would be comical if I wasn't still feeling it myself.

"What the hell, Molly! Why didn't you say something?"

Laughing gaily, Molly takes two mugs to the kitchen table. "Are you kidding? Besides, I doubt you two would have heard me knocking."

A pitiful noise squeaks from my throat.

Molly's laugh turns to a cackle. "Ah, to be young again."

"Kill me," Finn whispers.

"Me first," I whisper back.

"I'll get breakfast started while you two have your coffee," chirps Molly as she returns to the kitchen and opens cupboards. "Go ahead now, don't be shy."

Finn and I sit opposite each other. He sips his coffee. I sip mine. We avoid each other's eyes.

"This is not how I pictured this morning going," he mutters.

He sounds so disgruntled, a smile twitches my lips. "Oh yeah?"

Looking up, his gaze takes a slow path from my mouth to my eyes. "Yeah." Eyes darkening, he adds, "Good morning, princess."

I want to fly over the table and rip his clothes off. And from the gleam in his eye, he knows exactly what I'm thinking. He wants it, too.

What have I gotten myself into?

"Breakfast!" Molly drops a heaping pile of scrambled eggs and sausage between us, along with two forks and a bowl piled high with strawberries and blueberries. "The sausage is microwaved. Best I could do on short notice."

"It's great, thank you."

"Thanks, Aunt Mol."

She settles in the third chair with her coffee cradled in her hands. "Eat, then we'll talk."

I look at Finn and see in his eyes the same knowledge that's in mine. What we saw at the ranch. My appetite flees.

I manage a few bites of egg and some berries, forcing myself to eat that much. Finn eats only a little more than me before he gives up, too.

"That bad, huh?" asks Molly.

"It's not the food," Finn begins, setting down his fork.

At his nod, I tell her what led us to my uncle's farm. When I'm done, he tells her about the skull.

She listens, coffee forgotten in her hands, and at the end asks, "Dear God, what are we doing to do?"

It's another three hours and several refills of coffee for all of us before we have a plan we agree on. A good one that ends with Vivian, and most likely my uncles, going to jail for a very long time.

You can't kill an octopus by cutting off a leg.

So we're going for the head.

I can't spare my sisters this. Any way I slice it, their lives will be forever altered. I can only hope someday they'll understand why I had to do this.

I'm clear now. I finally understand why I came back. Not for something as petty as revenge, or proving to Vivian I'm better or stronger than her, or a vague need to save my sisters from their fates, but for the poor souls resting in unmarked graves thanks to my family. And for the simple reason that doing what's right isn't always easy, but at the end of the day, our choices define who we are.

And we are not them.

34

Callisto

FINN DROPS me off around noon. As soon as the front door closes behind me, a scathing voice asks, "Where the *fuck* have you been?"

I was ready for it—Lizzie sent me a text this morning telling me Uncle Franco stopped by and lost his shit when he realized I wasn't home.

"Hello to you, too." I kick off my shoes in the foyer and brush past him.

He grabs my arm, halting me. "You know the rules, Calli. What the hell were you thinking? Do you know how much trouble you're in when Vivian finds out?"

I meet his beady gaze. "I'm not fifteen anymore. You can take your rules and choke on them."

Lord, it feels good to stop pretending. Like a weight

has been lifted. Still, I'm surprised by the vehemence that drips from the words. Until this moment, I didn't truly know I had it in me to fight back.

Franco releases me, more from shock than an awareness of how hard his grip was. "What the fuck is wrong with you? Where were you?"

"None of your damn business," I say with a smile, then continue toward the kitchen.

Lizzie sits at the kitchen table, a magazine spread before her and headphones in. I give her a wink, then grab an apple from the basket on the island and take a satisfyingly loud bite.

Franco appears in the doorway, flushed and furious. He's so focused on me, he doesn't notice Lizzie.

"How dare you walk away from me like that! You'd better explain yourself right now."

"No, thanks."

"You snotty bitch," he snarls. "I've never trusted you, Little Bear. Didn't trust you back then, and definitely not now. You're up to no good, and this proves it."

I finish chewing. "An astronomy lesson for you, Uncle—I'm not named after the *little bear*, as you've so charmingly and demeaningly called me all my life. Callisto is the Great Bear. Ursa *Major*. So back the fuck off, because I'm not in the mood to play nice."

His neck flushes dark red. "Wait until Vivian hears about this."

"Vivian, Vivian, Vivian," I sing. "Do you have a mind of your own, or are you just a lap dog? I'm thinking lap dog. You're certainly small enough."

Okay, maybe that was too far, but damned if it doesn't feel good to see him struggle for control.

"You're done," he hisses.

I examine my half-eaten apple. "Not yet, but you are." I meet his livid gaze. "Get out."

He storms off, cursing under his breath. A few moments later, the front door slams.

"That was awesome and scary," Lizzie says in a hushed voice. "What just happened?"

The first step.

"I'm just tired of dealing with this shit. I'm a grown woman and spent the night at my boyfriend's house. It's not like I was robbing a bank."

Lizzie whistles. "Man, I wish I had your balls."

I toss my apple core into the trash and sit beside her. "And if you did? What would you do?"

Fear alights in her eyes. "Nothing," she says quickly.

"Lizzie, tell me. What if you were free to do whatever you wanted?"

After a furtive glance at the doorway, she takes a swift breath. "I want to be a fiction writer. I love mysteries, thrillers, that sort of thing. Don't say anything to Mom, though, okay?"

"Why? If it's your dream—"

"Just don't." She closes the magazine, dropping her earbuds atop it. "You don't understand, Calli. If you did, you wouldn't ask. I gotta go."

She's gone before I can think of something to say to bring her back.

THE NEXT WEEK passes with excruciating slowness. Lizzie gives me the silent treatment, going so far as to leave any room we both occupy. At least Franco stays away, though I notice two new guards prowling outside at night.

Selina doesn't show up for work three days in a row —her replacement says she has the flu. And when she does return, she avoids me like the plague. Molly never spoke to her on Thursday, which now I'm grateful for. Apparently when Selina returned home from work, her little boy and husband were waiting outside for her. I'm still not convinced—like Finn is—that she's an under-cover cop or an informant. It's much more likely she's here for the same reason Finn is: a vendetta.

Tired of banging my head on a wall where both

women are concerned, I give up and spend the rest of the week pretending to relax. Reading in the shade of a backyard umbrella, swimming laps until my muscles are lax, and texting with Finn to keep up the ruse that we're a normal, newly dating couple.

I miss *him*. Not the canned charm of our messages, but the acerbic, sarcastic man. I miss the possibility of us that was sparked last week, so much that sometimes I wonder if it really happened.

Then, at 9:00 p.m. every night, he calls the burner phone and reminds me it was real.

———

NEAR MIDNIGHT SUNDAY NIGHT, after lying sleepless for hours in dread of Vivian's return tomorrow morning, I finally break, giving in to the curiosity that's been on simmer since I came back.

Now or never.

I don't creep through the house. Wearing pajamas and a robe, I clomp barefoot down the shadowed hallways toward the kitchen, veering right instead of left when I reach it. A short hallway ends with a door. I try the handle—locked.

"Dammit."

"What are you doing?"

I gasp, spinning to find Lizzie in the archway of the kitchen. She's in boy shorts and a tank, her dark blond hair in a messy bun, her face clean of makeup and glowing with youth. Though she doesn't necessarily look happy to see me, at least she isn't avoiding me anymore.

"You scared the shit out of me," I say with a short laugh. "Why are you awake?"

"Same reason you are, I guess. Couldn't sleep. Came down for a yogurt." She glances behind me. "Why are you trying to get into the basement? You know it's always locked."

A lie comes easily. "I wanted to see if Vivian kept anything from my mom's marriage to Dad, or if she threw it all away when she said she did."

Lizzie watches me another moment. "Hang on." She disappears into the kitchen. I hear a thud and a tinkling sound like water, then she reappears holding a set of keys. "She keeps them in the rice. Don't tell her I told you."

The keys arch my way. I catch them.

"Thank you, I won't."

"There's nothing down there, anyway. Everything was cleared out to a storage unit years ago."

Well, that answers the question of my father's files.

"I'd still like to take a look."

"Suit yourself."

The third key I try fits, and the door opens on cool, musty air. Fumbling on the interior wall, I find the light switch and flip it. Track lighting buzzes on, illuminating the long room at the base of the stairwell.

Wood creaks as I make my way down, keys tucked in my robe pocket. When I get to the bottom, I stare, struggling to absorb what I'm seeing.

"That's weird, huh?" Lizzie whispers behind me.

That is a single chair bolted to the floor in the center of the room.

Cold skates over my neck. "We shouldn't be here," I say, turning and clasping Lizzie's hand. "Let's go."

She pulls away, frowning. "No." She walks closer to the chair, head swiveling left and right as she scans the room. Besides the chair, the space is bare save for a narrow table against a wall with a toolbox sitting on it.

Lizzie reaches the table just as I see the blinking red light poised near the ceiling.

"Lizzie, stop!"

She freezes and looks back. I point to the camera and watch comprehension sweep her expression. But just as swiftly it shifts to determination and she turns away.

"Please, Lizzie, let's just go."

She ignores me, opening the toolbox with a flick of her wrist. Something long and shiny emerges in her hand, and she turns to face me.

"You know, I've never understood the point of torture." She holds up the scalpel. "How do you actually know if someone's telling the truth or simply telling you what you want to hear? People will say anything to stop the pain."

Ice crawls through my extremities, seeking my heart. "Just put it back," I tell her with forced calm. "I'm sure there's an explanation for this. We can ask."

"Oh, I already know what it's for. Don't you?" She gestures to the chair. "It's been neglected since you came back. Poor guy, he must be lonely."

Blood rushes in my ears, drowning all thoughts. I watch, mute and rooted to the spot, as Lizzie saunters to the chair and runs the scalpel gently across the back. When her eyes flicker up to mine, there's nothing in them I recognize of my little sister.

"Uncle Enzo is my teacher. He's a true master. He always knows just what to do to get them to tell the truth."

Horror darkens my vision. Swaying on my feet, I rasp, "How long has this been going on?"

"I think what you're really asking me, Calli, is when was the first time. Right?"

My throat closed, I nod.

"You remember David, don't you?"

My knees buckle, slamming against the concrete

floor. But I don't feel any pain. Just freezing darkness spilling into my world, leeching light from my heart.

David Willis was my first boyfriend. He might have been my first love, but he died before I could find out. A freak mugging. No one knew why a high school athlete was in that part of downtown in the middle of the night, but the cops dismissed it as gang violence and a stupid kid in the wrong place at the wrong time.

My family's specialty.

Lizzie was only fourteen at the time.

"Why?" I gasp.

She shrugs, regarding me impassively. "Why not? Mom and Dad didn't like him. He wasn't good enough for you. So I called him pretending to be you, crying about how I was lost in a bad part of town."

Bile rises in my throat. *She's sick. She needs help.*

"And Vivian? Did she know?"

"She found out later, but by then she'd already realized what an asset I was." She grins, but just as swiftly the smile falls. "Imagine how proud Dad is of me. I only wish I had a chance to tell him before he died, but Mom wanted me to wait."

I make my way to standing, pins and needles searing the soles of my feet. "I know he's proud of you," I tell her. "You have a gift."

She snorts. "Don't patronize me, sis. I get enough of that from Ellie."

Oh, Ellie... no wonder you stay away as much as you can.

I take a small step backward. "So what you told me earlier, about writing being your dream, you were lying?"

Her brows lift. "Throwing stones, really? We all play our parts, wear the masks we have to in order to be who we need to be."

"Why tell me now?"

She shrugs. "I liked how you handled Franco today. Sure, he's family, but he's also a snake. Seeing your true colors made me want to take the risk of trusting you. And if you're serious about following in Mom's footsteps, someone had to tell you the truth. I'm your baby sister, so I figured it would be best if it came from me."

I take another step back. "And what is the truth, exactly?"

"The same as it's always been. We live in service to this family. And if someone betrays us... Well, that's where I come in." Twirling the scalpel deftly in her fingers, she walks back to the toolbox and tosses it inside, then closes the lid.

I breathe a silent sigh of relief.

"Now that that's out of the way, wanna make cookies?" Skipping to my side, she grabs my hand. "Last year I found Grandma's old recipe for double chocolate buried behind the cookbooks. That was your favorite, wasn't it?"

I smile while my heart shatters inside me.

"It was, and I'd love to."

35

Callisto

MY FIRST INSTINCT when I return to my room an hour later is to call Finn and scream at him to get me out of here. Instead, I stumble to the toilet and throw up the three cookies I managed to swallow past a dry throat. When there's nothing left, I sink to the cool tiles, curl into a ball, and weep.

I can't call Finn. Not now, when there's a risk he'll be targeted like David was. *David.* He went out that night because he thought I needed him. All the possibilities of his young life... snuffed out. By Lizzie.

My empty stomach roils, rebelling, trying to eject what I've learned. Denial rises—it can't be true. *She was playing with me. There's an explanation. Maybe she knows I faked my abduction and is getting back at me.*

But I know it's real. I felt her wrongness. My skin

crawled with the primal recognition that the person across from me was fundamentally *off*. It's the same way I feel when I'm alone with Enzo, and exactly why I've avoided him most of my life.

Oh, Lizzie...

My thoughts cycle inward, all my pain focusing into self-loathing. How could I have missed the signs? I was seventeen when she killed for the first time. Between navigating early adulthood, high school, hormones, and increasing displacement in the family, I was, in a word, self-absorbed. When did she start changing? Did she try to reach out to me? Did I brush her off one too many times, causing her to seek support elsewhere?

No.

No.

This isn't my fault. As far as my own young mind could ascertain, Lizzie was normal. Charming and precocious. She didn't hurt animals—that I know of. Sure, she was sometimes shockingly blunt in her opinions and hurtful in her lack of empathy. There were more than a few times Ellie or I were reduced to tears by her assessment of our hair or fumbling attempts at makeup. But that's sisters, right?

No.

That whispered voice builds, gaining power. *No.* Lizzie needs help. A place where she'll be given the professional attention she needs. Somewhere she'll be safe—and somewhere the world at large will be kept safe from her.

And there's only one way to do it.

Stick to the plan.

I TAKE special care with my appearance in the morning, smoothing concealer under my eyes, applying mascara and lip gloss, and pinning back the sides of my hair. I wear a casual summer jumpsuit picked by Vivian's stylist and nude heels. Dab perfume at my wrists. Practice my smile in the mirror until it doesn't hurt so much.

You are strong.

You are brave.

For better or worse, you're an Avellino.

Lizzie, Ellie, and Franco are already waiting when I step outside into the balmy morning air.

My smile is ready, my steps steady. Ignoring my uncle, I kiss my sisters' cheeks in greeting. "Good morning, Lizzie. Ellie, I'm so glad you made it."

"Not like I had a choice," she mutters, casting a venomous glance at Lizzie.

Lizzie rolls her eyes. "Spoiled brat. Mom needs to

tighten your leash."

Ellie turns away, arms crossed. Since I'm standing right beside her, I hear her whisper, "Psycho."

My heartbeat trips. A quick glance Lizzie's way tells me she didn't hear. What I once thought was normal bickering between siblings takes on new meaning.

"You're delusional and paranoid. Keep at it and you'll end up in a padded room."

Ellie knows. What that means, I'm not sure. Does she even care? Heartsick, I focus on the driveway as a limo moves slowly through the gate, down the long drive, and finally stops before us.

I hazard a glance at Franco and find him scowling at me. With effort, my welcoming smile holds as the limo's back door opens.

Vivian emerges first, cell phone to her ear. "Hold on," she tells the caller. "Girls! So wonderful to see you. You all look lovely. Lord, I am so glad to be home!"

She embraces each of us in turn. Air kisses for all. Then she sweeps toward the house, her conversation about Senator Whoever floating behind her.

"So glad I got up early," murmurs Ellie, watching her mom disappear inside. Lizzie, Franco, and Enzo follow, the latter two pausing to give me similar, dark looks.

"What did you do?" asks Ellie.

"What do you mean?"

"The uncles only look at someone like that if they're on their shit list, so what did you do?"

"I told Franco off last week. He's not happy with me."

Her eyes, green and sharp and so like Vivian's, narrow in interest. "Huh. Maybe you're not as hopeless as I thought." Her head tilts. "I've been trying to figure out what your game is, Calli, but every time I think I have you pegged, you do something unexpected."

"So do you," I tell her frankly.

Shadows darken her eyes. "That's the only way to survive, isn't it?" she murmurs. "Play by the rules as much as we can, try to carve out a little slice of happiness for ourselves. And when we can't, run. Some of us even make it out."

With everything that's happened, I'm not even surprised.

"You knew all along, didn't you?" I ask softly.

She shrugs, her soft smile ironic. "Everyone thought you were too stupid to live, but I guess I knew you were too smart to die. What I don't understand is why you came back."

"To stop them," I whisper.

Ellie nods, like my answer was a foregone conclusion. "I guess they were right, after all. Too stupid to live."

My laughter surprises both of us. Ellie's lips quirk. "Or maybe not. You've definitely changed."

With a glance at the front door, I ask softly, "Does Vivian know? What you think about..."

She shakes her head. "I never told her. I'm the flashy airhead, remember? The prize mare. They don't care what I think."

Dots connect in my mind. "That's why Lizzie was talking about being married off. She was trying to get under your skin."

Her sigh is my answer. "It's what we do. The only normal we have."

"You know she's not well."

"Yes." She blinks hard, eyes reddening. "I'm not saying I think you'll succeed, but if you do..."

"I'll do everything in my power to get her help."

"Okay." With a bolstering breath, she visibly calms, slipping back into her role in the family—the one that allows her to survive. "Tell Mom I'll call her later. I have a study session this morning."

I grab her hand before she can leave, waiting for her to meet my gaze. "I love you, Ellie."

Tears shimmer. "I know. Even though I wish I didn't, I love you, too. Be careful."

She walks to her BMW convertible, not giving me another glance.

"Callisto?"

I turn to find Vivian on the stoop, cell phone still to her ear, her eyes hard on me. *Smile. Everything's fine.*

I join her. "What's up?"

"I'm sorry to say you have an appointment with Detective Willis... Wilber... whatever her name is at ten this morning. My driver will take you and Hugo will meet you there."

My heart leaps. Outwardly, I'm serene. "Why?"

"I don't bloody know. Follow-up on the physical or some other nonsense. Trust me, I tried to get you out of it, but apparently that woman you spoke to has the ear of the Chief of Police. She's making a stink. Hugo has advised us to play nice."

I nod. "Whatever you need."

"Good, thank you."

She ends the phone call without saying goodbye—Hugo's used to it, I'm sure—and smiles. "I heard you had a spat with Franco."

"He overstepped."

"Hmm. According to him, you overstepped."

I shrug. "I don't take orders from him."

Her expression hardens. "And me? Those were my rules you broke."

"Only to show you they weren't necessary."

"For you, perhaps. But maybe they weren't for you. Don't defy me again."

On that parting note, she sweeps back into the house.

36

Callisto

"GO ON IN," says Detective Wilson, opening the door of an interview room, "I'll stall Barnes a bit."

Before I can ask why, I see Finn rising from a chair at the metal table, his worried expression melting to relief. In seconds I'm in his arms, babbling—mostly incoherently—about what happened last night and this morning.

All the fear and fury, helplessness and grief comes surging out of me until I forget where I am. The camera blinking in a corner. The smoky mirror on one wall.

"Hey, princess, breathe. Slow down."

Holding me by the shoulders, he searches my tear-streaked face. "We're talking about your youngest sister? *Lizzie?*"

I nod.

His jaw ticks. "You're not going back there. This isn't a vague threat anymore."

"I know, but—"

"No *buts*, Callisto. This is your life on the line, and if you won't keep yourself safe, then I will."

"She's sick. You have to believe me. She'd never hurt me. They've done something to her."

Even as I say it, I wince at the denial in my voice and remember her face. Her words: *If someone betrays us... Well, that's where I come in.* And suddenly I don't know whether or not she would take my life if she needed to. Or was told to.

Finn sweeps his thumbs over my jaw. "I get that you want to find a way to defend her, to make this anything but what it is, but your sister admitted to murder. Whether or not she was groomed by your uncle, she's a psychopath. You can't go back."

A sob tears out of me, barely muffled by my fist. "She's only n-nineteen."

A voice behind me, firm but not callous, says, "Old enough to be cognizant of and responsible for her crimes."

I spin on Detective Wilson, the door swinging shut behind her. She's alone.

"You heard everything?" I ask weakly.

She nods, glancing at the mirrored wall. "Mr.

McCowen was very forthcoming this morning, too. I'll admit, what he had to say was hard to swallow. Sounded more like a Hollywood movie script than truth. Until he showed me the photos on his phone. It's my strong recommendation you do as he suggests and not return home."

Finn's lips press softly to my temple. "Please, Callisto. I can't risk losing you like I lost my father. It's over. We're stopping this now."

The finality—and reality—of his words sink in. He's right. My hope for this ending a different way died in the basement last night with Lizzie. The plan had been to convince my sisters to take a trip with me. A bonding vacation. To get them far away for when Finn laid everything out to Detective Wilson and their worlds were upended.

Too late. It was always too late. There's no going back for any of us.

The door swings open on a fuming Hugo, whose gaze lasers each of us, stalling on Finn. "Who the hell are you?" Without waiting for an answer, he turns to the detective. "Please tell me you're not questioning my client without her lawyer present."

Before she can respond, I say, "Hugo, you're fired."

He turns ashen. "Now wait a minute—"

"You heard her," says Detective Wilson, no hint in

her voice of the satisfaction she likely feels. She takes his arm and guides him back to the door. "Time to go."

"You're making the biggest mistake of your life," he growls at me, right before the door closes in his face.

"Well done, Calli."

Not sharing the detective's smile, I sink into an uncomfortable chair. Finn clasps my shoulder, squeezing gently.

Wilson sits opposite me, dropping a thick file and notepad onto the table.

I nod to the file. "What's that?"

"Until today, it was my pet project in conjunction with a friend at the Bureau. Now, it's a case file on your family's extracurricular activities."

All my capacity for surprise has been scourged. I merely nod. "When we first spoke, I had a feeling you knew more than you let on."

She gives me the barest of smiles. "It wasn't a coincidence that you spoke to me, although I felt damn lucky I was working the night you came in." Her keen gaze shifts between Finn and me. "I only wish I'd made more of an impression—maybe you would have invited me into your little troupe of vigilantes."

"It was my idea," Finn says quickly. "Like I told you, I wanted revenge and blackmailed her into helping me."

She gives his hand, still on my shoulder, a pointed

look. "So you say. It's time for you to step outside, Mr. McCowen. Don't go anywhere. I'm sure I'll have more questions for you."

Finn crouches beside me, his gaze heavy on mine, full of pride and a touch of worry.

"I'll be okay," I whisper.

"I know."

His lips meet mine only briefly, but the moment itself expands like a ripple in water. Endlessness wrapped in our shared breath. And when he draws away, I'm left with the same feeling of having hiked through the forest outside Solstice Bay.

Rooted.

Strong.

Calm.

The door closes softly behind Finn, and Detective Wilson asks, "Are you ready, Callisto?"

"Yes."

"Let's start with events leading up to you staging your own death."

37

Callisto

AFTER CLOSE TO eight hours of interviewing, with only minimal breaks for food, I'm the kind of tired that runs into walls and misses steps.

When Finn suggests we spend the night above a sex club in the owner's private loft, my eyes almost fall out of my head. But after he tells Detective Wilson the owner's name—Dominic Cross—to my surprise, she agrees it's a good idea.

"He's ex-military special forces," she says, then adds with a dry tilt, "I'm sure his place will be more accommodating than where we'd put you up tonight."

Finn tells me a bit more on the drive over—how Dominic and his wife, London, were attacked at the loft some years ago, and despite the threat being laid to rest, he had a state-of-the-art security system installed.

"No one's getting in there but us."

Despite my fatigue, a thrill dances up my spine. *No one but us.* Given I spent the day offering the police not only the means to ruin my family, but also the ability to bring me up on charges for faking my own abduction, it feels blasphemous to look forward to a night alone with Finn. But with Molly in a hotel downtown under an alias, I can't help my relief. We'll be safe. At least tonight. I don't think about tomorrow—it's too painful.

"Here we are."

After parking in a small back lot off Wilshire, Finn leads me through the deepening dusk to a nondescript back door. The building is square, two stories, and though I know the ground floor is some infamous club, I don't hear any music.

"The club's not open yet," says Finn, reading my mind.

"Ah, okay," I answer, shifting from foot to foot as he punches in numbers on a keypad I hadn't noticed.

There's a soft beep and a click. The door swings open. Finn leads me through a dim hallway to another door. Equally nondescript. Another keypad, this time requiring a thumbprint. It takes seconds, then there's a series of *thunks* as bolts snap away from their sockets. Finn pushes the heavy door open, revealing a narrow staircase framed by pristine white walls.

"This is…" I trail off, biting my lip on the words *over the top*. Because it isn't. It's exactly what we need.

Finn slants me a humored glance before he steps inside. "Members are fingerprinted these days. A few clicks on his keyboard, and Dominic can give limited access to the loft."

I consider the implication, not sure how to feel about it. "You, uh, come here a lot?"

He chuckles, planting a kiss on my forehead. "Not in the way you're thinking. I've been for drinks a few times. It's actually my best friend, Gideon, who's friends with the owners. I called him yesterday, and he called in a favor."

I nod like that makes sense, while a funny tingle in my stomach reminds me how little I actually know about Finn. His likes and dislikes. Habits and aversions—aversions besides my family, that is. Does he like oysters? I hate them. Does he play sports—I'm not coordinated enough.

Are we even compatible? Do we have anything in common besides my family?

Finn, oblivious to my mental spiral, waves me inside. I wait as he closes the door and resets the keypad. *Thunk thunk thunk.* Immediately my anxious thoughts fade away, security melting the edges of the bone-deep stress

I've carried since stepping foot inside my childhood home.

I'm safe here. No pretending. No overthinking. I can be myself for the first time in what feels like forever. And when we reach the top of the stairs and Finn flips on a light switch, my gratitude doubles.

"Wow," I whisper.

"Right?" Finn agrees, tossing his wallet and keys on a sleek side table and heading for the open-concept kitchen. "Something to drink?"

"Yes, please."

"Sparkling water, wine, or liquor?"

A shot of something strong sounds magical, but I also don't want to pass out in twenty minutes. "Wine, please."

"Coming right up."

I wander through the space, drifting past an elegant seating area, dining table, a console with a beautiful record player and saliva-inducing record collection, and admire several beautiful, bold pieces of art. On the other side of the kitchen is a bedroom—I can glimpse dark bedding on a massive bed.

I stall beside one section of the wall where a giant cross leans. I almost ask if the owner is very religious—then I see the cuffs. Blushing at my own naiveté, I spin and almost knock the wine glasses from Finn's hands.

His eyes twinkle at me. "Never seen one of those before, have you?"

I take a gulp of wine, not tasting it. My second sip is more measured—it's excellent.

"Definitely not. I mean, I kind of understand the appeal—allowing yourself to surrender control in a safe way—but the only way someone would get me on there is kicking and screaming. I don't like being restrained. Or confined. It's, um, an old fear."

Locked doors. Sightless dolls as company.

I turn away, embarrassed, but Finn captures my free hand in his before I can flee. "Hey, don't hide from me. I want to know about you. *Everything* about you."

I meet his gaze with effort, unsteady even though I'm wearing flats. Maybe it's the wine on an empty stomach, but I know it's more. It's *him*, blue eyes fixed on mine, frank with interest and something else. A darker current.

I've never had a man look at me with such raw possessiveness. Like I belong to him. It fills me with equal parts fear and longing.

"I don't know how to do this," I murmur, the honesty nearly splitting me apart. "My only boyfriend was murdered by my *sister*"—I almost choke on the word —"and I've been running since I was nineteen. I don't know anything about normal relationships. Is that even what this is? What are we, Finn?"

I bite my lips shut.

A smile flickers over his face. "I love it when you blush."

Releasing my hand, his fingers graze my hot cheek. "I don't know how to answer your question, but I'll try. I've been single-minded for so long, focused on preparing and waiting for the perfect opportunity to make the Avellinos pay for what they did to my family…" His fingertip traces my lower lip, igniting nerve endings all over my body. "All I know now is that I want *you*, Callisto Avellino."

More questions slip out, high-pitched, riding the wings of insecurity. "Because we have shared trauma? Or because it's a different type of revenge against my family?"

He can't actually want me, can he?

"Oh, princess." His smile grows, edged with that same darkness.

My fingers tremble on the stem of my wine glass, wishing to touch him. Here, now, with no great threat hanging over us, no bones in the dirt or adrenaline to level my inhibitions, I wish I were brave enough to show him how much I've come to need him. *Rely* on him. But he still hasn't answered my questions, and doubt keeps me rooted to the spot.

Finally, he says, "At the risk of sounding like a perv,

I've wanted you in some capacity since I was eleven and saw you for the first time at Rafael's sentencing. You looked so lost and out of place. I wanted to protect you and didn't know how to handle that. I decided to be angry instead."

So he was in the courtroom that day. I try to imagine Finn at eleven, having recently lost his father, and my heart squeezes.

He takes my hand again, threading our fingers together. "I'm so sorry for how I treated you in Solstice Bay. I was a complete ass. I guess in some ways I was eleven again—I couldn't reconcile how I felt about you with how I thought I *should* feel. If that makes sense."

I nod, a delicate hope blooming inside me. "It does. But you forgot to apologize for blackmailing me."

He winces. "I was never going to blackmail you. It was a stupid, spur-of-the-moment idea because I wanted to pull your clothes off like a caveman in that fucking closet and I hated it. I hated that I was so affected by you, that I wanted you, that you'd been under my skin for years. And that you were braver than I'd ever been."

"And now?" I whisper.

My pulse skitters wildly. I'm afraid of dropping my wine, but before the thought has fully formed, Finn takes my glass and sets both on a nearby table. He moves close, until our chests are a hairsbreadth apart. His body radiates heat and life and strength, a vital vibration that calms me as much as it arouses me.

Cupping my face, his fingers sink into my hair and clench lightly. I almost moan.

"I know who you are," he murmurs, then kisses me softly. "And who you are has nothing to do with your name." Another kiss, long enough to curl my toes. "You are brave. Stunning. Smart. Sexy. Kind. And I know you don't see it, but you're strong. So fucking strong, because despite your family and everything you've been through, you are *good*."

I don't know I'm crying until he kisses my tears, then my mouth. I taste the salt and more—the truth. His faith in me. My forgiveness of myself. And desire, burning bright and pure, unclouded by the past and future.

"Take me to bed, Finn McCowen," I say against his lips.

He lifts his head, distress in his face. "There's something I need to tell you. About this place. I want to be honest with you. A few years ago, I was here with—"

"I don't care."

To punctuate, I shut him up with a kiss. My fingers find his hair and tug, pulling his mouth more firmly to mine. But it's not enough. I want *moremoremore*. Releasing his hair, I fumble for the button on his pants.

"We can slow down," he whispers, strained.

"No!"

"Thank God."

I yank the button free and lower his zipper. My hand dives under the waistband of his boxers, finding hot, silky skin, thick and hard for me. He grunts, his head falling back as I wrap my fingers around him. My name comes from his lips as a whisper of supplication.

Staring up at him, the tight brow and closed eyes, the strong, smooth column of his throat that swallows convulsively, I revel in my own power and the deeply feminine knowledge that I'm not just any woman. His surrender and pleasure at my inexperienced touch mean one thing.

He's mine.

What we are or aren't doesn't have to be defined. This is enough. This is everything.

His mouth finds mine again, breath sucking breath, our tongues entwined in lazy exploration. My body's tight, needy hum reaches a painful pitch. I'm barely aware of my begging whispers, of him taking control, undressing me, stroking my newly bared skin like an unearthed treasure.

We stumble into the bedroom. Fall naked to the sheets. My limbs receive him. My body and heart welcome him home. Each thrust of his hips drives past the limits of my body into the fabric of my being. Creates a permanent space for him. For *us*.

His voice in my ear murmurs, "I need you," but my heart knows what he can't say and whispers it back.

I love you, too.

38

Finn

I WATCH HER SLEEP. Sometimes she twitches, or a small frown puckers her brow. I wonder what she's dreaming about. If she's having nightmares or if her mind is finally resting. But I know.

Neither of us will rest peacefully until this is over.

Her head is on my bicep, a leg thrown over my thigh. Soft, thick hair drapes over the pillow. She breathes low and deep, her lips slightly parted.

And it hits me.

I'm in love with the daughter of the man who killed my father. And there's not a damn thing I want to do to change it.

I've probably always been a little in love with her, a seed planted that day in the courtroom. We were both lost and alone. We were the same.

My obsession was an angry, uncomfortable one through my teenage years. Via late-night Internet searches, I watched her grow up. Become beautiful in a way my hormone-soaked brain couldn't handle. Unable to reconcile my shameful desire with my loathing, she became central to my plans to destroy her family. I told myself—*believed*—she was as evil as her father. I would use her, betray her, and be justified in doing so.

The lies I told myself...

When the news of her abduction broke, I drank for a straight week. Twenty-five years old and devastated for a reason I couldn't confront. Couldn't believe. How could I grieve a girl I'd never met, whose family had ruined mine?

My father's voice comes into my sleep-deprived mind. The last words he spoke to me before he left that night, before I snuck out of my room and into the back of his car, then witnessed the last minutes of his life.

"I need you to do something for me, son."

"What?" I was curt. Annoyed with him for working crazy hours lately and forgetting he promised to take me to batting practice yesterday.

His hand rested heavily on my back. I almost pulled away, but even with how mad I was, I liked how it made me feel. Like nothing could hurt me.

"Always take care of your mom and sisters. But don't tell them. Strong women don't appreciate men thinking they need protection."

"Abby doesn't need protection," I scoff. I still had a bruise on my arm where my oldest sister had punched me for laughing at the big zit on her chin.

Girls were dumb.

"Maybe not," my dad agreed with a smile in his voice. "But look out for her anyway. For all of them."

"Fine," I groused.

"Promise me."

"I promise. Goodnight, Dad."

The heat of his hand faded as he stood. I wanted to ask him to stay but couldn't.

"I love you, bud. Sleep tight."

What a shit job I've done making good on that promise. I barely know my sisters as adults, and they barely know me. I send texts on birthdays and Mother's Day, and presents to their kids at Christmas, but that's been the extent of my involvement in their lives.

After Dad's death, there was a nonstop stream of police, lawyers, child therapists, and family counselors. Silent dinners eating mushy casseroles gifted by neighbors. Nights spent sleepless, listening to my mother sob in her bedroom. My sisters had each other—always close, they banded together even more tightly in their grief. And the promise I made to my father was forgotten.

It's not their fault—not anyone's fault, really—that I was left alone. They didn't understand what it was like to hear him die. They didn't *want* to understand, not that I could blame them. I wasn't Finn anymore. I was the Witness. An unlikely spear of justice to be thrown at Rafael Avellino. I embraced that identity with everything in me. It was all I had left of my father.

Finally close to the end of my long journey toward retribution, I don't feel anything I expected to. No triumph or vindication. No catharsis.

Instead, I'm raw soul matter. A foal on newborn legs. Who I've been, what I've done, all the hatred I've nurtured so long... I see it now, the tragedy of it. My hatred kept me from love—the only necessary ingredient for living a life that matters.

Family is everything.

I turned my back on my family, and now all I want is to see them. Hold them and tell them I'm sorry. Meet my nieces and nephews. See their bright, excited faces on Christmas morning.

With Callisto at my side.

BUZZ. Buzz.

Sheets whisper. There's a small sound, like a scrape, on the nightstand.

Fighting the thick bands of sleep on my mind, I mutter, "What's that?"

A small pause. Her hand on my shoulder. "Nothing. Go back to sleep."

WHEN I WAKE UP, she's gone.

39

Callisto

I KNEW it couldn't be that easy. Despite all the reassurances from Detective Wilson and her thick file on my family, she doesn't know them. Not like I do.

Where there's one good cop, there are five more open to persuasion.

My father's words. And he was nothing if not a master of persuasion. He must have been truly flummoxed by Charles McCowen, a man who wouldn't bend from what was right.

I doubt the family's views on having friends among the police have changed in Vivian's reign. She probably received transcripts of my interview within hours of me leaving the station. But I expected it—I played my hand when I fired Hugo.

"'We live in service to the family.' What does that mean, Uncle Ant?"

I looked away from the dirty plaque I found on the ground, half buried by sawdust. It was heavy in my small hands and felt old and important.

My uncle looked up from his whittling. "It means there's only one way to leave the family, and that's feet first."

Sometimes he said the weirdest things. Sometimes those things scared me. But he was still my favorite uncle. The only one who always had time for me, a funny story to tell, or a game to play. Lately, though, he'd been frowning more than smiling.

"Bury it in the garden," he instructed after a moment.

His tone frightened me, so I hurried to gather my small shovel. Cradling it with the plaque, I headed toward the open doors of the stable.

Behind me, my uncle muttered, "Let the worms come for it as surely as they're coming for me."

Two days later, he was dead.

THE STREETS ARE EMPTY, golden-orange under the glow of city lamps until I exit the freeway and the lights come fewer and farther between. The hills of Calabasas rise around me in the dark.

I think of Finn waking to find me gone and hope one day he'll understand.

I always knew I'd be alone in the end.

When I make the final turn onto our street, I see the gates standing open. The house beyond is dark; it's the middle of the night, after all. But they're waiting for me.

You know what we want

The text message from an unknown number came with an image attached of a woman. She's gagged, her hands bound before her with nylon, and sits on the foot of a familiar bed, in a room that's a time capsule of the past. Floral wallpaper. Pink and white gingham bedspread with ruffles and matching pillowcases.

Vivian lied when she told me my childhood room had been repurposed, which I'd taken to mean gutted. From what I could see of the image's background, nothing has changed. Even the row of creepy-as-fuck, oversized dolls remains on the window seat. I hated the dolls, their blank eyes and perfect curls. Vivian didn't care—or more likely, enjoyed tormenting me—and gave me a new one every Christmas.

My palms are clammy on the steering wheel as I pull

to a stop before the front door. My heart, conversely, is preternaturally calm. No more self-doubt. No fear or anger. This isn't about revenge anymore, but about wiping the slate clean. Cutting away the roots of obligation, ambition, and corruption that have held my family down for generations. Purging the poison that infected my little sister.

That infects us all.

As I exit the car and walk up the steps, a figure steps outside to greet me. Slim. Blond hair. Trembling shoulders.

"They said I can't kill you yet." So much betrayal and rage in her young voice.

My calm shivers but holds. I pause on the step beside her and look into her shadowed eyes. "You shouldn't be the one to do it," I say softly.

"I *want* to," she snarls.

Tears glisten on her cheeks, touched by starlight. I don't know if they're real or not. Is she crazy? A sociopath? Or was she simply fed the milk of violence until it changed her?

"I never meant to hurt you, Lizzie. I love you. I didn't know—"

"That's enough," rumbles Enzo, his bulky figure shifting into the doorway. "Let's go. Traitors first."

Though I know my end isn't imminent—Vivian still

needs something from me—I don't like having my back
to them. My skin itches, anticipating pain, as I walk
down the hall and up a flight of stairs. The door to my
old room stands open, soft light spilling into the hallway,
tinged pink from fabric lampshades.

I pause on the threshold, absorbing changes I
hadn't been able to see in the photo's narrow field.
The decor is the same, yes, but there's signs of occupa-
tion. An open closet filled with adult, feminine
clothes. A dresser, new and white, with framed photos
on top. *Recent* photos, including one from the garden
party of the three of us—Lizzie beaming between me
and Ellie.

Vivian's sigh brings my gaze to where she sits on the
window seat. The dozen or so dolls are in a pile on the
floor, lidless eyes staring, arms and legs bent at weird
angles in a macabre display. Franco leans against a
nearby wall, his smile vulpine, a toothpick bobbing
between his teeth.

"It's rather odd, isn't it?" asks Vivian. "I told her it
was disturbing behavior, wanting to live in your room
with your hideous things around her day in and day out.
But you know Lizzie when she puts her mind to
something."

I give the dolls a pointed glance. "You were the one
who forced all these hideous things on me."

She smiles, slight and cruel. "I enjoyed the look on your face every time you unwrapped one."

"I imagine you did."

Finally, I glance at the woman on the floor. She stares up at me, her eyes wet and terrorized. "Please," she slurs around the gag in her mouth, "Please help me."

"Enough games, Vivian. Let her go."

"I thought we'd have a chat first. You know who she is, don't you?"

I do. Her curly hair is dark, peppered lightly with gray, bedraggled and wild from a struggle. I recognize the shape of her nose and eyebrows. She's younger than Molly, with a thinner face and brown eyes instead of blue. But there's no mistaking the resemblance.

They took Meredith McCowen.

Finn's mother.

Since she lives in Solstice Bay, they must have taken her days ago, which means...

"The ranch," I deduce, focusing on Vivian.

"Smart girl. Of course, when Franco showed me the video of your little adventure up there, I'll admit I was surprised by your choice of guests and venue. Whatever made you want to visit stables?" She waves away the question. "No matter. By dawn the bodies will be gone, that decrepit place burned to the ground."

By dawn.

Dread sneaks through the cracks in my composure. Grinding my molars, I stay the course. "So you knew all along who Finn was? Who his father was?"

"Do I even need to answer that?"

"No," I acknowledge.

She answers anyway, the invitation to hear herself talk too tempting. "He's been sniffing around for years, but he wasn't a nuisance until recently."

I think of the private investigators Finn hired, one of whom disappeared without a trace. "His PI found something," I muse.

Vivian sniffs. "Like I said, a nuisance. Does he really think we didn't know he was the protected witness in Rafael's case?"

Margaret whimpers, her eyes squeezed closed.

I make myself ask, "Why didn't you kill him, then?"

Her features rearrange into a wounded expression. "You really think I'm heartless, don't you? I'd never touch a child."

More likely, she spared Finn because my father going to prison aligned with her plans to be head of the family.

"Any more questions?" asks my stepmother.

"Yes. Before today, did you know I staged my abduction just to get away from you?"

Her answer is a startled laugh. She looks away, but not before I see the truth in her eyes. A glance at Franco and the toothpick hanging limply from his lower lip confirms it—they never suspected. They were merely relieved fate had stepped in on their behalf, taking me off the game board.

All that time, I was safe and didn't know it.

"What happens now?" I ask, looking around the room at my family. Lizzie won't meet my eyes, but Enzo and Franco spear me with a clear message of what they'd like to do to me.

Turning back to Vivian, I muse, "When I wind up dead, you'll have a pretty big mess on your hands. Especially with my detailed statement to the police today. Even if you manage to get rid of the evidence at the ranch, what do you think the public will say about the timing? About my eye-witness account of a human skull buried on your property? They might like you, Vivian, but they *love* me. Say goodbye to politics, your social calendar, and your famous friends. You're done."

Fury flashes white-hot in her eyes. "I should have killed you when I killed your mother."

The room goes silent with shock.

And not just mine.

Lizzie gasps, "You killed her mom? That's cold even for you!"

"She was spineless, just like her daughter. Not worthy of the Avellino name."

I find my tongue. "She died of an aneurysm."

"Right," Vivian scoffs, "just like your father died of a heart attack."

Lizzie jerks forward. "You killed *Daddy*?"

"No. You can thank Enzo for that gift. And you should. Rafael wanted to have you committed."

"He did? Why?" she whispers.

"Because he found your trophies, you imbecile! I told you to get rid of them!"

Enzo's bulk moves in my periphery. "We're getting off track."

Vivian fluffs her hair, visibly calming herself. "Yes, right, we are. Callisto, it's time for you to call your troublesome boyfriend and have him join the party." Almost as an afterthought, she nudges Meredith's leg with her shoe. "She can go once we have what we want."

She doesn't bother sounding sincere.

"No," I answer. "Let her go now, and I'll write my suicide note myself. I'll make it ten times more convincing than whatever bullshit you've come up with."

Vivian's eyes narrow, glittering with twisted humor. "Tempting, but no. I don't negotiate." She nods at

Franco, who tosses me a cell phone. "Don't make this difficult. Do it, or I let Enzo play with our guest."

Bile burns my throat.

I'm running out of time.

Think, Calli. Think.

"Since it doesn't matter anyway, what did you want me to find at Uncle Ant's ranch?"

"Curious till the end, aren't you? I guess there's no harm in the truth. Your father, sentimental as he was, wrote Anthony a letter from prison. It's rather inflammatory. A lot of false accusations."

I nod, understanding. "It was about you."

She clicks her tongue. "It's irrelevant now. Wherever it is, it will be smoke and ash soon. Just like you."

It takes everything I have and then some to keep my expression neutral. "Ahh, so that's how it's going down. Let me guess—I've been hiding a secret drug addiction. Finn must have gotten me hooked. We went to the ranch to partake, only we ended up burning the place, and ourselves, to the ground. Tragic story with a tragic end. The press will love it."

Vivian only smiles.

I make myself look at Enzo. "Dad didn't give the order to kill Anthony, did he?"

Enzo stares at me coldly, unblinking, which is answer enough.

"Of course not," Vivian supplies. She's gleeful. Gloating. "Rafael didn't have the balls to do what needed to be done. None of them did."

"But you did," I tell her. "You rose up from nothing, didn't you?"

"You're damn right I did." She points at Lizzie. "You should be proud of your mother. Imagine how many Avellino men are rolling over in their graves with a woman in charge of the family!"

"You're not a feminist, Vivian," I say flatly. "You're an egomaniacal, delusional bitch."

Enzo takes a threatening step forward, but Vivian shakes her head. Moving close to Meredith, she gives her dark curls a brief pat, then wiggles her fingers at Franco.

He hands her a gun.

"I'll make this easy for you," she coos. "Call your boyfriend or I blow her brains out."

With practiced ease, Vivian points the gun at Meredith's head, her finger steady on the trigger. My heart lurches into my throat. Meredith closes her eyes, lips moving in a silent prayer.

Lizzie mutters, "On my bedspread, really?"

"I'll do it!" I gasp. "Please, just put the gun down!"

Vivian nods. "Put the call on speaker, if you don't mind."

I can barely breathe, oxygen struggling to reach my

lungs through a vise of sheer terror. Fingers shaking, I punch in memorized numbers and hit Send. Three rings resonate in the room before the line opens with a click.

"Marlow's Pizza, what can I getcha?"

For a second, I can't remember what I'm supposed to say.

"What the—" begins Franco, pushing away from the wall.

It comes to me in a flash.

"Spaghetti!" I yell, then dive toward the door.

I don't see anyone's reaction, because the window nearest Vivian explodes inward. Something hits the floor with a *thump*. There's a low, whooshing noise and smoke pours toward the ceiling.

"Get down!" yells Enzo.

More glass shatters, this time when Franco—arm over his face—grabs the canister and chucks it back outside. But the damage is done. Everyone's coughing, the room thick with acrid smoke.

"No! No! No!" screeches Vivian.

"Lights, Elizabeth!" hollers Enzo.

Seconds later the bedroom goes dark. *Now or never.* Holding my breath, I lunge for where I last glimpsed Meredith. Thankfully she's not far, having dragged herself halfway to the door. I grab her, pressing my lips to her ear.

"Come with me," I whisper, my throat on fire from the gas. I feel rather than see her nod. Under the cover of smoke and chaos, we make it into the hallway.

Into the collar of my shirt, I wheeze out, "I have her. We're out of the room." Then I haul Meredith to her feet and shove her toward the stairs. "Go!"

She runs awkwardly, her bound hands held to her chest. At the head of the stairs she glances back, her eyes widening when she sees me not following. She hesitates a moment, then disappears down the stairs. *Smart woman. Smarter than me, that's for sure.*

I flatten myself to the ground outside the bedroom.

Gunshots and yelling form a gruesome symphony inside. I can't hear the answering shots from the police, but I can see them—chips of wood and puffs of plaster raining through the air.

My legs itch madly with the need to run to safety, but I can't. I'm glued to my spot by guilt and desperation. Eventually, the bullets taper off and stop, replaced by loud ringing in my ears. I edge closer to the doorway, knowing full well what I'm doing is foolish. Reckless. *Crazy.* But I have to try to get Lizzie to come with me.

Floodlights blast light through the bedroom's windows, so intense the hallway is illumined too. My uncles curse. Lizzie cries out in pain. I almost do, too, and bite down hard on my hand to stay quiet. My eyes, still sensitive and streaming from the gas, feel about to burst.

From outside, a tinny, amplified voice calls, "This is the police! We have you surrounded. Come out with your hands up!"

"Fuck, fuck, fuck." *Franco.* "The yard is crawling with SWAT. They've gotta be in the house by now. What are we going to do? How do we get out?"

Lizzie starts crying.

"Shut up," snarls Enzo, then to his brother, "You told me Calli didn't make any calls or stops on the way here!"

"She didn't!"

"Then how the fuck is this happening?"

"You must have missed something," Franco hisses back. "Did you even check her for a wire? She was asking all those questions for a reason, getting Vivian to spill her guts. We're fucked. So fucked."

"Mom?" whimpers Lizzie. "Mom, wake up! Oh my God, she's bleeding bad. *Do something!*"

"Serves her right for waving a gun out the window," snaps Franco. "She got too big for her britches. Idiot thought she was bulletproof."

"Shut your mouth," growls Enzo, "or I'll shut it for you."

Franco's voice only rises, panic mounting with every word. "Vivian screwed us over big-time. *Big-time.* And you know what? I'm not going down this way. I'm not taking the fall for you psychos."

"Don't even think about it, brother."

I've never heard Enzo's voice so cold, so *empty*, and I shuffle back from the doorway on instinct, knowing something bad is about to happen.

"Fuck you," says Franco. There's a burst of movement in the room. Glass crunching, shifting.

"No, don't—" Lizzie's words are interrupted by a gunshot and a *thunk* as something—someone—hits the floor. I cover my mouth with my hands to stifle my whimper.

Enzo spits loudly. "Coward."

Lizzie's tears intensify, then cut off abruptly. My body goes cold. *No...* Then she sniffs loudly, and I sag against the wall with relief.

"I know you don't like guns, kid, but take this. I thought if we could get to the garage..." Enzo sighs heavily. "That time has passed. They'll be on us soon. Let's give 'em everything we got on our way out."

Lizzie sniffs again. Her voice comes soft and hoarse, "You murdered Anthony and Franco. My *daddy*. All three of your brothers. Who does that? I'd never hurt Ellie or Calli, no matter how mad I was at them."

Silent, man-shaped shadows spill into the hallway from the stairs. Narrow red beams flash over the walls, over me. My extremities are mostly numb, but a trickle of adrenaline allows me to lift my hands over my head. *Don't shoot. I'm unarmed.*

"You told me David raped Calli." Lizzie's voice is stronger now. "You said killing him was the right thing to do. But he loved her, didn't he? They loved each other." She pauses. "I hurt good people because you told me to."

"Come off it, kid. You like it—no, you *love* it. You're just like me." He snorts. "And you can stop it with the *my poor daddy* shit. You know damned well I'm your father." There's a small pause, then, "Elizabeth, stop right now. Don't make me shoot you!"

The first set of boots pass me, then another. They move fast, so fast, a dark wave surging into the bedroom.

"Please," I whisper. "Please don't hurt her."

"Drop the knife! Don't move! Hands up!"

"Clear!"

"Clear!"

"Three down, one in custody—"

I don't hear anything else.

40

Callisto

MY EYES CLOSED, I listen to the steady *beep, beep* of the monitor, underlaid with the low hum of an air-conditioning unit near the window. Doors open and close, muffled by walls. Voices rise and fade—nurses and doctors, moving with purposeful footsteps. Tireless in their commitment to saving lives.

Even hers.

Although she's out of the woods, I haven't left her side. I want to be the first face she sees when she wakes. I want her to know she isn't alone.

The sun rises. There are other visitors. Some

new, some familiar. Doctors, detectives. Shift changes for the armed officer stationed outside the door. Even handcuffed to a hospital bed and recovering from a twelve-hour surgery, she's considered a flight risk.

The sun sets. I sleep off and on, my head pillowed on a sweatshirt, my legs beneath a thin blanket. Night nurses come in intervals, work quietly, then leave. I sleep again, lulled by the *beep, beep* of her heart.

When the sun has begun another ascent, I jolt awake at an unfamiliar noise.

She's coming around.

Pale light filters through the blinds, striping her face with gold. Scooting forward, I reach for her cold fingers. They squeeze back, the handcuff clinking against the bedrail.

Her bruised eyelids flicker at the sound, then open. "Where—" Her face contorts as pain finds her.

"Hey, it's okay. I'm here."

Some of the confusion leaves her eyes. "Callisto?" she croaks.

I stroke the blond hair from her brow. "You're going to be just fine."

"No," she whispers, jerking her head away from my touch. "No."

"Don't worry," I soothe. "They had to take out your

spleen and some of your large intestine, but you'll be right as rain in no time."

She moans, eyes rolling in panic. She tries to yank her fingers from mine, but the handcuff stops her.

"Enzo?" she whispers.

"He's gone. So is Franco."

The beeping intensifies as her heart rate spikes. Any minute, an alarm will sound and a nurse will come.

But I don't need long.

"I'm so glad you made it through surgery. It would have been a real tragedy if you'd died."

She whimpers, chin quivering. Tears leak from her closed eyes. "Just kill me," she whispers. "You want to, I know you do."

I shake my head. "I'm not like you. And thank God for that. Plus, that would be too easy. You don't deserve easy."

I gather my purse, sweatshirt, and the small bag with my change of clothes and toiletries, then head for the door.

"Please."

My hand on the doorknob, I pause. The officer outside sees me and stands, a question on his face. At my nod, he waves to someone down the hall.

"D-don't leave me like this. No matter what's happened, we're family."

"No, we're not." I meet her gaze a final time. "I hope you enjoy a long, healthy life in prison, then spend eternity rotting in Hell. Goodbye, Vivian."

The door closes behind me, and I take my first deep breath in a week.

Detective Wilson strides toward me, two nurses on her heels. At Wilson's nod, the officer opens Vivian's door and follows the nurses inside.

"Finally awake, huh?"

I nod, fatigue rolling heavily across my shoulders. "She didn't even ask about her. Whether or not she survived. What kind of mother..." I trail off, blinking rapidly.

Wilson touches my arm. "A shitty one. You can spend a lifetime trying to understand the pathology of a criminal like her, but you never will."

I nod again. "You're right. Thank you for everything."

She smiles. "I couldn't have done it without you. Do you want to go now, or do you need some downtime?"

I suck in a breath. "I'm ready. Unless you want to stay? You've been waiting days to question her..."

Wilson smiles gently. "She's not going anywhere."

"Okay. Let's get this over with."

As we walk toward the elevator, it opens on another detective and two more uniformed officers. My stomach tightens as I scan their faces. *Can they be trusted?* Wilson exchanges a few low words with the detective, then follows me onto the elevator.

As the doors slide closed, she says, "There are officers stationed at every entry and exit point in this hospital. No other patients are on this floor. And no one I haven't personally vetted is allowed anywhere near her room."

I smile halfheartedly. "Am I that transparent?"

"Nah. I'm that paranoid. Until Vivian Avellino stands trial and is sentenced, we'll be watching her like a hawk."

"Any word on Hugo Barnes?" To no one's surprise, Hugo went MIA the morning after what happened at the house.

Wilson grins. "I got word last night that customs nabbed him on his way out of the country with a suitcase full of cash."

Another knot inside me releases. "Good."

The elevator doors open and we walk side by side toward the hospital's entrance. My gaze trained on the floor, I don't notice Wilson slowing until she clears her throat.

I look up.

Standing near the entrance in a pool of golden

sunlight, with a bouquet of flowers in one hand and an extra-large cup of coffee in the other, is Finn.

When our eyes meet, he smiles. A little hesitant. Mostly hopeful. I haven't answered his calls or returned his texts, even the one telling me his mom was okay, that she and Molly were on their way back to Solstice Bay.

It's not that I haven't wanted to see him, or haven't missed him. The opposite, in fact. He's never far from my dreams and waking thoughts. But I needed time to process, to accept. To come to terms with the fact he might hate me for what I did. Disappearing in the middle of the night—doing exactly what I said I wouldn't. What I put him through... he *should* hate me.

And yet here he is.

Wilson murmurs, "I hope you don't mind. I thought you might want some extra support for this."

"I don't mind," I tell her.

My madly thumping heart leads my feet forward, but I can barely meet his too-blue eyes. "Hi, Finn. It's good to see you. I—uh..." My throat closes.

I'm sorry. I love you. Please forgive me.

He hands me the flowers. "These are for you."

"Thank you. They're beautiful."

As I lower my face to smell the bouquet, he asks, "Are you done yet?"

Registering the playful tone, my head snaps up. I see his smile. Look into his bright, laughing eyes.

"Done with what?"

"With pretending we're over." His smile grows. "Because, princess? We're just getting started."

41

Finn

DESPITE CHUGGING HALF HER COFFEE, Callisto spends the drive asleep with her head on my chest. I'm content to suffer pins and needles in the arm wrapped around her and wedged against the hard seat.

I'm not letting her go. Not for anything.

Holding her is my reward for the herculean level of patience I've demonstrated for a week. Not seeing her, hearing her voice, or touching her has been the single most difficult test of my life. I've been an emotional mess, alternately angry with her, afraid of losing her, and mad with longing.

If not for my mom and Aunt Molly repeatedly laying it out for me—*you're in love, dummy*—I might have done something stupid like flee the country.

"First time in the back of a police car?"

I meet Detective Wilson's amused gaze in the rearview. "Actually, no. I was arrested at fifteen. I swear we didn't know our principal's car windows were open when we threw all those eggs."

She smirks. "And you look like such an upstanding citizen."

I grin, well aware that with my tattoos on display and my hair a week past the boundary between *disheveled* and *derelict,* I look like I belong back here.

"Now now, Detective, by this point in your career I'm sure you've learned not to judge a book by its cover."

She sobers immediately, her gaze flickering to Callisto. "Damn right I have." She shakes her head, eyes back on the road. "She sure doesn't look like undercover material, but I gotta say her performance that night was flawless."

"So you've said."

I'm still sore about Callisto leaving with no word and putting herself in massive danger, but I'm learning to live with it. She saved my mom's life and probably mine. And she did it the right way, calling Wilson from her burner phone after she left the loft.

But there's still a lot I don't understand.

Seizing the opportunity, I ask, "How did you know?"

Her brows lift. "What do you mean?"

"You had to have known something was going down

that night. Don't bother trying to convince me you called the cavalry and had them in place within twenty minutes of Callisto calling you. So, how did you know?"

After a weighted pause, she says, "This stays in the car, understood?"

"Absolutely."

"A tip came in a few hours before Callisto received that text. It came to my desk because the call was placed from the Avellino home. The person identified themselves as a member of the staff and said they'd seen an unconscious woman being dragged upstairs, and that Enzo and Franco Avellino were carrying guns."

"Selina Hernandez?" I guess.

Wilson scowls. "I'm not going to ask how you know that."

"Good idea," I agree. "And I'll forget her name."

"Good." After a long silence, she adds softly, "It's not her real name, actually. She came to the station a few days ago to give her statement, and apparently you're not the only would-be vigilante with a grudge against the Avellinos. Her mother nannied for the girls for almost seven years. Most of her childhood. One day, her mother didn't come home from work. When she and her father raised hell, the family's lawyers released a statement that the nanny had been fired for stealing and probably run off. The missing person's case was buried."

"Christ, that family is fucking evil."

Callisto stirs in response to my sudden tension. I force my shoulders to relax and stroke her soft cheek until she settles.

"They are," agrees Wilson. "But at least Los Angeles is free of them. And we won't have an Avellino in charge of our state."

Her words make me think of Callisto's second cousins. One murdered for being gay, the other for running away from the family.

"What about the other Avellinos? In Chicago?"

Wilson shifts in her seat, putting on the blinker. I recognize the area—we're almost there. Sure enough, when we turn a corner, I see a row of news vans. Reporters and cameramen mill thickly near a chain-link fence.

"I know you're worried about them retaliating, Finn, but trust me, you don't have to be. Even before Rafael's death, the families rarely spoke. And since Vivian has been in charge there's been no contact. I don't think they approved of her." She must notice my frown, because she adds, "That's classified information straight from the FBI wiretaps, by the way."

It helps. A little. I still want to take Callisto away. Chop off her hair. Change her name. Tattoo her face.

Okay, maybe not that. But I might make her wear fake glasses again. Be my Nerdy Snow White.

Wilson passes a police barricade and navigates the long driveway, then pulls to a stop between two police cruisers. Car in park, she turns to face me.

"I want you to know that when Callisto called me and told me what she was doing, she wouldn't listen to reason. I was livid. I would *never* put a civilian in that kind of position willingly."

I smile in spite of myself. "She's kinda stubborn, huh?"

"To put it mildly." Glancing at Callisto, her gaze softens with admiration. "She knew she was being tracked via the cell phone Vivian gave her, so I had to jump in the car with her at a stoplight to get the wire on her. It wasn't pretty, but it did the trick. Her idea, by the way. Thanks to her, we have a crystal clear recording of Vivian's multiple confessions."

I kiss the top of Callisto's head.

Fucking brilliant, fierce, fearless woman.

Wilson turns off the engine, sighing. "I wish I knew why she wanted to see this."

Outside the car is a freaking circus. Tons of uniformed and forensic types in white coats swarm Anthony Avellino's ranch. As I watch, a body bag is carried from the stables and loaded into the back of a white van.

"How many so far?" I ask Wilson.

Her lips thin. "Eleven and counting." She opens her door, letting in a wave of heat and noise.

Callisto lifts her head with a yawn. "Are we here?"

I kiss her temple. "Yep."

She looks up at me, bronze sparking in the dark depths of her eyes. "Thank you for being here, even though you're still mad at me."

I chuckle. "I'm not *mad* mad. And I'm getting over it."

Wilson pokes her head back inside, her gaze swinging between the two of us. She winks at me. "Just a little bruised ego. He wanted to be your hero, Calli, but you didn't need one. Right, Finn?"

I roll my eyes. "Way to rub it in."

Callisto laughs, the sound rusty. She hasn't had much to laugh about recently—a fact I plan on remedying for the long-term.

But first, we're digging up a garden.

42

Callisto

THOUGH THE STABLES stand between us and the news cameras on the street, Wilson still had a tent erected over the raised garden bed. I don't need to ask why—helicopters crisscross overhead—I'm just grateful we won't be featured on the evening news.

The three of us are alone in the tent, Wilson standing nearby as Finn and I dig methodically in the bed. While the work in the stables and house continues loudly outside, we're in our own little world, undisturbed to a level that points to pulled strings.

I don't think about what's happening outside, though. It's enough to know that the bones of the wrongfully dead are finally beginning their journey to rest. There will be weeks, months, and years ahead for me to think about the families reunited with the remains of missing loved ones. The reopened wounds and bitter-sweet closure.

Perhaps Selina's mother, our former nanny Adele, will be found in my family's vile graveyard. For Selina's sake, I hope so. After all the risks she took, she deserves to know what happened to her mother.

It was Selina who put the pieces together. Months ago, she overheard Enzo suggesting to Vivian that they "clean the stables." Since the family didn't own horses, the conversation struck her as odd. Then, a week later, she heard Lizzie and Vivian talking in the kitchen.

"I miss visiting Uncle Ant's stables, Mom. When are you going to bring home a new horse for me?"

"I told you already—the stables are off-limits right now."

"But my horses are getting lonely! They need a new friend."

"Good God, Elizabeth. You know I hate it when you talk like that. It's so morbid."

"Do you think I can show Calli my horses someday?"

"Maybe someday, sweetheart. Fetch me an orange, will you?"

Selina's face should be the one on front pages and

news reels nationwide, not mine. But Wilson said she doesn't want any recognition, only to put this all behind her and live a quiet life with her family.

I wish I had that choice.

Maybe someday...

Beside me, Finn sits back on his heels and wipes sweat from his brow. "Anything?" he asks.

I shake my head. "Not yet."

I'm sure most of the people outside the tent think I'm nuts for requesting this. At least a few probably resent me being allowed here at all—a civilian digging through a potential crime scene. I'm lucky Wilson has the clout she does, regardless of whether she attributes that clout to me.

Finn hands me a water bottle, a not-so-subtle suggestion to rest. The tent is a sauna. I'm dripping sweat. Despite the small hand shovel I'm using, my fingers are raw from the old, dry soil, my cuticles near bleeding.

"Are you sure you don't want a metal detector?" asks Wilson for the umpteenth time.

I shake my head. "He wouldn't put it in something that would rust or with seals that might degrade."

Wilson shoots Finn a concerned glance. He touches my shoulder. "Maybe we should take an actual break—grab some lunch. What do you say?"

"Ten more minutes. Please."

He scans my face, eyes soft. "Okay, princess."

We dig.

When my shovel hits something plastic, I don't immediately rejoice. Old drip lines run inside the bed, most of them damaged, and we've had several instances of false hope this morning.

Dropping my shovel, I dig with my fingers, brushing and scooping until I see white PVC.

The drip lines are black.

"Finn."

Registering the excitement in my voice, he joins me just as I pull a sealed tube from the ground. Wilson is a second behind him. Once she sees what's in my hands, she whistles.

"Would you look at that. Don't open it. I'll be right back." She runs from the tent.

Laughing, I hold up the thick, six-inch tube. "Thank you, Uncle Ant, for being so paranoid."

Finn grins. "What do you think is in it? The letter?"

"Maybe." I shrug. "Vivian wanted that letter my father sent from prison, and she believed I knew where it was. Plus, Ant said that something in my head—my memory—was a danger to the family. This was the only place I could think of. It was special to me. To us. Before my visits, Ant would bury little trinkets in here. Digging for treasure was the highlight of my weekends as a kid."

"He sounds like an awesome uncle."

My eyes sting with tears. "Yeah, he was. I just wish he could be here."

Finn strokes sweaty hair from my temple. "I know."

"Here we go," Wilson says, jogging into the tent. Two detectives and a forensic tech follow.

The tech squats beside me. "May I?" he asks, holding out a gloved hand.

I give him the tube. Wilson hands him pliers. With one strong tug, the cap pops off. The tech trades pliers for tweezers, and seconds later removes a small, rolled piece of paper. Brows lifting, he looks at Wilson.

"This is all that's in it."

Wilson pulls on gloves and takes the piece of paper. I grab Finn's hand as she carefully unrolls it.

"What is it?" I whisper.

A moment later Wilson looks up, her eyes wide and... *laughing?* "Take a look," she says, her lips twisting comically. "No gloves necessary."

She hands me the paper.

If you're reading this, it means you've uncovered the final, biggest treasure of all! Your prize is a bowl of cotton candy ice cream, courtesy of your favorite uncle. Don't forget to clean your feet before you come in the house. And put away your tools!

UNCLE ANT

I'm laughing.

And crying.

And when the tears are gone, left in their wake is a small, tender kernel of peace.

"Should we head out?" asks Finn gently.

I glance around the tent. We're alone, though I can see Wilson's silhouette outside and hear her muted voice on a phone call.

"In a minute," I tell him, picking up my shovel one more time. "There's one more thing I have to do."

I know where to dig, of course. I was the one who buried this particular item all those years ago. Two nights before Ant died. The very last time I saw him.

Bury it in the garden. Let the worms come for it as surely as they're coming for me.

I can't say why, exactly, I need to find the plaque. More closure, maybe. I want to know what Ant meant when he said the biggest threat to the family was in my head. Though I'm prepared to accept he didn't mean it in any concrete sense but a more philosophical one, I don't want to look back in ten years and regret not going the extra step.

Finn watches me as I shovel out dirt from the southwestern corner of the bed. He's dangerously distracting —blue eyes electric, hair damp from sweat, tattooed arms on display. With effort, I tear my eyes from him and dig.

The moment I touch a tarp-wrapped bundle, I know I've found what I'm looking for.

I didn't bury the plaque in tarp.

Which means Ant dug it up after I last saw him.

"What is that?" asks Finn, moving up behind me.

I'm too taut with nerves to respond. Setting the bundle on my lap, I unwrap it quickly to reveal the familiar plaque. *We live in service to the family.* It looks the same, old and battered, once a treasure and now trash. Disappointment surges toward me. Maybe he got drunk and nostalgic that night and wrapped it to protect it, thinking I might want it one day.

When I lift the plaque to show it to Finn, something flutters to my lap. A Ziploc bag with paper inside. I shove the plaque into Finn's hands and grab the bag, barely believing what I'm seeing.

A letter. *The* letter.

Lined pages are folded in half and filled with my father's distinct handwriting. On the visible page, my eyes jump from word to word.

Vivian—evidence—storage unit.

"Oh my God," whispers Finn.

I nod, giddy, and yell, "Wilson!"

43

Callisto

MOONLIGHT, full and bright and demanding, pierces the gaps in the blinds over the bed. Finn sleeps beside me, his arm locked over my waist like he's afraid I'll disappear again. I lie awake. On edge. My mind racing.

The relief and closure I felt three days ago when I found Uncle Ant's note and the letter from my father has faded. Now all I feel is heavy and heartsick. Stuck in endless limbo as I wait for the debris of my blown-up life to settle. For Ellie to return my calls, for word on Vivian's court date. For the coroner to release Enzo's and Franco's bodies for burial...

My sisters. My uncles. My mother, father, step-mother. Broken or dead, each and every one of us.

I got what I wanted, but it still hurts.

As children, we shape our world through the lens of

our immediate family. They are our first teachers in lessons of love and fear, our very foundation of security. As we grow, that lens widens to include others. Friends and romantic partners. Classmates and teachers, colleagues and employers. But in crisis, I've found that our view of the world defaults to our beginnings.

Unless we break the foundation.

Rabbit was the first person I trusted enough to share details of my childhood with. A lifetime of secrets, suspicions, and fears came out. It was a miracle she believed me at all, but she had her own difficult story to tell. She understood the unique burden of being born at odds with your bloodline, and she helped me take the first step in freeing myself.

Neither of us could have known that the final step would be up to me, and that I would have to come home to take it.

Perhaps my mother, had she escaped Vivian's ambition, could have changed the Avellino foundation. Gentle, a dreamer and artist, from my father's rare stories and those old albums, she was in all ways the antithesis of Vivian. Would she have altered the family's dark fate? Would her gentleness have softened my father in time? Or would she have shattered her own foundation and replaced it with theirs?

I'll never have the answers I want, the questions

themselves intangible. I'll never know my mother or her family. She was an only child, her parents dead before I was born. Perhaps someday I can learn more. Find more stories from her life before the Avellinos.

The full moon buzzes in my blood, whisking me from one thought to another, one unknown to the next. I can't change the past, nor who I was in it. Life will never be what it *might have been*, only what is.

But that knowledge doesn't make the present any more bearable.

Only *he* does.

Rolling to face him, I read his features with my fingertips. Absorb his breath with mine. Revel in the tragic twists of fate that brought us together.

"Stay with me," I whisper.

His eyes open, the depths too clear for someone who was supposedly asleep. "Always, princess."

Shifting forward, I fit my nose beside his, my mouth to his mouth. "You're awake."

His lips curve. "Guilty. You've been flopping around for hours. How's a man supposed to sleep through that?"

But there's worry beneath the words, and I know he was afraid I'd leave while he slept. *All of us broken.* Will we ever rebuild? Or is this our fate—to see the world through a veil of fear and uncertainty put in place when we were too young to defend ourselves against it?

"What's on your mind, princess?"

I blink, focusing on his voice. "Will this heaviness ever go away?"

His arms come around me, rolling us until I'm settled on his chest. "It will. I promise." The words are punctuated with soft kisses, and end with a deeper one.

I love the taste of him, the effortless way we kiss, like our bodies aren't learning but remembering each other. The strength and dependability of his arms. The pleasure his touch gives me.

But it's not enough.

Finn breaks our kiss. "What's wrong?"

I shake my head. "I don't know."

The truth is, what I want I can't speak. And what I need I can't name.

"Does this feel wrong?" he asks carefully.

"No," I say quickly. "It's nothing to do with you. I think I'm what's wrong. I'm *wrong*."

He tenses beneath me, brow furrowing. "That's bullshit. You're everything that's right."

He can't see it. Feel it. This shifting inside me. The broken pieces of my foundation fighting to find new alignment.

I move off him, swinging my feet to the floor and cradling my head in my hands. "I'm sure it's just everything catching up with me. My head won't shut up.

Maybe I just need a drink. Something to take the edge off."

The sheets move as he does. "Do you trust me?"

I lift my head, glancing back. He's sitting up, moonlight dancing on his bare torso, shadows nesting happily in cuts of muscle. Awed, as I am nearly every time I look at him, I offer a distracted, "Yes, of course."

He flings the sheet and pillows from the bed, leaving the mattress bare of everything but our naked bodies. Lowering onto his back, he tucks his arms behind his head.

"Use me."

Despite everything we've done together, I blush and laugh nervously. "What?"

"As much as I'd like it to be true," he muses with a wicked glint in his eye, "sex with me won't be the answer to all your problems. But I think, *maybe*, if you can be in control here, it will make you feel less out of control in here." He taps his temple, then resumes his supine position. "You're a pressure cooker ready to blow. What you've been through... it's a fucking miracle you haven't lost your shit yet. I want you to let go safely, right now, with me. I'm not in charge, you are."

My cheeks and chest burn, my eyes flickering unconsciously to his cock, already hard against his stomach. It jerks under my gaze. My thighs squeeze together, my breath catching. I want him. *God, how I want him.* But I don't know how to do what he's asking.

"I always let go when I'm with you," I say, mortified by the tremor in my voice. "Don't I?"

His gaze stays steady on mine, accepting without judgement. And he gives me the hard truth. "Our lives aren't in danger anymore, Callisto. It's just you and me and this space between us. I want you to find her—the woman I met in Solstice Bay, who accepted an invite for a one-night stand. Who dared me to feel how wet she was."

I welcome the rush of heady anger that drowns out my vulnerability. "Sorry to disappoint, but that version of me is gone. She was a fucking child. She knew *nothing* about pain or sacrifice."

"I disagree," he says calmly. "We don't shed skins, princess, we layer new ones on top of the old. And the fact you're angry right now means I'm right."

"You're not right—you're delusional."

He grins. "How do you feel right now?"

"Like I want to slap that smug smile off your face."

"See? There's the spunk. You can't hide who you are from me. I see you. I *know* you. Just for tonight, I want you to let go and remember who you are. And if you can't do that, remember who you want to be."

I'm so angry I can't speak, so I act instead. I curl my

fingers around the base of his erection and squeeze. His eyes roll back, his whole body shuddering. I stroke him firmly up and down, my anger melting into something barbed and velvety.

After my hand shuts him up, my mouth gives him back his voice. He pants and groans, whispers how good it feels when I take him as deep as my throat will allow. His body speaks even louder—jerking at the graze of my teeth, hissing when my nails scrape down his abdomen.

In time I replace my mouth with my body, using him like he invited me to. When he tries to touch me, I slap his hands away. When he laughs, I stop moving until he apologizes.

I take and take. Unrepentant and defiant. Unhinged with my need to reclaim, rebuild, redefine this broken life by any means necessary.

He lets me fuck him like he's my revenge.

Maybe he is.

When I collapse onto him, replete and finally empty of thought, I welcome his arms around me as I drift toward sleep.

He whispers into my hair, "Sex therapy. I'm a genius, right? Just call me Dr. Finn."

And there it is...

Light shining in the darkness.

44

Finn

"OH MY GOD. I did that? Let me see. Are you okay? Does it hurt? I'm so sorry."

Callisto is horrified, her eyes comically wide as she gazes at the marks her nails left on my chest. She's blushing from her neck to the roots of her hair.

"These are my love stripes," I tell her, tugging a T-shirt over my head to conceal my grin. I take a few seconds longer pulling it down because her reaction makes me want to roll on the floor laughing. Which I'm sure she wouldn't appreciate.

I don't want her to think I'm laughing at her when in reality I'm still riding an endorphin high from last night. Callisto Unleashed equaled the longest, most intense orgasm of my life. I'm wrecked and slaphappy.

"Are you sure they don't hurt?" she asks, squinting and skeptical.

They do sting a bit, but I rather like it. I catch her fluttering hand and draw her toward me. Looking down into her gorgeous, worried face, I almost blurt the words that have been on my mind for days. Weeks. Months. Years...

I love you.

But I chicken out.

"Princess, last night was amazing." I pause, frowning. "No, amazing isn't big enough. Meaningful enough. Last night was *more*. I've never felt as close to another person as I did to you when you let go and trusted me. At the risk of sounding like a loser, I felt wanted. Needed."

"I *do* need you, Finn. So much. I'm sorry if I haven't told you that." Sighing, she rubs her cheek against my chest. This time, instead of my dick perking up, my heart does. "I wouldn't have made it this far without you. Thank you for being here, for shocking me back to life. I know I've been distant the last few days. Not myself."

"With good reason," I assure her. "And listen, I know healing from everything you've been through is going to take time. I don't want to rush that process. But I do want you to remember that there's life here, too. Happiness, even. And no matter what, you don't have to hide your pain from me. I'm sorry I was an asshole, though."

I'm lying. I love her feistiness.

She looks up with a mischievous grin. "No, you're not."

Feeling utterly in love and dizzy with it, I laugh. "You're right. I like angry sex with you. A lot."

She shoves my chest, then gasps when I wince. "Oh God, you *are* hurt!"

I grab her face and kiss her hard. "You can hurt me anytime you like."

An alarm sounds on my phone, plugged in near the bed. Callisto set it on mine since both of her phones were bagged as evidence by Detective Wilson. Releasing her reluctantly, I fetch the device and turn off the alarm.

"It's time?"

I take in her suddenly pale complexion, the way she hugs her arms protectively to her chest, and wish more than anything there was a way to talk her out of what she's doing today. But I won't diminish her courage by trying.

Not that she would let me convince her, anyway.

God, I fucking love her.

Because I can't help wanting to protect her, I ask, "You still don't want me to come with you?"

She shakes her head. So stubborn. So brave. "I won't

be gone more than a few hours, I don't think. If it's looking that way, I'll borrow a phone and call you."

I chuckle. "I can't believe you're comforting *me* right now."

Unable to resist, I pull her into my arms and kiss the top of her beautiful head. And standing there, with the world in my hands, the truth no longer seems scary. Just inevitable. Freeing.

"I'm in love with you, Callisto. I was lost until I found you."

She sighs, but it's a happy one. I can tell. It's confirmed when she lifts her head and I see her smile. The glisten in her eyes.

"I love you, too. If we get lost again, let's do it together."

I kiss her. Then I kiss her some more, peppering her face and neck until she giggles and eventually bats me away.

"To be continued later," she says, dancing out of reach and grabbing my car keys off the dresser. "See you soon." Then she's gone, and moments later the apartment door opens and closes.

To avoid making myself crazy waiting for her, I finish dressing. Have coffee. Make some breakfast. Call my mom to confirm that she and Aunt Molly made it safely to Solstice Bay. We talk about the drive, the weather. We joke that her visit to Los Angeles was a drag and agree that being duct-taped in the trunk of the car isn't a comfortable mode of travel.

When we run out of stupid shit to talk about, instead of my usual hasty goodbye, I hesitate.

"Finn?" asks my mom, a thread of worry in her tone.

Thinking of Callisto, I push past old habits and find the person I want to be. "There's something important I need to tell you, Mom. I wanted to tell you in person, but it can't wait."

"What?" she barks. "What is it? Did you finally tell Callisto you love her?"

"Yes, but that's not—"

My mom squeals and yells, "He told her!" to someone on her end. Aunt Molly screams like a teenager. *Women.*

"Mom, that's not what I wanted to tell you!"

"What? Oh. Sorry, honey." She shushes Molly. "What is it?"

I suck in a breath, then let what I feel coat my words, "I'm sorry." There will be more words later—many, many more—but for now, these two are all I have. And all I need.

There's a beat of silence, then my mom, tears in her voice, whispers, "I know. I'm sorry, too. You're coming home soon?"

I don't bother reminding her I've never lived in Solstice Bay, because I understand what she's saying. Home to her. Home to my family after years and years apart.

"Yes. I'm coming home."

She sniffs. "Good. That's really good."

In the background, Molly yells, "Tell him he's not welcome unless he brings my girl with him!"

"He heard you. And I second that."

"McCowen women." I sigh. "So bossy."

"True enough," my mom says with a chuckle. "Can't wait to see you, Finn. I love you."

"Love you, too, Mom."

I hang up with a strange mix of sadness and lightness. But maybe that's what making amends feels like— regret is still there, but it's fading as I shift the direction of my life. Now, instead of moving away from love, I'm moving toward it.

I do the dishes with a goofy smile on my face. Then I grab the spare apartment key and head to the manager's office to break the lease on this craptastic apartment.

I've never been so ready to leave Los Angeles.

45

Callisto

FLUORESCENT LIGHTS FLICKER along the walls of the bland hallway. Shoes squeak on faded linoleum as people pass me. All types of people, with passive faces, angry faces, withdrawn faces, brave faces... The children are the worst. After the first few, I can't look at them anymore.

If my expression reflects what I feel, too, then I look terrified and twitchy. My heart jumps every time the distant door opens, hoping for a familiar face, but time is running out. I have to accept that she might not come.

"Miss? The inmate is ready."

With a final glance down the hallway, I nod and follow the officer through another door. He leads me down a row of cubicles truncated by thick plexiglass. When we reach the third cubicle from the end, my knees turn to jelly. I half fall onto the chair, my hand instinctively grabbing the phone receiver on the wall.

Lizzie picks up on her end, smiling broadly.

"Oh my gosh, Calli, it's so good to see you."

When Wilson told me about the preliminary evaluation of Lizzie's mental state, I didn't want to believe her. *Undiagnosed adolescent-onset conduct disorder. Antisocial personality disorder.* But looking at her now, being confronted with her lack of appropriate emotion, severs the final tentacles of denial. The last time I saw her, she threatened to kill me.

My baby sister is a sociopath.

"Aww, Calli, don't cry. I'm fine. I'll be out of here in no time."

I shake my head mutedly, choking on the debris of my broken heart, until someone removes the phone from my ear. Looking up, I see Ellie beside me. She came. She's here. *Thank you,* I tell her with my eyes. She nods, then faces Lizzie and speaks into the phone.

"You're not getting out." Her voice has a veneer of calm, but her hand trembles. "You've killed innocent people. You slit Enzo's throat in front of six cops. Even if you're found guilty by reason of insanity, you'll be imprisoned in a psychiatric hospital the rest of your life."

Lizzie isn't smiling anymore, her eyes hard as they

shift between our faces. When she speaks, Ellie holds the receiver out so I can hear her.

"I was coerced," she says with a shrug. "Brainwashed as a child. Killing Enzo was self-defense, anyway. He was going to shoot me. Call Hugo. He'll figure it out."

Ellie shakes her head. "Hugo is in jail."

"Then hire someone else. It's not like we're short on money."

"You really don't get it, do you? Mom is going to prison for life. Franco and Enzo are dead. The police dug up Uncle Anthony's ranch and found *seventeen bodies*, Lizzie! There isn't enough money in the world to buy you out of this, and the sooner you realize that, the better."

Lizzie dissolves into a raucous fit of laughter, the sound so out of place that she earns wary glances from the other inmates. Then she stops, so suddenly the hair on my neck stands up. Ellie shudders and grabs my hand, her fingers clammy.

Our little sister leans toward the glass, her eyes flat, and hisses into the receiver. "The only thing you two had to do was shut up, prance around in pretty clothes, marry rich dudes, and have babies. Mom was right— you're both stupid, ungrateful brats. You have no idea how hard I've worked for this family, for *you*." She turns her focus to me. "It's your fault I'm in here, so get me the fuck out and I might forgive you."

With a muffled sob, Ellie drops the phone. It thumps into the raised shelf beneath the plexiglass. "I'm sorry," she whispers to me, then flees, disappearing through the exit.

I pick up the receiver, calmer now that I finally understand Lizzie can't be saved, treated, or freed. She stabbed my high school boyfriend twenty times, killed God knows how many other people, and slit her own father's throat.

There's no rehabilitation for that.

I'll always carry guilt—misplaced or not—for leaving her at the mercy of Vivian and Enzo, for not noticing signs of psychopathy when we were young, for not being a better big sister. What my mind can accept, my heart still regrets.

The *what-ifs* and *maybes* will haunt me forever. But I can live with them. What I can't live with is another person dying because of her.

"Ellie has always been the weakest, hasn't she?" asks Lizzie on a yawn.

"I think she's the strongest of us all."

She scoffs. "Yeah, right. Anyway, what's the plan? I know you've talked to a lawyer. No plea deals—we'll definitely want a trial. I'll charm the socks off a jury and do a few years somewhere. Easy-peasy. Then it's you and me running shit, Calli. Bosses. Sounds good, huh? I bet you're glad Mom's out of the way. I think we'll make Dad super proud."

She grins expectantly, eyes sparkling, and the familiar expression coupled with the insane words lift goose bumps all over me. The sister I loved all my life was just a face the monster inside her learned to wear.

My options in the moment are few, but it doesn't take me long to decide. For her, for me, I'll be an Avellino one final time.

So I smile and nod.

And I lie through my teeth.

"I'll talk to Ellie and calm her down. We'll figure this out. Just hang in there, okay?"

"Okay." She relaxes, smile softening. "I'm not mad at you anymore, Calli. I was only mad because Mom was, anyway, and she was just peeved that you were smarter than her. They all got what was coming to them, right?"

"Right. I have to go, Lizzie, but I'll be back soon."

"Cool. I'll be here." She blows me a kiss. "Love you, big sis."

"I love you, too."

I hang up. Stand up. Walk away.

One foot in front of the other, I abandon my sister for the second time. Only this time, I'm not coming back.

When I walk outside, I'm surprised to find Ellie waiting for me. Dark sunglasses conceal her eyes, but there are tear tracks on her cheeks. She's on the phone, but says goodbye and hangs up when she sees me.

"Hey, Calli."

"Hey back. Thanks for waiting. And for, uh, coming."

I'm nervous again, unsure of where we stand. Whether or not she hates my guts. Were our situations reversed, I'd probably hate me.

I dismembered everything that was normal in her life, and our names will be forever associated with our family's crimes. As Vivian's eldest daughter, Ellie is already under incredible scrutiny from the media. Depending on the reputability of the outlet, either she was stupidly ignorant, threatened to silence, or she's some sort of criminal mastermind who orchestrated everything in order to take over the family.

"I'm sorry, Ellie. I ruined your life."

"You didn't. That happened when I was born an Avellino." She clears her throat. "I'm sorry I didn't return your calls. The last week has been...." She trails off, staring into space.

"It's okay. Really."

She laughs, brief but genuine. "What a mess. The only thing that got me out of the fetal position this morning was Xanax. Thank God for my therapist and the fact my boyfriend's dad is a lawyer."

I blink. "You have a boyfriend?"

For a moment, her features soften. "Yeah. We met on campus last year."

"Then why were you upset about Finn?" Before she can answer, I understand. "You didn't want the family to know you were seeing someone, did you?"

"Hell no. They wouldn't have cared how smart, driven, or kind he was—all they would've seen is the color of his skin. And now that I know what actually happened to David, I'm extra fucking glad I never brought him around."

"Me too."

Her fingers find mine, link for a moment, then release. "That must have been a huge shock, finding out Lizzie killed David." She nods toward the jail. "I'm glad she's alive, but I hope they lock her in a padded room and throw away the key."

Misery tightens my lungs. "I just wish..." I shake my head. Too many wishes, all of them ash. No going back.

Ellie murmurs, "You saw only the best of her. She worshipped you. Me? Hot sauce in my shampoo and dead squirrels in my bed were the very least of it."

I pinch the bridge of my nose. "Jesus. Where the hell was I when this was going on?"

"Oh, I don't know, withstanding ongoing emotional abuse and alienation?" She touches my arm. "I'm sorry, Calli. For what a bitch I was to you."

"Same."

We share a smile—sad and small.

"What now?" I ask.

"My boyfriend's dad says we need to make a plan for the house and businesses and whatever else."

"I don't care what you do," I tell her honestly. "I don't want anything, any money."

"Good, because after Mom's trial and all the lawsuits coming our way, there won't be any left. And you know what? I'm kind of looking forward to it. No more blood money."

"Do you think Vivian will..." I swallow the words, afraid to even say them aloud.

"Not a chance. She's my mom, so yeah, I'm getting her a lawyer, but I heard the tape from that night. What she did to your mom, our dad, the shit she said..." She shakes her head. Her lower lip quivers a moment before she squares her shoulders and lifts her chin. "It's about time someone in this family besides you did the right thing. She'll pay for her crimes. I promise."

For all that we share a father and grew up under the same roof, Ellie and I are cut from separate cloth. We might never be close, or even friends, but I'm suddenly overwhelmed with deep love for her. For the woman she's become in spite of our family.

"I'm proud of you," I tell her.

She smiles softly. "I'm proud of you, too. You turned out to be a total badass." An SUV pulls up to the curb beside us. She waves to the driver, a handsome African American man who smiles back. "This is my ride. Don't be a stranger, okay? Or disappear again."

"Deal."

"Oh, I almost forgot—this came to the house for you." She pulls an envelope from her purse and hands it to me. No return address. My name and the Calabasas address handwritten on the front. Ignoring it for the moment, I hug my sister.

This time, she hugs me back.

When she's gone, I walk to a small shaded area on the outside of the building and lean against the stucco wall to open the letter. Inside is a single sheet of paper with only a few lines of text, penned by the same masculine hand that addressed the envelope.

AFTER MUCH THOUGHT, WE'VE DECIDED NOT TO SEEK RECOMPENSE FOR YOUR DEEDS. CONSIDER YOUR LIFE AS PAYMENT FOR RIDDING US OF YOUR TROUBLESOME FAMILY. LET THIS BE THE LAST TIME WE HEAR YOUR NAME.

D.A.

My arm falls, leaden, to my side.

D.A. can only be one person—Dimitri Avellino. My father's cousin, head of the Avellino family in Chicago, who had his own son murdered for being gay and his niece killed for trying to escape. Who, with a single order, could make me disappear for good.

My head drops against the wall. Hysteria bubbles in my throat, but I choke it back, swallowing repeatedly until the sensation passes.

Inflaming the other side of the family was always a risk, of course. One I weighed against the likelihood they wanted Vivian gone as much as I did. Having a woman in charge of the family out here must have been a thorn in their side.

Until this moment, though, I don't think I realized just how real the threat was. Or maybe deep down I believed I wouldn't make it out of this alive. Either way, I'm glad I never met any of the Chicago family, and with luck I never will.

For a few minutes, I stay where I am and breathe. In for four seconds, out for six. In. Out. Until the tremor in my hands fades. Until my heart rate lowers. Until the haze clears from the edges of my vision.

Wilson said having anxiety, and more specifically

panic attacks, is normal given the circumstances. That in all likelihood, I have post-traumatic stress. She thinks I'd benefit from steady therapy, potentially some medication to help me through the next few months or years.

I know she means well. And there's a solid chance she's right. But for now, I'll breathe.

And be thankful for my life.

For today.

Finn and I are having dinner tonight with Rabbit and her boyfriend. I can't wait to see her and meet her love—have her meet mine. Hug her and actually see what color her hair is.

And then?

I'm going home.

EPILOGUE

Finn

FIVE MONTHS LATER

"HERE, you look like you need this." My mom pushes a frosty bottle of beer into my hands, then sits beside me on the bench. "I've never seen them take to someone so fast."

Across the backyard, I can barely see my girlfriend's head beyond the three-woman wall of my sisters. Compared to Callisto, the lot of them are Amazons. But I hear her voice, clear and confident. Her laughter, unrestrained, with that touch of smoke that makes me think about things I shouldn't be thinking about while sitting next to my mom.

"She's holding her own."

My smile is smug. "That she is."

"If you want to head inside, I'll take over out here for a bit."

All three of my brothers-in-law are watching sports. They're nice enough people, but I'd rather stir-fry my own balls.

"I'm good, thanks."

This is exactly where I want to be.

On the other side of the backyard, Aunt Molly is teaching my oldest nephews—eight and ten years old— how to grill the perfect steak. Two more boys and three girls, all under the age of seven, are destroying Mom's garden as they chase butterflies and squeal over earthworms.

I'm technically in charge of the tiny savages. Five minutes ago, they were shoving dirt clumps under my shirt and spitting on my shoes. Since no one's bleeding and no one's crying, I decided I'd earned a little break.

If I keep this up, I'll be Uncle of the Year in no time.

"Did she see the news last night?" asks my mom, her voice pitched low.

And just like that, I'm not thinking about the kids anymore. After a heavy swallow of beer, I nod. "Detective Wilson called before the story broke."

"Is she okay?"

"Define *okay*."

"Fair enough. How about you? How are you doing?"

I shrug. "It's a mixed bag. I'm relieved, and I'm pissed she won't stand trial. She deserved to suffer more. Does that make me a shitty person?"

"No. It makes you human." She takes a swig from her bottle, her eyes soft on her grandkids. "I feel the same way, but mostly I'm glad she's gone."

Yesterday morning, Vivian Avellino was found dead in her cell from an apparent suicide by hanging. Good fucking riddance with a side of *enjoy roasting marshmallows in Hell*, right?

If only the heart were so simple.

Luckily we have a routine in place for when the past bites us in the ass. And it has. Repeatedly. Like when Ellie made the decision to withdraw from UCLA due to several instances of violent harassment. Consequently, after spending a week with us she decided to reenroll and change her major to prelaw. I kind of like her now. She reminds me a lot of Callisto.

More fallout came, heavy and spiked, when families of victims found at the ranch began to step forward publicly to condemn the Avellinos. Even Callisto wasn't spared the vitriol. And when Lizzie refused an insanity defense. And a week after that, when Wilson informed us that six of the seventeen bodies had been conclusively linked to the youngest Avellino.

We've accepted that the emotional shockwaves will continue, possibly for years. And though we're insulated somewhat in Solstice Bay, there's no umbrella for emotions.

So, when the past hits, we keep to our routine. We don't immediately talk about our feelings or dissect our thoughts.

We hike, bike, or run.

After news of Vivian yesterday, Callisto needed to run. I let her set the pace, push herself as hard or as little as she wanted to. Six miles later, we ended up deep in her favorite forest, and then we ended up naked. I have nail marks on my ass, and she has bark-burn on her back.

In a few days, we'll do the so-called normal communication stuff. Hash out our conflicting responses to Vivian's death. Be honest with each other. Move forward.

Maybe our method isn't the most conventional, but it's ours.

"Are you going to tell her you bought the house? The one she's been talking about for weeks?"

I give her the stink-eye. "No, and you can't let it slip, okay? It's a surprise. No telling Aunt Molly, either, because she can't keep a secret to save her life."

My mom nods in agreement, smiling as she gazes across the yard at my sisters and Callisto, all of whom are laughing.

Her eyes well up, smile fading. "I wish..." She trails off, shaking her head. "Don't mind me. Senior moment."

"Stop," I say gently, shifting closer so I can put my arm around her shoulders. Squeezing her to me, I kiss her graying curls. "You don't have to do that anymore. Not with me. I wish he were here, too."

Looking up at me, she whispers, "He'd be so proud of the man you've become."

"Shit, Mom." I wipe my leaking eyes. "Way to pull out the big guns."

One of my nieces—Jessie, I think—screams like her arm's being sawed off. It's horrible. Bloodcurdling. I leap off the bench like an Olympic sprinter and run full tilt down the grassy hill. Ten feet from the kids, my sneaker catches a root and I trip, slip, and slide the rest of the way. Seconds later I'm crouching before Jessie, whose face is bright red as she wails. Tears roll down her chubby cheeks.

"What's wrong? What happened?" I pant at the other kids, who stand nearby shrugging and wearing various *It wasn't me* expressions.

Jessie lets out another mind-numbing scream and holds out her thumb.

"Boo-boo! Boo-boo!"

I take her hand gently, examining her finger for a wound. Bee sting, splinter, cut... There's nothing. I turn her hand over. Then examine the other hand. All perfectly unharmed—if dirty—skin.

Jessie shoves her thumb back in my face.

"Kiss the boo-boo!"

I carefully kiss the tip of her thumb. She pats my head like I'm a good boy, then jumps up and runs to join her cousins. I gape after her.

From the other side of the yard comes a chorus of feminine laughter.

"So gullible!"

"Wrapped around her little finger!"

"You'll never learn!"

I salute my sisters with a middle finger before falling onto my back to admire how the late afternoon light caresses the branches of a nearby elm. Here, surrounded by my chaotic, colorful, forgiving family, with the distant rush of the ocean in my ears and fresh air on my face, I have no regrets. Everything is fucking perfect.

Sunlight fades as the main reason for my happiness bends over me, her smile hitting me right in the heart. *Brave, beautiful woman.* My fingers twitch for my camera—an impulse that's been coming with increasing frequency.

"I think I might try nature photography," I tell her. "Trees are cool."

Eyes narrowed, she sees right through me. "Are you ever going to take my picture?"

"What makes you think I haven't?"

Her nose wrinkles. "Creepy."

"Only creepy for you."

She laughs and offers me a hand. I make it to my feet, then tip up her chin and kiss her soundly.

"Little Jessie has your number," she says when I release her.

"I know." I hang my head. "I thought I'd finally found a woman who needed a hero."

Callisto smirks. "You'll always be the hero of my heart. Does that count?"

"It sure does, princess." I kiss her again. "I'm going to take your picture tonight. And tomorrow, and the next day, and probably every day for the rest of your life. The only rule is you have to be naked."

She giggles. I grab her ass and lift her into me, angling my head for better access to her mouth.

From behind us comes exaggerated gagging and vomiting noises. My oldest nephews. They're little fuckers, just like I was. But I have the upper hand—their mom told me my tattoos scare them a little. Setting Callisto down, I face them.

"Run," I growl.

They scream and take off at a sprint toward the house. My arm draped around Callisto's shoulders, I watch them disappear.

Eventually, she asks lightly, "You're not going after them, are you?"

"Nope. Suckers."

Head thrown back, she laughs and laughs. Her dark eyes shining, cheeks rosy with life. Her spirit so fucking bright it hurts to look at her. But I look at her anyway.

My fierce princess who didn't need a prince.

Thank you so much for reading Finn and Calli's story! Reviews help readers find new authors and books, so if you have a moment, I'd be grateful for a brief review on Amazon, Goodreads, or wherever you like!

Don't want to say goodbye to Finn and Calli? You don't have to! Sign up for my reader list to receive a bonus epilogue.

Finally, are you itching for a look inside Crossroads, the BDSM club featured briefly in TGH? ***Turn the page*** *to read the first chapter of PERFECT VISION, Dominic and London's story >>*

PERFECT VISION

"A heart-poundingly twisted tale of love and betrayal."

BOOK CLUB GONE WRONG

1

A few of my mental screws are loose. Why else would I be sitting on a bench in a brightly-lit hallway beside two women doing sexed-up Edward Scissorhands impressions? Halloween was four months ago.

Their black latex bodysuits have cutouts around the shoulders and waist, highlighting their toned, tanned bodies. I can't even imagine the crotch-sweat happening right now. What if they have to pee? Is there a zipper down there?

Defying logic, they don't look uncomfortable as they chat and laugh quietly. In fact, they look like they're exactly where they're supposed to be. Like they belong here. I'm clearly missing a big piece of the puzzle. Did I overlook some fine print in the email? Was there a specified dress code?

Here to interview for a bartending position, I'm wearing skin-hugging black pants, my comfiest ankle boots, and a tight black T-shirt—a nice one, flattering and new. Black on black, but actual, practical clothing. I look good. Sleek and professional, my dark blond hair pulled back and my makeup perfect thanks to YouTube tutorials.

What I saw of the newly constructed nightclub on my walk through was modern and on trend. White walls. Discreet lighting. Various seating areas—tables, couches, chaises—that in my former life I wouldn't mind enjoying on a night out. A huge, sleek bar I can definitely see myself behind. Zero indication that the intended clientele are people with latex fetishes.

The online job advertisement had been oddly obscure, the description of the club vague and heavy on words like *exclusive* and *private*. God willing, the club's exclusivity doesn't translate to obligatory background checks for employees. Either way, the gamble is one I have to take. Despite working part-time at two other bars, I have fourteen dollars in my bank account. Living alone in Los Angeles is *not* cheap.

The fluorescent lights overhead are giving me a headache, and the presence of four closed doors in the hallway feels increasingly ominous. Clearly television has rotted my brain, because for several minutes I entertain the possibility I'm in a horror movie. Any second one of the doors will open and a clown with a chainsaw will jump out.

To distract myself, I stare at the tantalizing glow of the Exit sign at the end of the hallway and fantasize about running away. Far, far away where no one knows my name. Maybe I should have left the country when I had the chance, before my savings disappeared into the pockets of impotent lawyers.

Among other things—like grief and rage—what stopped me then was one of my mom's favorite catch phrases. *No matter where you go, there you are.* In our childhood home, a sign with the words hung in the entryway where it couldn't be missed. And it's true.

There's no running from the past—it comes with you. Nearly three thousand miles between me and the past, and it's with me all the goddamn time.

"I'm sorry, we're being so rude! We don't mean to ignore you, we're just super excited."

Grateful for the reprieve from my chaotic thoughts, I

turn toward the voice. The latex women are smiling at me. Besides the dominatrix gear, they look... normal. Gorgeous, polished Los Angeles women. *In latex.*

"I'm Maggie, and this is Beatrix," says the woman closest to me.

I force a smile. "I'm London, nice to meet you."

"You too," gushes Maggie. "What are you interviewing for?"

"Bartender," I reply, but it comes out like a question. "Is that, uh, what you guys are here for, too?"

They giggle like schoolgirls. "Oh no," says Maggie. "We're auditioning."

Auditioning?

As I open my mouth to ask for what, the door just past our bench opens.

A smooth, deep voice says, "Maggie and Beatrix, come in."

Their immediate nervousness is palpable. I have a feeling—a bad feeling—about what they're auditioning for. They stand up, smoothing nonexistent wrinkles in their latex, and turn toward the open door.

My desperation for this job takes an immediate step to the back shelf. I blurt, "You don't have to do this."

Hair flies as the women's heads whip around. Instead of the embarrassment or affront I expected, they wear twinned expressions of anger.

"Honey," snaps Beatrix, "you have no idea what you're talking about."

"That's enough," says the man, still unseen in the room beyond. "Come in, ladies." When they hesitate, he says calmly, "Now."

His tone holds no edge, no emotion, but the power of it echoes down my spine.

"Yes, sir," the women say in unison.

They slip into the room and the door closes.

Dive into PERFECT VISION, available on Amazon and Kindle Unlimited!

ACKNOWLEDGMENTS

I'd like to thank caffeine for allowing me to write and finish this novel while packing a house and driving a thousand-plus miles with a nervous dog and a four-year-old and finally reaching our destination only to unpack the bajillion boxes so recently packed, none of which contained my husband's beloved cutting board (much to his everlasting dismay) and if he ever reads this he'll know that I didn't misplace that old, stained, bacteria-ridden piece of wood but cackled as I threw it away.

But the real hero is Summer Camp.

Dearest Summer Camp, I see you. I appreciate you. I owe you my sanity, my husband owes you his life, and my readers owe you for this book. Never stop, Summer Camp. We need you.

To my betas for *The Golden Hour*—Lee, Dawn,

Patricia, and Danielle. Thank you for helping me make TGH the best version of itself. Judy and Emily, for meticulous editing and proofing.

To my writer tribe—you know.

To all the unbelievably selfless bloggers and readers who took the time to share, read, review, and in general support this book, THANK YOU. Never ever think I don't see each and every one of you.

And you, too.

Bold, brave, beautiful you.

ALSO BY L.M. HALLORAN

ILLUSIONS DUET

Art of Sin

Sin of Love

THE VISION SERIES

Double Vision

Perfect Vision

THE RELUCTANT SERIES

The Reluctant Socialite

The Reluctant Heiress (*novella*)

STANDALONE NOVELS

The Fall Before Flight

The Muse

Breaking Giants

ABOUT THE AUTHOR

When not writing or reading, the author enjoys walking barefoot, subjecting her husband to questionable recipes, and chasing her spirited daughter. She's a rabid fan of coffee, moon-gazing, and small dogs that resemble Ewoks. Home is Portland, Oregon.

lmhalloran.com

Made in the USA
Middletown, DE
29 July 2024